Moonlight City Drive

BRIAN PAONE

Dedicated to all my fellow Dog Fashion Disco fans
and to the *real* Mushroom Cult.
(You all know who you are.)

Editor: Denise Barker
Copyeditor: Nina Johnson
Chapter artwork: Amy Hunter
Author photo: Elisabeth B. Adams
1947/1984 Handwriting Segues: Ashley Mayer
Front Cover, Back Cover, & Title Page artwork,
and 1947 & 1984 ads: Kyle Lechner

Published by Scout Media
Copyright 2017
ISBN: 978-0-9979485-8-5

May 2, 2017 — August 24, 2017
(New Bern, NC / Kingsland, GA)

For more information on my books and music:
www.BrianPaone.com

LAS VEGAS, NEVADA; 1947

1: The Darkest Days

The tall and broody man hid in the shadows of the looming trees and glared at the single-story building in front of him. He shook his head in disgust and thought, *In 1945 this brand-new subdivision brimmed with hope for families buying their starter homes, the World Wars over thankfully. Then, somehow, some city official allowed this, this, this travesty to invade our peaceful community less than a year later. Just a few months afterward people are evacuating, leaving their homes whether sold or not—which makes no difference with the market prices quickly diving and dying there.*

His shoulders were hunched, and his chin almost touched his chest. He could see unruly wisps of his eyebrows as his eyes strained to their maximum leverage. His teeth were clenched, grinding against each other. The fingernails in his right hand drew small speckles of blood inside his tightly closed fist.

He quickly brought the inside crease of his elbow to his mouth to stifle a cough. He knew he had to be careful. He knew he had to be silent. Any careless noises could sound the alarms, and they'd be on him quicker than moths to flames.

The man flipped the hood of his long black cloak over his head, and the fabric covered most of his face. He raised a fist in the air to signal the scores of figures behind him that they were about to begin. He heard their excited chatter rise from the silence of the night. He scowled at them, then raised a single finger to his lips. The murmuring ceased immediately.

He turned toward the building and bounced his outstretched hand up and down, gesturing for them to move slowly behind him. The herd of figures followed the man, all hunched down to stay underneath the path of the spotlights. He reached the large purple sign that directed family members when they visited their teenage delinquents.

The Siegel Home for Wayward Children: only the best of the best gets to call this hellhole home. Only the most well-behaved are allowed to leave when they turn seventeen and forever have bragging rights to their hooligan friends downtown that they "survived Siegel" with only a black eye, broken arm, or maybe violated genitals. And that's just from the staff's doings. They'll be rewarded to live another day in Technicolor and amphetamines, destroying everything they touch. The best of the best.

The man placed his hand atop the wooden sign, and his thumb slipped into the engraved *G*. The disciples huddled around him, breaking their ranks and waiting for instruction as a searchlight swung across the parking lot toward Siegel's main entrance. The man curled into a ball and pressed himself against the wood for concealment. The beam of light scanned across the top of the sign, and the sea of followers disappeared, leaving the man alone to cower as he waited for the light to continue panning left. As soon as the beam cleared the main entrance, the rows and rows of figures materialized again.

He pointed to a female three rows back and motioned for her to come to him. She low-crawled past the first two rows and giggled excitedly.

"Can you handle leading the charge?" he whispered.

She bounced her head up and down and clapped as a small droplet of drool trickled from the corner of her mouth.

"*Shh!* I'm trusting you, Nikki. Don't let me down. You know what'll happen if you do."

Nikki nodded.

"Good girl. I'll stay here to catch the . . . difficult ones." He straightened his back to see over the heads of the first few rows. "You, you, you, you, and . . . you three. Stay here with me. The rest of you will go with Nikki."

The pack of followers faded quickly as the spotlight swept across the main entrance again. He ducked and pulled his hood farther over his head. When the light cleared the area, he shook his finger at the side wall of Siegel's.

"Go! Go! Go!"

Nikki and the rest of the Mushroom Cult corporealized and stormed the walls of the detention center like a tidal wave. The man pressed his back against the main entrance sign and silently counted the seconds before the stragglers escaped through the doors, screaming in terror—maybe in even more terror than their victims had screamed.

One can only hope, the man thought as he smoothed his brown mustache.

When the first explosion ripped through the silence, he constricted his neck into his shoulders, like a turtle retreating into its shell. He giggled and placed a finger to his lips to signal the disciples with him to stay quiet. His command was futile, as the handful of cult members chattered and cheered.

He stood up, abandoning the safety of the sign, and motioned for them to charge. A deafening secondary explosion projected him backward, and his body contorted around the stump of a tree. He hit the ground and counted the stars in his vision. One, two, eight, thirteen, twenty-six, four hundred . . . and out.

The followers at the sign pointed to his motionless body while they shook and jumped up and down. One female disciple pointed to the fire and smoke, accompanying the screams erupting from the building. The rest of them continued to flail their limbs as they gawked at the man at the base of the tree. She grabbed the wrist of the follower beside her and yelled a single-toned scream.

The cult stopped panicking and turned their attention to the one who had taken control. She squeezed the disciple's wrist tighter and shook a finger at the building. They nodded in understanding and crouched in a defensive stance.

Black smoke and bright orange flames enveloped Siegel's Home for Wayward Children. The frantic screams of the dying children engulfed the stillness of the night outside and excited the waiting ghouls. The roof, completely consumed, slid from the top of the building, exposing the screams of the staff burning alive.

The man shook his head and rubbed his eyes. "Cyana . . ." He cleared his throat and brushed dirt off his pants. "Cyana!"

Cyana diverted her attention from the burning building to her master and clapped excitedly, jumping up and down.

"Come here, my child."

Cyana gripped the hands of another Mushroom Cult member, gurgled an unintelligible command, and bounded toward the man like a kangaroo.

He clasped her face. "Cyana, I need you now more than ever. Are you ready to prove yourself?"

Cyana nodded with such ferocity he thought her head would pop off her neck.

"Any second now some of the children and staff will escape from the fire and spill into the street. They'll think they found safety outdoors. They might think they were strong and courageous, but they're really just the overachievers. Sentenced to the same fate as their burning brethren. I'm trusting you to pick them off, one by one, as they come out."

Cyana clapped and bounced up and down.

The ashes and smoke rising skyward momentarily distracted the man. "Good, good," he continued. "We burned down the temple where they were sleeping. We woke them up and showed them the truth of their ways. Now you can feed on their fears."

Cyana clicked her heels together and sprinted toward the rest of the disciples hiding behind the sign. The man watched as she grunted a few commands to the group, and then he walked toward the sanctity of the entrance sign.

"You're putting a lot of faith in a half-wit," Anya said, materializing beside him. A black veil hid her face and stringy white hair. "Cyana is a few hay straws short of a scarecrow."

"I don't need her to be smart. I need her to be effective."

"You worry about collecting. I'll worry about facilitating. They're my girls," Anya retorted. "Plus I've made it perfectly clear how unhappy I am about what you're doing here. This is a useless cleansing. I'm not getting compensated. I'm not adding *any* new girls tonight."

"That might be true, but I thank you, Anya, from the bottom of my heart for letting me use the girls tonight. A blanket of fire when the hellions are young is so much more effective than picking them off one by one when they're adults."

"This is your one freebie from me, Mr. Covington. The girls are mine again starting tomorrow," she sneered and vanished. "And we get back to the mission."

"Always a pleasure," he mumbled.

The detention center's front door burst open, and waves of terrified children spewed into the street. Covington laughed as he watched them fall over each other, trying to reach safety from the flames. "Not so tough now, are you?"

He glanced at the building and saw charred children pressing their bodies against the closed windows, screaming—begging—for anyone to open the windows. Like a waterfall of dripping flesh, the children trapped inside piled atop one another to escape. Covington placed his hand over his mouth to hide his smirk of satisfaction.

"You hoodlums deserve every moment of pain. I'm cleansing the world of your filth!"

He felt a hard tug on his cloak and looked down. Cyana pulled at the seams of his disguise and pointed to the front of the building.

"Ah, yes, my child. Very good. Do what you must. If they escape the building, then they're fair game."

Cyana nodded and rallied a battle cry. All the followers hiding behind the entrance sign stood up and screamed. They fell in behind Cyana and raced toward the juveniles leaving their burning home. The children's eyes grew larger in fear as they saw the Mushroom Cult descend upon them. The disciples chased the terrified children in and out of every shadow.

One by one, the ghouls brought down the children as their maniacal cannibal teeth sank into the flesh of the children's backs. The escapees scattered, like cockroaches in sunlight, but the cult moved faster. Veins were ripped from necks while the screams pulsated from the ones burning inside the building. Pounding and pleading, the trapped staff and juveniles slowly and painfully paid for their indiscretions.

A boy loosened a brick from the entrance wall and situated it firmly in his palm. Fire had singed the left side of his hair, and his scalp still smoked. "C'mon, you rat bastards!"

Cyana stopped gnawing on a crisp child's thigh and diverted her attention to the infidel taunting her perfect clan.

"Yeah, that's right. You. I'm talking to you, you hoochie-broad."

Cyana rose to her feet and pointed to her chest. She tilted her head in confusion.

"Are you that dumb? I'm talking to you," he yelled, repositioning his grip on the brick. "Come get me!"

Cyana grunted and closed the distance between herself and the heathen.

Covington shook his head in disappointment. "Cyana!"

She stopped and glowered at him.

"Have you forgotten everything? How can I trust you with

more responsibility if you let your emotions impede your ability to use the tools you have at your disposal?"

The boy with the brick stared at Covington with his mouth agape. The screams of the children trapped inside the inferno slowly dissipated as they perished in the heat.

"You stupid bitch!" the boy said and charged Cyana with the brick held above his head.

"Now, Cyana! Call them now!" Covington said and leaped into the air. He collided with the boy, knocking the brick from his hand. He stood up and stepped on the boy's wrist, breaking it under the pressure.

The boy screamed and flung his head side to side in pain.

"Cyana, what are you waiting for? Call them! Finish this!"

Covington grabbed the discarded brick and brought it down with full force into the boy's face. Again. And again. And again. Blood splattered all over Covington's cloak and trickled over the pebbles on the ground. With each strike, he grunted in satisfaction. Winded on the final swing, he stood up to inspect the carnage below. The lifeless, bloodied body of the preteen did not move. A gurgle of blood erupted from the cavity where his nose should have been.

Covington dropped the bloodied brick and turned toward Cyana. "Have you called them yet?"

Cyana nervously shook her head. Her eyes were large, and her gaze appeared distant, like a deer caught in headlights.

Covington leaned over the hill and saw another swarm of children making it safely from the burning building. "For Heaven's sake, Cyana, some of them are getting away! Now do I have to hunt them down myself and then come back and decommission you, or will you step up to the plate and prove your worth?"

The sound of distant sirens reached them.

"Damn it, Cyana. The cops and firemen are just around the corner. If you don't take care of this, I will."

Cyana stumbled backward from his tirade and kneaded her

hands together. She dropped to her knees and placed her palms skyward.

"Good, good," he said, flipped his cloak around his waist, and headed down the hill toward the screaming children.

She flexed her fingers and closed her eyes. She released a continuous series of grunts until she felt the talons grip her index and middle finger. Slowly opening her eyes, she smiled in accomplishment. "Har!" she commanded, and the vulture took flight.

The cult would love her now, like she wanted. Now that she could summon the vultures, the followers were sure to find her irreplaceable.

A swarm of black death crowded the sky. Feathers, wings, and talons filled the heavens. One by one, they swooped downward and picked off the children outside the burning building. Beaks impaled the backs of necks, the soft tissue between shoulder blades, and the squishy, overweight midsections. Vultures speared and carried the smaller children into the sky—up, up, up, until fear or atmospheric pressure knocked them out.

A gaggle of birds stayed grounded and created a roadblock, aligning themselves wing to wing to prevent the emergency vehicles to pass. The remaining vultures carried away the dead, and Covington wondered if the birds would use—or not use—the deceased's bones and meaty flesh for nest building or feeding practices. It was hard for Covington to know for sure.

After the screams from inside the detention center were completely silenced and the vultures had neutralized all the fleeing children, Covington called for the ghouls to convene outside. The crackling of the flames slowly consumed the caws of the vultures as they flew farther away, carrying a handful of prizes to their hungry young.

"How many perished?" he asked Nikki.

She grunted and held a fist into the air.

"All of them? Well, that is good news. Congratulations, everyone. You just rid Earth of a plethora of society's scabs. I know they looked like children, but trust me. They deserved what we gave them."

Cyana pointed to the main roadway.

"Ah, yes. I guess we should let the coppers and fire-stoppers come in and act like they are important. Release the vultures from the street."

Cyana flung her arms above her head, and the vultures lining the roadway took to flight in unison. The patrol cars and fire trucks lunged forward, attempting to reach the burning detention center before there were too many casualties.

Covington laughed. "A little too late, don't you think?"

The rest of the Mushroom Cult, now congregated around his feet, laughed along with him.

"We did a good thing here. The world is better off without these degenerates. But the law is almost upon us, so we must make haste."

Nikki glanced at Cyana and nodded.

"Go, my children. There's always another night. Although this night will live in infamy."

The disciples faded quickly, one by one, until he was left alone on the hill, overlooking the singed and smoking home for wayward children. He clapped in triumph and flung his cloak over his face.

Glancing one last time at the torched center, he whispered, "This is just the beginning. It's too late to turn back now."

"I'm home!" the man called as he set his keys on the dining room table.

"You're home early," his wife responded, taking a sip of coffee. "It's not even five thirty yet."

"*Mmm*, boss man cut me loose. We were overstaffed. Sometimes it pays to be the most tenured technician." He bent down to kiss his wife. "How're you liking those pajamas?"

"Cozy and comfy."

"Good. Kids not up yet?"

"Not yet. Another half hour and I'll get them ready."

Covington reached into the cupboard to locate a coffee mug and noticed the dirt and soot trapped underneath his fingernails. Glancing into the next room to confirm she couldn't see him, he turned on the hot water in the kitchen sink and scrubbed his hands as roughly as he could. He used a butter knife to remove the evidence of the Siegel Home fire from under his fingernails. Quickly checking his wife's location again, he inspected his clothes.

The cloak should have prevented any ash or blood from soiling his work clothes, but he needed to make sure. She was the one who did the laundry, after all. He picked at a small stain just above the knee of his work pants that could have either been chocolate or blood. But he couldn't take any chances.

"Hey, Maggie. What time are we heading to your parents on Saturday?"

"I'd like to leave before lunchtime," she called from the other room. "I think they're planning on feeding us."

"Hi, Daddy."

Startled, Covington spun to face his daughter. Her curly blond pigtails had loosened while she slept, creating thin wispies resembling spider webs escaping from the hair ties.

"What're you doing up so early, sweet pea?"

She raised her hands for him to pick her up. "I couldn't sleep."

"You didn't wake your brother, did you?"

"Cross my heart."

"I'll cross your heart," he said and then shoved his lips into the crook of her neck and blew a raspberry. "And then I'll tickle your face!"

She giggled uncontrollably and flailed to get away.

He put her down and smoothed his mustache. "Can you help me make my coffee, please?"

"Sure, Daddy."

Covington lifted her and placed her on the kitchen counter.

"What's that on your ear, Daddy?"

Covington's hand shot to his earlobe to rub away whatever she might have seen.

"The other ear, silly."

He caught his reflection in the dark kitchen window and noticed a large gray smear across the top of his ear. He licked his fingers and wiped away the smudge—soot and ash.

"Hey, baby. What would you like for breakfast?" Maggie asked her daughter, entering the kitchen and brushing her platinum-blond hair behind one ear.

"Did you get your hair cut?" Covington asked his wife.

"Just the bangs. You like?"

"Daddy likes!" he said, giggling and tussling Maggie's hair.

"Oatmeal, please," their daughter answered.

"Coming right up." Then to Covington: "Do you work tonight?"

"Yeah. But I doubt I'll be let go early tonight. We have a new batch of techs starting tonight."

After Maggie made the oatmeal, she turned the knob of the large radio sitting on a cabinet in the kitchen.

"Firefighters were dispatched to the scene, however, not before the detention center was fully engulfed. The casualty count is unknown at this . . . We are being told now that both children *and* staff members are among the deceased—"

Covington quickly reached up and silenced the radio. "She doesn't need to hear about that."

"My God," Maggie said. "What a terrible tragedy. I heard the sirens about an hour ago, but I didn't think anything of it. Imagine all those parents losing their children like that."

"Yeah, imagine," he replied, rubbing his hands together. "I'm sure they'll find out it was some electrical fire in the walls or some faulty construction."

"Could you imagine if it *was* arson though? Jeez. We really might be living in the darkest days, for someone to do that to children."

"What happened, Mommy?"

"Nothing, sweet pea. Just eat your oatmeal," Covington said. "It's not table talk for little ladies."

His daughter giggled.

"All right, I'm turning in," he said and kissed Maggie on the lips. "I'm gonna crash. I'm exhausted."

"I'm going downtown today with Evelyn," she called as he walked toward their downstairs bedroom. "I need to find some new shoes, and Matt wants to open a second lounge. She told him that she'd scope out some locations for sale. She might come back here for some tea. We'll be quiet and try not to wake you."

"Matt wants to open another Rippetoe's lounge? Isn't he worried about overextending their revenue?"

"With prohibition over, she said some of their friends are making stacks of moolah opening multiple bars."

"It won't last," Covington said as he entered the bedroom. "Prohibition ended about thirteen years ago now. The novelty of speakeasies has almost completely worn off. The Rippetoes should invest in savings bonds instead and focus on their one lounge."

"Maybe. But I do like her company."

"Well, say hello to her for me."

"G'night, Daddy!"

"Have a good day at kindergarten," he replied and closed the bedroom door.

He stripped off his clothes, put on his pajamas at the foot of the bed, and tucked himself underneath the covers. He flipped to his right side, facing away from the edge of his side of the bed, and felt a hand stroke his hair.

"Your girls did good tonight, Anya," he said and reached back without looking. Then he lovingly placed his fingers over her cold, lifeless wrist as she continued to massage his head.

"As long as we continue to do great things, all of us, together, the world will one day thank us," she said, her words sounding more like a gurgle from the back of her throat than a voice.

He turned his head to face her. "Good night, Anya. Get some rest. The next opportunity is just around the corner."

She vanished from the room, leaving behind the only remnants that she had been here at all: a stench of mildew and a single fly taking flight from where she stood.

"Daddy!" she squealed and jumped on his chest.

He rubbed the dried crust from the corners of his eyes. "Hey, sweet pea."

"Is it time for you to get up?"

He looked at the pocket watch he kept draped over the corner of the headboard. "It is now."

She peeled the blankets and sheets off his upper body. "Why do you have to work at night and sleep during the day? Me and Ray miss playing with you."

"I know, Rose. But Daddy's job is to make sure the dam is working right, and everything is safe at night. You don't want the dam to break or any nice people to get hurt, do you?"

Rose shook her head.

"That's my sweet girl."

Maggie gently pushed open the bedroom door and peeked in. "I'm sorry, hon. Did she wake you?"

"Nah. I love having my little dumpling in bed with me," he said and consumed Rose with his arms, tickling and kissing her until she couldn't breathe through her hysterics anymore.

Maggie smiled and stepped from the room.

"Honey!" he called.

She poked her head back in.

"How did it go today with Evelyn?"

"Good. Looks like Matt is buying that lounge we looked at."

He nodded and slid from bed.

"Do you *have* to go to work tonight, Daddy?"

"Yes, he does," Maggie said, entering the bedroom and scooping up her daughter. "Daddy works very hard so you and Ray can have all those nice clothes and new toys."

"I love you," he said to his wife.

"I love you more," she replied and planted a puckered kiss on his lips. "Go take a shower. Dinner will be ready in a few."

He waited until Maggie and Rose were gone before walking toward the master bathroom with its interior closet. He closed the door behind him and stripped off his pajamas. He collected them and turned to toss them in the hamper; a shadowy figure stood motionless in the shadows.

"*Gah!* You can't keep scaring me like that," Covington said, placing a hand over his chest.

Anya stepped forward, her face shrouded behind the black veil.

"Is everything okay?"

She reached up and slid a maroon-colored book from the top shelf of his closet. She offered the book to him, holding it out and cocking her head to one side.

"Not tonight. I have to work. Real work. At my job. Put the book back."

Covington noticed Anya furrow her eyebrows behind the sheer black lace of the veil as she opened the metal cover of the book. She fingered the yellow-discolored pages, letting each brittle page flop lazily from one side to the other.

"The guilt trip won't work on me tonight, Anya. I can't call out sick tonight too. Even last night was risky. And think of how many souls we freed in just one night. I think we met our quota for the year just within last night."

"We went there only because *you* wanted to disinfect a bunch of snot-nosed kids. Not to add to our ranks. Last night was a pointless endeavor for me and the cult. Last night was a favor to you—your last one, I might add. So don't come boo-hooing to me about how much work you're missing when it doesn't benefit me at all."

"You want to do something to *benefit* your cult?" Covington retorted. "Why not stop lollygagging and get in touch with our guy tonight or tomorrow morning?"

Anya closed the book and fingered the insignia on the metal cover. "I've already mailed him the package. Are you *sure* he's the right one?"

"He's not only the right one but he's the *only* one. Have some faith in me. He's exactly who we've been waiting for."

She placed the book on a shelf, eye level, and turned to face him. "Fine. I'm just not used to being dictated to about decisions this pivotal. And, just so you know, your antics didn't please the vultures. They wanted to create, not destroy."

He waved her off. "Look. I'm in control here. Not the vultures. Not any other disciple. I hold the book. That's what you told me. I don't take suggestions or threats from—"

Knock, knock. "Daddy?"

Covington directed his gaze to the closed bathroom door. "Hey, bud! Give me a minute, okay?"

He looked back where Anya had stood, but she was gone. He sighed and jumped backward when an invisible hand flung the book from the eye-level shelf, and the book landed on the closet floor with a *WHACK!* He collected the book and returned it to its designated location, then opened the bathroom door and forced a smile for his son.

"Mommy says you have to work tonight."

"Yeah, Ray. Sorry. I have to work every night this week. But I'll be off for your birthday. We're going to Grandma and Grandpa's."

"Will we have ice cream?"

"Do you want ice cream?"

"I want two kinds of ice cream!"

"Then we'll get two different kinds of ice cream."

Raymond clapped and scooted from the bedroom.

"Hey, Ray! I love you, bud!"

His son answered from the living room. "Love you too, Daddy!"

He turned and glanced into the closet. Anya did not seem to be returning tonight.

2: The Uninvited Guest

Smith kicked his office door again while he jiggled the keys stuck in the dead bolt. He slammed the doorframe with the palm of his hand hard enough that one of the nails securing his nameplate to the door fell to the floor. He quickly grabbed the swinging sign before it dislodged from the second nail.

"C'mon, you good-for-nothin' bastard. Turn!"

Smith twisted the key as hard as he could and heard a popping noise as the locking mechanism finally gave way. He pushed open his office door and entered the dark room. He tossed his keys onto his desk; they slid a short distance before a stack of time-faded papers and case-file folders abruptly stopped them.

Flicking the light switch, the room illuminated with an anemic-brown glow from the single dusty bulb. He took a step toward the coffee percolator on the windowsill, and his toe caught the corner of a tied-up pile of newspapers dating back at least ten years.

Smith exhaled loudly with a frustrated grunt and kneeled beside the newspaper bundle; the air escaping from his lungs carried the stench of day-old consumed alcohol, topped off with more last night that led to closing time this morning. He really hadn't slept.

He napped for a couple hours, then came here. He removed the Swiss Army knife from his pants and cut the twine, freeing the newspapers, watching as they avalanched to the floor.

He used his palm to shuffle and smear the newspapers around his office floor. His gaze quickly scanned his name plastered on all the headlines, praising the ex-deputy-now-turned-private-eye for all the scum he had gotten off the street, as well as locating abducted kids, reuniting long-lost biological parents of orphans, and exposing spouses who may have forgotten their vows. Smith had seen more than he cared to remember while he had been a sheriff's deputy and could now safely check the box marked Seen It All since becoming a private eye.

He burped without opening his mouth, letting the stale odor of alcohol find its way out through his nostrils instead. He vigorously rubbed his nose to lessen the sting.

His gaze landed on a more current newspaper on his desk chair. He grabbed the paper and unfolded the front page, sighing as he scanned the article's first few paragraphs, describing the tragic torching of the Siegel Home for Wayward Children two nights ago, now deemed an arson case by the Las Vegas fire chief; the newspaper chronicled the event as one of the worst tragedies in the city's recorded history. The beginnings of a smirk—maybe even a real smile—formed on the corners of Smith's lips as he silently applauded whoever had torched the place, ridding the city of the imminent release of dozens of hooligans; their inevitable rescindment into society only to stain it further was good enough for Smith to commend the mystery arsonist.

Smith tossed aside the newspaper and snaked his way around the clutter blanketing his office floor toward the percolator, stopping to hang his brown fedora and gray trench coat on the coatrack. He scooped two heaps of coffee grounds into the brown-stained basket. After filling the reservoir with water—a handful of dried grounds slipped through the holes of the basket—he inserted the pump stem and plugged in the coffeemaker. Within seconds, the mixture of grounds and water comingled in the canister.

Smith pulled out his desk chair and sat down. The seatback gave out, and he flailed as he caught himself from flipping over. He grabbed onto his desk with one hand and tightened the adjustment knob of the chair with the other. He scooted closer to the desk, lit a cigarette, and removed his revolver from his shoulder holster.

He let his gaze wander through the thin trail of smoke to the skyline outside the window. The city was alive tonight. He could feel it. He leaned back and closed his eyes as he reveled in the wailing sirens in the distance mixed with the conglomerate sounds of buzzing neon signs and engines rattling the metal frames of cars below. This was his city. Down to the last bottom-feeder who walked the alleyways at night—this was his city. Always had been. Always will be.

The percolator gurgled, signaling its brewing had finished. Smith grabbed his coffee mug that his previous secretary—back when he could afford one—had given to him for his forty-fifth birthday. Wynn had even monogrammed the mug with TOP GUN FOR HIRE on both sides.

Smith tossed the remnants of yesterday's coffee into the trash can next to his desk and filled the mug from the freshly brewed pot. He sighed in pleasure as the warm liquid hit his stomach and then ran a fingertip over the stenciled words decorating the mug. "Oh, Wynn. You always were so good to me. Maybe one day I'll make this business into something worth a damn again, and it'll be like old times, you and me."

Smith opened the top folder on the pile atop his desk and balanced his lit cigarette on the edge of the ashtray. "Another missing teenager. Runaway cases are not worth my time for the money." He tossed the folder into the trash can and sifted through the pile. "These bimbos and their cheating husbands. So damn cliché."

An unopened yellow manila envelope addressed to him slid

from underneath the top file onto the floor. He picked up the envelope and noticed there wasn't a return address. Swiping his finger underneath the crease, a paper-clipped picture fell out with an attached letter, asking for help to locate a missing wife. Smith rubbed his temple in small circles to alleviate some of the pressure from his hangover and crumpled the stationery into a ball and tossed it at the trash can. It bounced off the rim and landed on the floor among the other numerous discarded papers and items scattered everywhere.

The first sign of dawn rose like pale death creeping in and ate the retreating shadows. The office slowly grew brighter with the natural light.

Smith's olive-green rotary phone rang, startling him as the sound cut through the silence. He used his fingertips to wipe a few beads of sweat off his brow and picked up the receiver. "Detective Smith."

"Good morning. I hope I'm not bothering you so early in the morning," a female replied.

"No, not at all," he answered.

"Good, good. I . . . I have a dilemma, Mr. Smith."

Smith heard a teakettle whine in the background. He rubbed the inside corners of his eyes and frowned. Everyone has a dilemma, or they wouldn't be calling him. He quickly scrolled through the roulette of social afflictions this woman might need his services for: adultery, fraud, missing family cat.

He took a drag of his cigarette. "I'm not taking on any new cases, ma'am. My caseload is a little hectic right now," Smith lied. Taking on *any* kind of trivial case would surely send him over the brink into complete and utter boredom and disgust.

"My grandson is the Boulevard Killer."

Smith's body stiffened as he swiped stacks of case files and inquiries off his desk to locate a pen. He opened the middle drawer of his desk and found a pencil. "Go on, Mrs. . . .?"

"Covington. Eva Covington. I have a photograph I'd like you

to see. I didn't want to chance sending it through the post. I imagine you're a very busy man, but I'd like to bring it by your office, if you're willing to take a look at it."

Smith made a mental note to maybe call Wynn sooner rather than later to offer her job back.

"I'd be very interested to hear your story, Mrs. Covington. Could you—"

"Eva. Please call me Eva, Mr. Smith."

"Could you come this morning?"

He heard the teakettle's scream abruptly silenced as Eva poured herself a cup.

"You come highly recommended, Detective. Even by some of your peers."

"You've talked to other dicks?"

"I've hired other PIs. None of them stayed on the case longer than a few days before quitting. They felt they weren't right for the job. But all of them said to contact you."

"I must admit, you have my attention."

"Would an hour from now be too early?"

Smith looked at his pocket watch. "That would be perfect."

Eva hung up with a goodbye, and Smith didn't respond before pressing the switch hook to activate a dial tone. He dialed Wynn's number from memory, listening to the pulse tone as the rotary wheel spun after each number was dragged in a circle. After a few rings, Wynn answered the other end of the line. Smith thought it sounded like uncoordinated hands fumbled the receiver and then dropped it.

"'Ello?" a sleepy Wynn answered.

"Wynn, I've been thinking—"

"Smith? What time is it?"

"I dunno. But I was thinking—"

"This doesn't sound like a party line."

"It's not. I paid to have a private line installed in the office."

"Why are you calling me?"

"Christ Almighty, if you'd let me finish."

She cleared her throat but remained silent this time.

"I want you to come back to work."

"Same rate?"

"Same rate."

"When do you need me to start?"

"In less than an hour. I have a new client coming in."

"Typical you. Some things never change. But I love you for it."

"So that's a yes?"

"You'll know if I show up or not."

Smith sighed. "I guess I deserve that answer."

Wynn hung up the phone, and Smith watched the sun peek over the top of the city's skyline. He took a sip of coffee from his Top Gun For Hire mug and thought about the scumbags going to sleep now that the day had broken, while the office zombies emerged from their castles to take over the city for the next dozen hours . . . until the cycle started again.

The city was only alive at night.

Wynn took a deep breath as she stood in front of Smith's closed office door. She heard him rummaging around, and the familiar sound of his neurotic tendencies made her question accepting his offer to return to work. She hung her chin on her chest and wrung her hands together in anticipation. She knew, once she knocked and was let back into the office, she would also be entering his personal world and everything—good and bad—that came with being in his life again. *Mostly the bad: He is still married. He is still a drunk. He is still spouting whatever hateful things that fall from his mouth because his brain is not in gear.*

"Okay, Wynn. You can do this. You can look him in the eye again. It'll be different this time. You'll make it different this time."

She raised her fist to knock and held her breath. Her heart

skipped a beat when her knuckles connected with the wooden door three times.

"Hold on," she heard him yell from the other side.

The door swung open, and he stood there, disheveled as always.

"Rough morning?" she asked, stepping into her old workplace.

He pivoted sideways to let her enter. "More like a rough night. Burned the midnight oil on both ends this time."

"Still haven't learned how to slow down, I see. I was surprised to hear from you."

Smith closed the door, making her decision final. "I might have a new case, and I don't think I can investigate this one alone."

"So you *need* me now?" she said and removed her coat.

Smith took it from her and hung it on the coatrack in the corner. "I've always needed you."

"Baloney," she retorted.

"Fine. Then you've always needed me."

"Oh, you'd love to believe that."

Smith took a step closer to her. "Tell me I'm wrong."

Wynn refused to answer. The silence electrified the space between them. Smith grabbed her blouse and pulled her into him, consuming her lips with his. Wynn put her hand on his chest, lightly pushing him away to break the embrace, but she found her lips didn't want to cooperate with her resistance.

An avalanche of familiar warmth spread over her body, comforting and relaxing her. Then she tasted the stale alcohol, and her stomach wrenched. Just as quickly as the warm memories had arrived, the taste of his breath flooded her with all the reasons why she had left in the first place. This time she pushed hard enough to separate their kiss.

"I can't do this again, Smith."

He wiped her leftover spit off his lips. "That one's on me, doll. I won't let it happen again. I won't muck it up again."

Wynn straightened her blouse. "Good. Now let's clean this pigsty before your client arrives, and you can tell me about the case."

Smith bent down and collected and organized the toppled stack of newspapers while he briefed her on the little he knew: for the first time ever, someone claimed to know the identity of the worst serial killer Nevada has seen in recorded history. After a few moments, he spied on Wynn in his peripheral vision. She hadn't moved.

"No offense, Smith, but why did she call *you*?"

"Thanks for the vote of confidence. She said she'd hired other dicks, but they don't stay on the case."

"Huh. Well, now I'm glad you called me."

"You weren't happy about it before? Well, that's just rich, now isn't it?"

"Smith, you're not the most pleasant of employers," she said with a smirk. "Let's stop dillydallying and clean up this place."

They started at opposite ends of the room and worked inward, organizing or tossing everything that seemed out of place, based on its relevance to his investigations.

"Aww, how sweet," she said. "You've kept my mug."

"I'm just too cheap to buy a new one."

"Don't lie. You love this mug," she said as she turned it back and forth, smiling when she noticed the TOP GUN FOR HIRE stencil had faded from all the times he had handled the mug.

"How many damn bottles are there?" Smith asked as he discarded what seemed like the tenth empty liquor bottle into the trash can.

The glass clinked as it struck the mound of others already piled inside the can.

"The good news is, you can see the top of your desk now," Wynn said, taking a step backward and admiring her organizational skills. "Are you responding to any of these other case files?"

Smith looked up from the floor. "Nah. You can toss them."

Wynn swiped the entire stack of folders into the trash can with her arm. "I'll take out the trash. It's full."

Smith gave her a thumbs-up and continued sorting through the disheveled stacks of paper on the floor. Wynn carried the trash can across the office and jolted backward when she opened the door.

"Oh, child. I didn't mean to startle you," Eva Covington said. "I was about to knock."

"I'm sorry, ma'am. I just didn't expect anyone to be there."

Smith stood up and approached Eva and Wynn. "Mrs. Covington, welcome."

"Please call me Eva."

"I'm sorry for the mess. We're in the middle of organizing my office."

"If you'll excuse me, Eva, I'll be right back after I dump the trash downstairs," Wynn said.

"Take your time, child. I'm in no rush."

"Sit. Sit," Smith said, motioning to a wooden chair on the other side of his desk.

Eva sat down and eyed Smith as he walked around the desk and took his seat. She removed her flowery wide-brimmed hat and placed it next to his desk lamp. Her white hair drooped and rested gently against the roadmap of wrinkles adorning her cheeks and forehead. She extended a withered and shaky hand across the mahogany desk.

Smith shook it, feeling her brittle bones underneath her scarred and papery skin.

"I'm pleased you've decided to hear my case, Mr. Smith."

"I gotta admit, Mrs. Covington—"

"Eva."

"—I'm not accepting new clients. But you said the magic words, especially with me being an ex-deputy. Any chance to get filth off the streets will become priority number one."

"*Aah* . . . yes. I knew leading in with my suspicions would garner your attention."

Smith offered his pack of Smolens to Eva.

"Thank you," she said, sliding one out. She leaned across the desk so he could light it for her. She quickly puffed a few times to ignite the rod and placed a Polaroid on his desk. "That's my grandson in the photo."

"What makes you suspect your grandson is a serial killer?"

"He frequents the motels with whores. I've followed him a few times. They seem to turn up dead near those motels. Plus, if you look at the picture, you'll see something incriminating, if not outright disturbing."

Smith picked up the photo and studied the image of a man standing underneath the red neon VACANCY sign of the Vertigo Motel. Dried blood covered the man's face; the whites of his teeth seemed even more exaggerated by the dark crimson stains. The far-left edge of the Polaroid halved the image of a woman's high heel lying on the sand.

Smith's eyebrows scrunched together as he tried hard not to let his confusion show on his face. "I don't understand—"

The office door opened as Wynn entered with an empty wastebasket. She placed the can next to Smith's desk. "Everything going okay?"

Smith handed her the photo. "The man in this picture is Mrs. Covington's grandson."

Wynn made a noise that sounded like she had just been asked to solve a complicated math equation.

Eva sat back in the chair, the cigarette balancing delicately between two wrinkled fingers.

"Okay, Mrs. Covington—"

"Please, call me Eva."

Smith leaned forward, placing both elbows on his desk. "Mrs. Covington, I don't like to become too friendly with my clients. Lines can blur too easily, too quickly."

Wynn snickered sarcastically and quickly covered her mouth with her hand, as if she could stop the sound that had already escaped from her throat. Smith shot her a hard glare and pursed his lips in disapproval.

"Sorry, Mrs. Covington, for my partner's outburst," he said without looking away from Wynn.

Partner? Wynn silently mouthed.

Smith ignored Wynn's question and focused on the Polaroid. "Was this picture taken on the date printed on the back?"

"Yes."

Smith swallowed hard. "With all due respect, Mrs. Covington, the Vertigo Motel burned down a long time ago."

"Ten years ago, to be exact," Eva added.

"How can your grandson be standing just last week in front of a building that has been gone now for over a decade? Is this some kind of prank photo?"

Eva took a long drag of her cigarette and readjusted herself in the chair. "I assure you, this is no prank. My grandson has been soliciting mistresses of the night—Velcro whores, if you will—right underneath the nose of his unsuspecting wife, violating his vows with these girls. He's been using the Vertigo to copulate with them and then kill them. As you can see from his jovial expression, he seems to take great pride in ending his victim's lives, smiling like a scarecrow in a burning field."

"More like a hunter bragging about his kill. But how could—"

"Don't interrupt me, Mr. Smith. The *how* isn't important. What is important is the *why*. And that's what I need your services for. You've come with the highest recommendations. Please don't let me down. I can't rely on his wife to do anything about it, even if she *did* find out. Maggie is a spineless jellyfish of a woman and would be too meek and scared to turn him in."

Smith made a note that the potential killer's wife's name was Maggie. "Have you gone to the police yet?"

Eva spit on the ground and grimaced. "You know as well as I do—and, if I'm not mistaken, even more than I do—law enforcement here can't be trusted and should be the last option in this county for someone who needs help. Hell, they'd probably either protect him, or offer him a job on the force."

Smith nodded in agreement, leaned backward, and folded his arms. "I want to know more about the Vertigo Motel."

Eva fiddled with her wedding ring. "The motel isn't important. I only brought that photograph because it's the only picture I have of him anymore."

"You'd want to start an acting agency if you only knew how many crackpots I have entertained," Smith replied, doodling on the corner of an envelope as he spoke. "People claiming they know who killed this person or who killed that person, or even people confessing to crimes they didn't even commit so they can bask in some national publicity themselves. In order to do my job effectively and to weed out the crazies who just wind up wasting my time, I need full cooperation and transparency with my questions. If you won't tell me about the Polaroid's origins, I'll have to decline accepting you as a client. Even if your grandson is the Boulevard Killer, I can't work with a client who won't trust me."

"I'm not ready to divulge the specifics of the photo yet, Mr. Smith."

"Very well. It's been a pleasure meeting you, Mrs. Covington. I wish you the very best in finding someone who can help you with your claims."

"So that's it? You're not taking my case? You won't get a cold-blooded killer off the streets because I won't tell you about the Vertigo?"

"No. I'm not taking your case because you've already established you're not willing to be 100-percent honest and forthcoming with me. How could I possibly give you my full expertise and leave no stone unturned if you refuse to answer what I feel is a pretty pertinent question about this whole situation? And one that seems to be straight from a Hitchcock flick to boot?"

Eva stood from the chair and looked at Wynn. "And your partner feels the same way?" she asked Smith, while staring at Wynn.

Wynn shrugged, walked to the door, and opened it.

Eva snuffed her cigarette in Smith's ashtray and covered her thinning white hair with her hat. "Well, I see both of you have made your stance clear. If you change your mind, Mr. Smith, here's my telephone number."

"And, if *you* change *your* mind, Mrs. Covington, you have mine as well."

She huffed and headed toward the door, neglecting to ask for the Polaroid back. "Do you have any leads on the disappearance of your own wife, Mr. Smith? It seems you're a magician when you're uncovering dirt on other people's families, but, from what I've heard, you can't seem to home in on your wife's absence."

Smith glared at Wynn. She understood her cue to get the old bitch out of the office as fast as possible.

"Thank you for your time, Mrs. Covington," Smith answered. "Trust me. I am doing everything in my power to find my wife. But that should be none of your concern, nor do I appreciate what you *think* you know about that case just because you might be upset at the outcome of our meeting."

Eva huffed and exited the office, and Wynn slammed the door behind Eva when she entered the hallway.

Wynn beaded her eyes on Smith. "Wendy's missing?"

He spun his wedding band around his ring finger, like he could start a fire with it. "I'm working on it."

"*Working* on it? Your wife has gone, what? Missing? And you're *working* on it?"

"Ex-wife."

"A *divorce* would make her an *ex-wife*. But you're too lazy to file for one, even with your so-called loss of love for her. You played me once, Smith. Played me real good, like a fiddle. Sucked me into the fantasy that you'd leave her for me. And we all know how that turned out. *I* was the one who wound up leaving. Whether you like it or not, she's still your wife—and you must find some comfort in it because you refuse to stop wearing that doggone ring of yours. Jeepers, whether *I* like it or not, she's still your wife, and I feel so pathetic saying that. But you have a duty to do right by her. You owe it to her and to yourself and, at the very least, to your twenty years of marriage."

"Wendy's not my priority. She's a grown woman who can do what she wants."

"But is she missing?"

Smith sighed and looked at his feet. "I'm figuring that out, okay? It's not for you to worry about. Wendy is my fight, not yours; regardless of what transpired between you and me in the past. What I need you for now is Eva Covington and her suspect Polaroid."

"Maybe you shouldn't have thrown her out of the office so fast. It's a shame," Wynn said, approaching the desk. "I was really hoping to hear how a motel that burned down when I was still in high school showed up in a photograph taken last week."

"Who said we aren't going to find out?"

"You think she'll cave and tell you?"

Smith tossed Eva's discarded cigarette into the trash. "Absolutely not. That old bag is guarding that secret with her life."

"Then how do you plan on finding out?"

"I'm taking the case. Mrs. Eva Covington just doesn't know it."

"What can I get you, Smith?"

"Whiskey."

"House or premium?"

"Whatever's the cheapest brown plaid you have."

"One of those nights again?"

"When Purgatory feels like home, every night is one of those nights."

"For you, sounds about right."

"Thanks for the vote of confidence, Matt."

"Hey, what are friends for?"

"Oh, so we're friends now?"

Matt laughed. "You're a snake."

Smith took a swig of the whiskey, and Matt walked away from him toward a small bachelorette party at the other end of the bar.

"I hired Wynn back."

Matt stopped in his tracks and faced Smith. "Now why would you do that? You *are* a glutton for punishment, you know that?"

Smith shrugged and finished the rest of his glass in one gulp. "Set 'em up, and I'll knock 'em down."

"Let me take care of the ladies first," Matt said and disappeared in the swarm of rowdy girls.

Smith pushed the empty glass toward the edge of the bar and removed the Polaroid from the inside breast pocket of his vest. He sighed and became distracted by the rhythmic pulsing of the neon sign advertising the lounge's name over the bottles of liquor behind the bar: RIPPETOE'S. Flash, fade, illuminate; flash, fade, illuminate—Rippetoe's—flash, fade, illuminate; flash, fade, illuminate—Rippetoe's—flash, fade, illuminate; wash, lather, rinse, repeat.

Looking down the length of the bar, Smith noticed Matt had become more entranced with socializing the group of tipsy bachelorettes than with serving a self-deprecating drunkard. Smith leaned over the bar and snatched the rolled-up newspaper Matt kept underneath the till. Smith unrolled it and scanned the front-page headlines.

He skipped the articles covering the continuing criminal activity of a local redneck biker gang and the rising popularity of Nashville southern rockabilly and stopped at a headline announcing the discovery of another dead, unidentified female. Smith shifted on the bar stool before immersing himself in the article.

"'Nother one?"

Smith jumped. "Christ, Matt. Don't do that to me!"

"Don't do what? Ask if you want another round? That's pretty much my job."

"No, sneak up on me like that."

"Must be something good for you to be distracted from the

view down the other end of the bar," Matt said, making eye contact with one of the bridesmaids. "Any news on Wendy?"

Smith looked suspiciously at Matt. "Why?"

Matt stopped wiping the bar. "I'm sorry. I didn't mean to pry. I was just curious."

Smith shook his head and fiddled with his wedding ring. "I'm sorry, man. Being a PI, I'm expected—by everybody—to solve the case of Wendy's disappearance it seems, like, yesterday. It doesn't work that way. I have a few leads, but they haven't panned out. Just because she's my ex doesn't mean I have some special, secret, detective superpower to figure out where the hell she is."

Matt tossed back his own glass of brown alcohol. "Didn't know you guys had gotten a divorce."

Smith waved him off. "Not officially, but it was coming."

"That's a shame. She's a good woman. Don't you think it's weird though? Wendy suddenly missing while all these girls are being killed? Have you been following these murders?"

"The hookers? Just what the news has been reporting. Sounds like we have our very own Jack the Ripper here."

"These are such godless days."

"I'll drink to that!" Smith said and tapped his empty glass, signaling the well was dry.

Smith watched silently as Matt filled another glass of whiskey for Smith, itching to divulge to the barkeep that he might know the killer's identity. Instead he just zoned out as the liquid splashed around the ice cubes. He wished Matt would remember that he despised ice cubes in his drinks.

"I'm thinking of expanding. Making Rippetoe's a chain."

"Oh yeah?"

"Evelyn and a friend of hers scoped out a new location for me. Might open a second location. What's new in your world?"

"I took on a new client this morning. Old broad. Knocking-on-death's-door old. Thinks she might have a tip on the killer. Says her grandson has a taste for the working girls, so she's convinced he *must* be our Ripper. Whole thing is weird. Weird enough for my radar to go up."

"Do *you* think this knucklehead might be the killer?"

"Not completely. Not yet at least. But something else is wacky. She brought a Polaroid of her grandson, get this, posing in front of the Vertigo Motel out there in Mesquite."

"The Vertigo burned down—"

"I know. Years ago. Yet it's a recent picture."

"What's there now? The . . . um," Matt snapped his fingers to help him remember.

"The Desert Palms Motel. Just as seedy as the Vertigo."

"That's right. Pay-per-hour kind of joint. A perfect place to bring vixens where no one will question—"

"Hey, chucklehead! You gonna get me another drink?" a man in the corner yelled across the lounge.

Smith whispered to the barkeep, "Get a load of that guy." Then took a long swig of his drink.

"That drip isn't worth my time. He's all high on cocaine and vitamins."

Smith laughed midswallow and snorted whiskey through his nostrils. "Don't do that! Damn stuff hurts coming out my nose."

"I guess I should go serve the master," Matt said, chuckling. "I'll be back. You have any requests? I'm gonna fire up the jukebox."

Smith swiveled on his stool and looked at the back of the pub. "You got ol' Loella fixed?"

"Nah. Way too expensive. I picked up this one refurbished from some bar called Sneakers. They were going under and selling all their stuff dirt cheap."

"How about something weddinglike? You know, for the girls down there? Isn't Sinatra's 'My Love for You' a staple at every wedding?"

Matt laughed. "So cliché, I love it. I'll see what I can do."

Smith threw back another gulp of whiskey and shivered as it burned his throat. He slammed the glass on the counter a little louder than he expected, garnishing a few looks from the bridesmaids.

"It's all right, ladies. Ol' Blue Eyes coming up. To get you in the mood," he said and belched loudly.

The bachelorettes ignored Smith's outburst, and a few of them leaned in to each other to whisper and giggle when the bride-to-be took her foam penis tiara and jerked it up and down in between her cleavage.

"Bimbos," Smith muttered.

"All right. So the Desert Palms Motel is where the Vertigo used to be," Matt said, returning to Smith's end of the bar. "And it's a hotspot for girls turning tricks."

Smith used his finger to scan line by line the article about the latest victim. "Right here. She was found less than one-quarter mile from the Desert Palms. Says she was buried, and a custodian found her."

"Either this is one elaborate ruse to mess with you or something heavy is happening in the desert."

Smith slid off the stool. "I'm gonna head downtown. They police themselves down there, and they trust me."

Matt wiped the residual condensation from the empty whiskey glass off the countertop. "Still, be careful, man. I'd love to hear what you find out about that photo."

Smith nodded and tossed a handful of crumpled bills onto the bar.

"Do you have it on you?" Matt asked. "The Polaroid?"

"Ah, yeah." Smith reached into his trench coat's breast pocket and removed the photograph. "Here."

Matt reluctantly took the picture from Smith, eyeing him with suspicion.

"Look right there. The sign is almost as big as he is in the photo."

Matt flipped over the Polaroid, examined the backside, then the front side again. "Are you feeling okay, Smith?"

"Yeah. To be honest, I haven't felt this intrigued by a case in, well, probably ever."

Matt let the Polaroid fall to the bar and leaned forward, using his outstretched palms as support. "This is a postcard of a Norman Rockwell painting."

"What? Give me that," Smith yelled and snatched the postcard from the bar and studied the image. "Are you insane? Look. That's my client's grandson covered in blood, and the Vertigo sign takes up almost half the picture. I don't think you're funny."

"Smith," Matt said cautiously. "Are you feeling okay? That is a postcard mailed from . . ." He ripped it from Smith's hands and flipped it over. "Maryland. It says right here, *Wish you were here. Having a swell time in Baltimore. Love, Maggie.* Who's Maggie?" Matt flipped over the postcard again. "This is a very famous Norman Rockwell painting. It's called *Walking to Church*, I believe. Evelyn took a modern art class at the community college and studied Rockwell."

"Maggie is his wife, and he's right there!" Smith retorted, pointing to the Polaroid. "What kind of chump do you take me for? And I don't appreciate being tricked like this so you can get your jollies off."

"You're pointing to one of the little boys in the painting. That's not her grandson, and there's no motel in this painting."

"And look. I don't see any writing on the back. Just the black photo-backing."

"The only Maggie *I* know is Evelyn's friend who she went future-lounge shopping with for me. And I don't think she's ever been out of Nevada in her life, never mind all the way to Baltimore. Plus her husband is some boring nightshift technician at the dam. I doubt he's the Boulevard Killer. Maybe you should take a few days off and collect yourself. I'm worried about you."

"It's not my fault you're blind," Smith huffed and tucked the Polaroid into his breast pocket. "Then how come Wynn could see it, huh? Looks like you're the only one with a problem."

"Smith, I don't know what to tell you. What you just showed me was an old postcard sent by someone's wife named Maggie, with a Norman Rockwell painting on the front. I think you should head home instead of going downtown and get some rest, clear your mind."

"I've been duped before, by hollow charlatans and fake bastards. I'm not taking the bait quite this easy this time, especially by the likes of you. Only fools believe they won't get fooled again."

Smith hastily navigated out of Rippetoe's and swung the exit door outward over the sidewalk. He didn't check if the lounge's door closed behind him or not before making his way downtown to ask about any sightings of Mr. Covington from the kind of scum Smith despised the most.

He patted the outside of his breast pocket where he had safely tucked away the Polaroid of Eva's grandson standing before the ghost of the Vertigo Motel. He removed the photograph and peeked at it, just to ensure it hadn't mysteriously transformed into a postcard. He returned it to his pocket, satisfied that Matt was the one who was hallucinating, not him.

3: Desert Grave

The woman staggered on the sidewalk and collided with the man's shoulder. "I'm sorry. You okay, mister?"

Covington patted her shoulders and nodded. "I'm fine. Are *you* okay?"

"Just a bit jiggered," she slurred.

"I can see that. Do you need help?"

The woman's eyes grew large as she looked over his shoulder. She took a step backward and raised an arm, pointing and shaking her finger.

The man chuckled and glanced behind him. "Everything okay?"

The woman turned and beelined for the street, tripping over the curb and landing face-first into a pile of leaves clogging the storm drain.

"C'mon. Let's see what fun we can get into," Covington said to the ghouls behind him.

The hordes of girls shuffled behind him as they approached the downtown area. Rows and rows of women—some with strangulation marks, some with gunshot wounds, some with fatally tilted necks—kept pace behind the man.

As they passed a run-down old brownstone, Covington haphazardly looked at the front steps and noticed a figure in the shadows, passed out with a needle dangling from the crook of his arm. He raised his hand to motion the cult to stop as he climbed the stairs two at a time. Covington reached for the needle and yanked it from the teenager's skin. He tossed it over the staircase railing and slapped the boy's cheeks. "Wake up!"

The boy stirred, cleared his throat, and tucked his hands underneath his thighs. When he opened his eyes, Covington sat down next to him and placed a hand on the boy's knee. The flock below on the sidewalk looked up, gawking at the affection.

"Get lost," the boy retorted.

"Stand up. You're coming with me."

A handful of followers below licked their lips as the man rose to his feet.

"I'm not queer."

Covington bent to eye level with the boy. "I never said you were. But you *are* a waste-of-space junkie. And you're coming with us."

The boy looked at the dozens of girls—all pale and rotting, like disfigured faces in Technicolor—staring at him with hungry eyes.

"What the hell is going on?"

"What's your name, son?"

"I ain't telling you nothin' until you tell me what's up with those crazy-looking broads."

Covington kicked a pebble off the stone stairs; it landed at the feet of the first row of girls. "Fair enough. Girls?" he said and stepped aside.

The Mushroom Cult stormed the staircase and descended upon the boy's body. Covington walked down the stairs and headed toward downtown, listening to the boy's screams fade as the gnashing teeth and clawing fingers slowly consumed him.

"Hey, baby. You lookin' for a date to the party?"

Covington glanced around to see if anyone else was watching. When he was satisfied, he took a step toward the girl standing underneath the ADULT FILM sign. She wore a man's blazer without a shirt or bra underneath. The buttoning point was open, revealing skin from her neck to her full cleavage and all the way down to below her belly button. Her shorts seemed to be only made of a few inches of fabric, elongating her legs from her thighs to the top of her obnoxiously tall high heels.

"Maybe. Depends on the party," he said and lit a cigarette.

The girl sashayed toward him, her straight blond hair rippling in the nighttime breeze, and fixed the lapel of his coat. "You by yourself tonight?"

"Just myself."

She leaned in closer, and he felt her breath on his earlobe. "Where's the missus?"

Covington spun his wedding ring around his finger. "Does it matter?"

"Not to me."

He laughed. "You got a name?"

"Maybe. Do you?"

"Maybe. You first," he said.

"Pum'kin."

He shook his head. "Right. Sure it is. And my name is Raymond Chandler."

"Who's Raymond Chandler?"

"Never mind. How much and for what?"

"You're funny. I like you. One-dollar blows, three dollars to shoot the moon. I don't usually go dog paddle, but, for you, if the price is right . . ."

"I'm sure you say that to all the guys."

She forced a laugh and placed her hand on his chest.

"Okay, Pum'kin. Lead the way."

She grabbed his hand, and they walked side by side down an alleyway. He glanced from the corner of his eye at the group of men huddled together, all trying to sleep on the same dirty, half-burned mattress. He thought he saw the bugs scurrying in and out of their long, unkempt hair. He was sure he smelled their body odor too.

"Doesn't this depress you?" Covington asked.

"Meeting guys like you makes it all worthwhile."

"Oh, hang it up. You can't possibly be happy down here."

"You're a real square. What're you, my dad?"

"Far from it. I'm here to save you."

"Oh, yeah? How are you gonna do that? You gonna tear off a piece of ass? Because I could use a good saving."

"Drop the act. You already have my business. You don't need to keep selling yourself to me."

Pum'kin didn't reply as they reached the end of the alleyway. She led him down a narrow side street lined with deteriorating apartment buildings and burned-down shacks.

"Where does your wife think you are tonight?" she asked with a hint of anger in her voice.

"What do you care?"

"None really. I just like to hear the excuses."

"My wife doesn't even know I left the house."

"Sounds like a healthy relationship if you ask—"

He grabbed her neck and forced her against a wooden fence covered in graffiti. She gurgled, catching her breath as he leaned in and licked the tip of her nose. "You want your money? Then shut up and work for it."

She nodded with urgency as he severed her air supply.

"And no more questions about my wife. Got it?"

"Uh-huh," she squeaked.

Covington released his grip and placed his hand, fingers splayed out, over her face so his middle finger rested on her forehead and his pinkie and thumb gripped her cheekbones. "Good. You're coming with me. This is my party now."

Pum'kin nodded in agreement, and he released his hand from her face.

"Everything okay, Pum'kin?" a guy asked from behind them.

"Everything's fine," she answered. "Just reviewing the terms of the job."

Covington glanced over his shoulder to see who she was talking to. The teenager from the staircase stood behind them.

"You know him?" Covington asked Pum'kin.

She took a step backward. "That's Johnny. Everyone knows Johnny."

"Johnny," Covington said, turning toward the boy. "Did you learn anything tonight?"

"Yes, sir. Everything makes sense now."

"Good, good."

"Johnny?" Pum'kin asked. "Are you okay? You're acting weird."

"I'd say Johnny's doing fine, aren't you?" Covington asked.

Johnny lowered his head in what almost looked like a bow and retreated around the corner.

Covington grabbed Pum'kin's hand and pulled her toward the end of street.

"Where are we going?" she asked with a tremor.

"My car."

They turned the corner, and he retrieved his keys from his pants pocket.

"You have a Rolls?"

He opened the passenger door for her, and she slid inside onto the leather seats.

"Who are you?" she asked. "You gotta be someone important to have a damn Rolls Royce Phantom. And what was all that futz with Johnny back there? How do you know him?"

Covington slammed her door without answering and walked

around the car to the driver's side. He shifted the vehicle into Drive, and Pum'kin reached over to rub his crotch.

"Tell me how you know Johnny, and this one's on the house."

He grabbed her wrist and flung her arm back to her side of the cab. "Not yet. All in good time."

She pouted and looked out the passenger window as the sand and palm trees that signified the border between civilization and sprawling nothingness were replaced in the span of the car's headlights with the slowly fading downtown landscape. She slapped both her thighs, like a drumbeat to some music in her head, and Covington remained silent and fidgeted with his wedding ring. He looked at her unimpressively as the car veered off the roadway, and the headlights exposed the sandy terrain. Pum'kin reached up and pressed on the headliner to keep from being tossed around the inside of the Rolls.

Covington pointed the vehicle straight ahead into the rolling dunes of the desert. When he looked in the rearview mirror and couldn't see any roadway signs behind them, he slowly eased the brake, bringing the car to a stop.

"Get out," he said, opening his door.

Pum'kin exited the Rolls; the car's headlights formed two perfect beams of light, illuminating the vastness in front of them and hiding the nothingness surrounding them. They entered the shadows at the back of the car, and Covington opened the trunk.

"Nice bumper sign," she said. "*Shit Happens?*"

Covington didn't give any indication she had spoken and removed a small bin with a cover from the trunk. He tossed it to the sand and unbuckled his belt.

"What's in the box?" Pum'kin asked.

Covington didn't reply; he sat on the closed bin and reached into his pants. "C'mon and earn your dollar."

Pum'kin smiled and swayed her hips exaggeratedly as she approached him. "Is that all I'm good for out here? I was hoping you'd order the deluxe package tonight."

Covington nodded and pointed to the sand in front of his feet. She kneeled and gripped him with both hands. He closed his eyes and placed one hand on the back of her head as he felt himself slide into her mouth. His fingers gently massaged her hair as she made sure he got his money's worth. He convulsed, bent forward, and shivered as he finished inside her mouth.

She wiped her lips and stood up. "That was fast."

He grunted instead of replying and reached into the vehicle's trunk.

"So what are we gonna do now?" she asked.

He gripped the shovel with both hands and spun around with as much force as he could, striking her across the cheek and nose. Pum'kin crumpled to the sand in an unconscious heap. He tossed the shovel beside her and opened the bin, reaching for a warm soda pop.

"Girls, you can come out."

Appearing from behind a lone palm tree, scores of followers materialized.

"What would you like to do with her?" the cult's queen asked as she stepped forward, studying Pum'kin's bloodied face.

"I'm going to bury her."

"May the girls play with her while you dig?"

He nodded in affirmation and grabbed the shovel. Dozens of gray ghoulish hands grabbed Pum'kin's ankles and legs as the flock swarmed the body. Covington inserted the tip of the shovel into the sand, placed his right boot onto the long edge, and drove the metal into the ground. The sun broke over the horizon, and beads of sweat formed on the man's forehead as the temperature climbed by the minute.

"Would you like some help?" Anya asked mockingly, alluding to the lines of moisture now falling from Covington's forehead.

"Sure, but I'll keep the shovel."

"Girls!" Anya commanded.

The group of tattered and bedraggled followers fell to their knees and frantically dug a hole, huffing and puffing like a pack of dogs excavating a bone. Covington continued to shovel heaps of sand from the hole; his efforts combined with the girls' accelerated the process. He glanced at Pum'kin's unconscious body and noticed pieces of her blazer had been torn and discarded.

"Hey! Careful with her. She's not dead yet!"

The disciples who had been ravishing Pum'kin stopped and looked at the man.

"I'm burying this whore alive, so please don't damage her any more than she already is."

A few girls whimpered and whined in protest.

"Fine. If she wakes up before I finish the hole, you can have your way with her."

Excited chatter emanated from the ghouls as they resumed fondling and squeezing Pum'kin's body.

"But once the hole's finished, playtime belongs to the vultures."

The sun had already climbed high into the sky well before the hole had been complete. Sweat soaked Covington's clothes, and, no matter how many times he wiped his eyes, the salt continued to sting. Satisfied with the depth of the hole, he jammed the shovel into the mound of sand beside it.

"Hey!" he yelled at the herd of disciples milling around the hole and still groping Pum'kin's body. "Come gather around, Mushroom Cult. It's almost time to induct another member."

The cult all faced him in unity.

Covington outstretched his arms and tilted his head, as if he were hanging on a crucifix. "Hear my words! Believe my message! You were all impure yourselves at one point in time and had lost your way before I found you. But I have saved you! Are you saved now?"

Murmurs of agreement not resembling actual words echoed through the ranks of the Mushroom Cult.

"All of you had slipped. All of your moral compasses needed to be recalibrated. All of you were sinners and adulterers, offenders to the sanctity of society. Until I found you—and cleansed you and made you pure again."

Anya placed a scarred hand on Covington's chest to signal him to stop talking and stepped forward. "It'll be my honor to accept tonight's offering as one of our own, to cleanse her, to make her pure again. She will walk with us forever."

A low rumbling of applause wafted from the flock.

"Now let's reward her with a baptism—a rebirth. Into the sand she shall go, a sinner and infidel, and she'll emerge purified."

The Mushroom Cult's applause grew steadily to a raucous cheer.

"She'll become your fellow sister! You're gaining a sibling tonight, reborn from the desert sand!" Anya added.

The excited hollering grew steadily.

"Eat, for this is my body," Anya chanted in monotone with her eyes closed, swaying side to side, as if the Devil himself possessed her. "Raise your glass and toast, for this is my blood. I am the pathway. Follow me downward into the void. I am the face of your fear. Salvation lives only through me."

The response was deafening. Anya knew her disciples were now ready to unbiasedly accept Pum'kin into their ranks. Covington lowered his arms and removed the shovel from the pile of sand.

"Please, if you would, place her in the birthing grave."

A dozen followers squealed in delight and grabbed Pum'kin's limbs and lifted her. The man wiped the sweat from his brow and shook his undershirt to fan cool air over his chest. His noticed none of Anya's girls had a drop of sweat anywhere on their bodies; they never had any reaction to the climate.

"Toss the impure body into the hole and help her reemerge lily-white, like all of you!"

One of the tenured cult members he remembered picking up as a hitchhiker, who had offered a hand job as payment for the ride many years ago, lost her grip on Pum'kin's wrist as they lifted her, and Pum'kin's balance of weight shifted to the ground. Pum'kin hit the ground hard and jolted awake. Her eyes sprung open in panic, and she leaped to her feet.

"Grab her!" Covington yelled as he lunged forward.

Pum'kin turned and ran, her high heels flailing spurts of sand into the air. Covington barged through the sea of followers, knocking some of them to the ground as he reached the fleeing whore. He grabbed her wrist and arm-barred her to the desert ground. She thrashed and struck him in the face as Anya swooped in like a tornado and bit Pum'kin's forearm, tearing a chunk of flesh off the bone. Anya and Covington kept their prey pinned long enough for the flock to swarm her body again.

Covington stood up, wiping a small smear of blood from his lip. "Get her to the hole! Bitch."

Pum'kin writhed and squirmed as the Mushroom Cult lifted her and carried her toward the awaiting grave. She forcibly yanked one arm from their grip, and her shoulder hit the sand with a *woomph!* She spun her body, using the ground as leverage, and snatched her other limbs free. Frantically getting to her feet, she shoved the followers backward as they encircled her like unified zombies. Covington clutched her wrist and spun her arm around her back, pinning her hand to the nape of her neck. Pum'kin cried in pain as he eased her to her knees.

"*Tsk, tsk*, young lady. Why the fight? Embrace your destiny."

He gently assisted her, facedown, into the sand and drove his knee into the back of her neck. She spit and blew bursts of air to clear a path so she could breathe through the sand.

"Nikki, today it's your turn to quarterback. Call the vultures!" he commanded. "This bitch has defied us long enough."

A follower, with matted brown hair and cracked spectacles, stepped from the herd and shuffled into a clearing. She cupped her hands over her mouth and released a series of short bursts of guttural noises into the sky. She rocked back and forth, directing her call to multiple spots upward. Nikki stopped after a few moments and pushed the top of her ear forward to listen closer. She nodded excitedly and pointed skyward.

"Are they coming?" he yelled.

Nikki jumped up and down, clapping.

"Oh, you bitch," he said to Pum'kin, touching his newly swollen lip. "The vultures are coming for you, and, when you return to us, you'll be mine forever."

"Go to Hell," Pum'kin retorted as loose sand slid into her mouth and nostrils.

Nikki retreated to the flock for safety as the morning sunlight darkened. Every member of the Mushroom Cult fell to their knees, bent at the waist, and lodged their faces into the sand. The ceremony was always more menacing when the lamb was still alive and kicking. They covered their ears as the sound of flapping wings became thunderous, and the sky blackened with diving vultures. Nikki whimpered in fright and scrunched her arms against her sides for added protection.

Covington flung himself off Pum'kin's neck to give the vultures a clear target. She felt him release and took advantage of her freedom by springing to her feet. She turned to run toward the roadway, but the first wave of vultures struck her behind her knees, causing her to bend backward and fall to the sand. In their second attack, the vultures used their beaks and talons to slice her shoulders and belly.

Pum'kin grabbed her stomach in pain and fell forward to use the ground as protection from any more injury. The final wave of vultures scooped her up midfall and carried her into the sky.

Covington glanced at Nikki and saw her stick her fingers into her ears to muffle the sounds of the screams that were about to follow. He chuckled, thinking about how many times the veteran disciples had witnessed a ritual similar to this.

Pum'kin screamed as a dozen vultures played keep-away with

her in the air, all taking turns pecking and stabbing her torso's soft flesh. Their beaks became jackhammers, picking and ripping her sides as they tossed her back and forth like a rag doll between their grasps. A large chunk of flesh fell to the sand, and her intestines peeked from the open wound on her side.

"Okay! That's enough," he commanded the flock. "Put her in."

The vultures congregated in a regimented formation, with Pum'kin screaming and draped across their wings like on a bed, and nose-dived toward the desert grave below. Within feet of hitting the discarded sand pile, the vultures banked sharply, dumping Pum'kin into the hole. She tumbled, her limbs flopping like a marionette, and blood from the open gash in her side permeated the brown sand.

"Cover her up," he yelled.

The followers moved like carpenter ants toward the sand pile. When the first row reached the pile, they pushed the sand into the hole; an avalanche of desert fell over the screaming whore below. Rows upon rows of the Mushroom Cult struck the sand pile, each contributing and sending more and more sand into the hole. The further Pum'kin fought against the incoming flood, the harder it became for her to move as the sand filled in all the empty spaces around her body.

She scrambled to free herself, but the vultures landed around the rim of the hole and pecked the top of her head, keeping her at bay as the followers finished burying her. Underneath the burning sun, the Mushroom Cult patted the last handful of sand; the hole now nonexistent.

Two vultures walked across the smoothed sand and stopped in the middle of the now-covered hole, their talons creating tracks on the perfectly placed desert ground.

"Can you still hear her?" the man whispered to the birds.

One vulture cocked its head, listening. Then it flapped its wing and took flight.

"I think she's ready to be reborn," Anya announced to her disciples.

A low gurgle of a cheer erupted from the rows of entities circling the tomb.

"Nikki, would you like to do the honors?" Covington asked.

Nikki stepped from the ranks and shuffled to the grave.

Anya placed a hand on Nikki's chest to stop her and leaned in to her ear. "Bring another child to our coven. You can do it."

Nikki's lips fluttered in what Covington thought would be a smile but then returned to the familiar lifeless droop which donned all their faces.

"Go get her, girl."

Nikki screeched and flung herself on top of the grave, digging with her fingers.

"Well, don't just stand there! Help her dig," he said, stroking his neatly trimmed brown mustache.

The herd moved forward, methodically falling to their knees and digging. Covington sat down and removed his shirt. He used the garment to wipe the sweat from the back of his neck and the cowlick constantly plaguing the front of his hairline.

"How're you doing?" he asked a few moments later.

Nikki grunted and pointed at the sand.

He stood and looked over the kneeling herd. "Stop!"

The followers stopped digging and looked at him. Covington walked to where Nikki had been digging. Four erect fingers were exposed through the sand.

"Nikki, test those."

Nikki stood and called for the vultures. Black wings swooped downward and landed in front of her. She grunted unintelligibly at them, but they nodded in understanding and waddled toward the hand sticking out of the sand. The first bird pecked Pum'kin's middle finger, driving its beak like a spear. It swiveled its head to look at Nikki. She nodded, satisfied with the results, and raised her hands with her palms facing skyward. The vultures fluttered and landed in a circle around Pum'kin's exposed hand, blocking its view from the rest of the onlookers. They squawked in excitement and urgency as sand and loose feathers fountained from the center of their circle.

Covington approached the vultures and peered over their black heads bobbing up and down with fervor. "Almost there. She's almost ready."

His voice had distracted one vulture, and it glanced backward for only a moment before returning to its task. The birds vigorously flapped their wings, fanning the loose sand and exposing Pum'kin's lifeless body. Nikki stepped through the circle of birds, causing them to stop excavating and to waddle backward. She kneeled next to Pum'kin and force-lifted her closed eyelids, exposing her pupils to the high-noon sun.

"You sure you'll be okay?" Covington asked.

Nikki grunted and smiled.

"Down you go, my child," Anya commanded.

Nikki lay next to Pum'kin and shimmied her body back and forth to get comfortable in the hot sand. She interlaced her fingers and rested her hands on her chest.

Anya kneeled next to Nikki's ear and whispered, "I'm so very proud of you. You're truly proving your worth to our mission." She clasped Nikki's folded hands. "And death will bloom like a garden around you. And you'll be that much closer to salvation."

Nikki smiled and closed her eyes. Covington and Anya walked away from the grave with the Mushroom Cult marching behind them in perfect rows of cadence. Only one set of footprints, matching the same ones marking their arrival to the area, was visible in the sand as Anya and her coven slowly disappeared one by one.

By the time he had reached his Rolls and headed toward civilization, the sun had already begun to lie down, to die over the dunes in the distance. Night was about to fall on the desert grave as a lifeless whore and a catatonic ghoul kissed the daylight goodbye.

4: Down the Rabbit Hole

"Smith!"

The detective couldn't decide if the knocking came from the other side of the door or from the pulsing inside his head.

"Smith!"

"It's unlocked."

His office door swung open, and Wynn entered, maneuvering around the empty bottles of booze littering the floor. He lifted his head from the stack of newspapers he had used as a pillow and wiped some residual vomit from his lower lip.

"Jeepers creepers, what happened?" she asked as she helped him to a sitting position.

"I went to Rippetoe's last night and had a few drinks."

"Looks like you had more than a few."

"Seriously. I only had a few. I left the lounge to head downtown to talk to some people."

"Well, what did you find out?"

"I . . . I don't remember. I don't even remember making it there."

Wynn collected the empty bottles and tossed them in the trash can. "You *must* have been drunk."

Smith placed his hand over his forehead to relieve some of the pressure and sighed. "I really don't know what happened." He made a smacking noise with his tongue. "Huh. I think I'm bleeding."

Wynn stopped cleaning. "Where?"

"There's blood in my mouth," he answered and stood up.

"Let me see."

Smith opened his mouth, and Wynn folded back his lips to get a better view of his gum line.

"I don't see any cuts or anything. Go rinse your mouth. I'm sure it's nothing."

Smith filled a paper cup from the mini bathroom's sink and swished the water inside his mouth.

"Any news on Wendy?" Wynn called from behind his desk.

Smith spit the water into the sink. "Nothing yet. She probably took off to Hollywood with some pipe dream of being a famous star."

"You don't sound like you're too concerned about her."

Smith exited the bathroom. "Our lives were clearly not on the same path anymore. You, of all people, should know that."

"Do I ever," she mumbled, then said louder, "I feel like I somehow became the victim of your fall out with Wendy."

Smith located an almost-empty bottle of scotch from the floor and, with the rim pressed against his lips, threw back his head, allowing the few remaining drops to enter his mouth. When he lowered the bottle, he noticed Wynn standing rigid and staring at him accusingly.

"You duped me into believing I meant more to you than your wife. You're the one who put these affairs in motion, Smith. By cheating on your wife with me!"

"The hell I did!" he said and threw the bottle against the top of his desk. "Who do you think you are, assuming it was me first?"

Wynn took a step backward. "You're right. I'm sorry. I just thought, with what had happened between us . . . I assumed she had found out about us when you fired me out of the blue that morning. I didn't mean—"

"Lying bitch cheated on *me* first. She's probably gallivanting around somewhere, hopefully far away, with her new play-toy knucklehead. Change the subject, Wynn. All this yelling is not helping my headache."

"So, if you don't remember going downtown, then you must've come here. Right?" she asked, on to another topic.

"Yeah. I mean, I must've. I don't remember exactly."

"Do you think you were drugged?"

"At Rippetoe's? Unlikely. But when I showed Matt the picture of the Vertigo Motel, something strange happened."

"Do you think that's smart? Showing people something we can't figure out yet?"

"He couldn't see the picture. He said it wasn't a photograph of anyone in front of the Vertigo. All he saw was a postcard with some Rockwell painting on it. Between that and blacking out, maybe I *do* need a vacation. Now I understand why other dicks have stopped working on the case. Mrs. Covington's under the impression I didn't take the case anyway, so no harm, no foul." Smith took the Polaroid from his pocket, crumpled it in his fist, and tossed it in the wastebasket.

Wynn shook her head. "Thank you for reminding me why I was happy when you let me go last time. Some things never change. *You* never change."

Smith opened a desk drawer and rummaged through some old hanging files. He found the unopened bottle of scotch behind the folders and headed for the door. "Maybe I made a mistake calling you back to work. Nobody deserves to deal with me on a daily basis."

Wynn crossed the room with lightning speed, slammed the door, and stripped his hand of the bottle. "Sit down," she ordered, pointing to his desk chair.

He smirked. "God, you're sexy when you take charge."

"Jeepers creepers, just go sit down," she said, slapping his hand from reaching for her blouse. "You gotta control your urges."

"Oh, if you only knew the movies that play out in my head."

"Just, sit," she said as she retrieved the crumpled Polaroid from the trash.

Smith pulled out his chair and plopped down, running his hands through his hair.

"See, it's fine," she concurred. "No Rockwell postcard. There's Maggie's husband, still smiling like an idiot in front of the Vertigo. I don't know what kind of sick trick Matt was playing on you, but I don't appreciate it, and it's inappropriate. I have a good mind to pay him a visit tonight so we can have words."

"Just let it be. I'm sure it was supposed to be a harmless jest."

"At your expense! Has this happened before? This . . . blackout? Or whatever you want to call it. Is this the first time you don't remember an entire night?"

"I think so. Well, at least the nights I know I'm not sauced."

Wynn folded her arms. "Let's go downtown now."

"Now? None of those scumbags will be awake. It'll be pointless."

She smoothed out the photograph on the desk and handed it to him. "We need to get to work on what's in this picture, and coming up with excuses about the time of day is a pretty amateur start to figuring this out."

Smith chuckled. "I hate when you're right. All right, doll, you win this time." He placed a cigarette between his lips. "Let's get this over with. I always feel like I need a shower after visiting downtown."

"Decent people live there too, you know."

"The Devil you say. They're low-down, dirty snakes. All of them. The whole place deserves to go up in flames. Cleanse the area of filth. Maggots."

"You're always a ray of sunshine, Smith. It's a pleasure to be back."

Smith slipped a small flask full of brownish liquid into his inner trench coat pocket. "You can go to Hell too."

Wynn held the door open for him. "You need me too much. Plus I think you secretly like me telling you what to do. A wise man once told me, 'Life's just a ride.' And I'm just along for the ride, baby. And your demons will quiet once you learn to take that advice."

Smith plopped his fedora over his brown hair and shut off the office lights. "Oh yeah? And who was this so-called *wise* man?"

Wynn placed her hands on her hips. "You, you idiot."

"Huh. I must've been drunk."

She playfully punched him in the arm. "You're such a wet rag. C'mon. Let's go visit some of your friends."

"You do realize I hate you," he answered as he stuffed his keys into his pants pocket.

"Yeah, yeah. You hate everything you can't drink. You know? The cure for clinical depression is a lobotomy."

Smith took a swig from his flask and grimaced. "Harsh but, with my recent outlook on humanity, probably true. Life's no longer a mystery to me."

"Such an optimist. Did you bring the picture of the Vertigo?"

"Got it right here," he said and removed it from his back pocket.

"Let me see it again."

They exited the tall industrial building that housed numerous small business and some satellite corporate offices. Smith shielded his eyes from the piercing sunlight and grunted.

"Welcome to the world of the living," Wynn said, taking the Polaroid.

"*Gawd!* How do you people stand the shininess of it all?"

"Stop being so melodramatic. You used to love to lounge around in the sun, getting all tan and whatnot. I remember."

"That was a different time. A different me."

Wynn slapped the photograph against her thigh as they turned up Fremont Street toward the downtown boulevard. "I really wish I had known you when you were still working for the sheriff."

"That part of me doesn't exist anymore. I never could have imagined being surrounded by so many corrupt human beings in one place. I entered a new chapter in my life the day I turned in my star."

"Yeah, more like an epilogue. So, instead of chasing real bad guys, now you just hunt down cheating wives and runaway teens—" Wynn abruptly stopped walking.

"You okay?" Smith asked and tossed back another gulp of liquor from the flask.

She handed him the Polaroid. "Look."

Smith snatched the photograph from her hand. "What am I looking at?"

"The Vertigo! It's not in the picture anymore."

Smith and Wynn entered the busy offices of the *Henderson Gazette* and headed straight for the back of the large open area. Smith dragged Wynn behind him, maneuvering around the plethora of reporters and interns bustling back and forth from their desks to the copywriters' or editors' rooms. Wynn's hip clipped the corner of a desk with such force that she jarred off center the typewriter the reporter clacked away on.

"Sorry," she whispered as she continued to be whisked through the rows of desks.

"Keep up," Smith spat, ignoring her collision with the reporter's desk.

"Stop pulling me so hard. You're hurting my wrist."

Smith released her hand and bounded through a doorway into an office surrounded by glass walls. The man behind the desk stood up and greeted them with a smile that touched his earlobes.

"Smith! Wynn! It's so good to see the dream team back together."

"We need to talk," Smith said.

"Sure," the head reporter said and approached the door to his office and closed it. "You guys haven't gotten yourselves into any kind of trouble again, have you?"

"I don't think so. At least not that we know of yet."

"Sounds intense," the reporter said, his rattlesnake cowboy boots echoing through the office with each step he took back to his desk. "But you've always been an intense kind of guy. Haven't you, love?"

"Hank, I'm not in the mood right now. We didn't know who else to go to with this."

Hank raised his shoulders to his delicate jawline and giggled. "*Ooooo*, flattered, as always."

Smith removed the Polaroid from his back pocket and handed it to Hank. "Tell me. What do you see?"

Hank picked up the item with his perfectly manicured hands and pursed his lips so tightly in concentration that the natural-red tint dissolved into a pale pink. He flipped over the picture and then looked at Wynn, raising one eyebrow in confusion. Letting the photograph fall to his desk, he placed his hands on the hips of his snug-fit jeans. "Tell me, Smith, what do *you* see? Is this some kind of wacky riddle? Because I don't want to get it wrong. You know I hate being wrong," he said, using his palm to smooth his meticulously gelled and combed bouffant.

"C'mon, Hank. Can you just tell us what you see?" Wynn interjected. "This is serious."

"Fine, fine," Hank answered, rapidly tapping the toe of his cowboy boot under his desk. "It's a postcard from some needy hussy, who obviously went on vacation in Baltimore. God knows why anyone would *choose* to voluntarily visit that cesspool. I wouldn't be caught dead there."

Smith glanced at Wynn and uncomfortably shifted his weight on his feet.

"Was that not the right answer? Oh, God, I just *hate* when I'm wrong."

"Hank, what do you see on the other side of the postcard?" Wynn asked.

The reporter flipped over the cardboard rectangle. "It looks like some propaganda realism, probably by some hoity-toity ar-*teest*."

"I've been told it's called *Walking to Church* by Norman Rockwell. But the problem is, that's not what Wynn and I see. What you're holding—what we *see* you holding—is a Polaroid of my client's grandson, covered in blood, standing in front of the Vertigo Motel."

Hank scrunched his brows together and flipped the postcard over and over, as if needing a magic number of times to manhandle it before the postcard's artwork morphed into the photograph. "I'm not following."

Smith updated Hank with what had transpired over the last thirty-six hours and what little they knew about the details.

"We were heading downtown," Wynn said, "to ask some of the locals if Smith had been there last night, since he can't remember anything from the blackout. Plus, when we looked at the picture again after his blackout, the Vertigo was missing."

"Blackout, huh? You gotta lay off the sauce, love."

Smith and Wynn exchanged a glance, and Smith decided not to elaborate on the blackouts just yet. Not discussing them was the easiest way for him to pretend they didn't exist or to pretend they weren't getting worse.

"Let me get this straight," Hank continued after the silence in the room became uncomfortable. "I'm looking at a postcard, but, when you guys look at it, you see a picture of a man standing in front of a motel that burned down ten years ago?"

"We *used* to see a picture of a man standing in front of the Vertigo. Now it's just a bloodied man standing in the desert. The motel behind him has been mysteriously erased."

Hank sashayed to his office door, opened it, and yelled, "Dougie, come here for a moment."

A large man with a red beard stood up from behind a desk and entered Hank's office.

"Humor us for a moment. Can you tell me what you think this is?" Hank asked, handing Doug the postcard.

"It's a Norman Rockwell painting."

"Thanks, Dougie. That'll be all, love." After Doug returned to his desk, Hank turned to Smith and Wynn. "Are you sure you guys aren't doing any drugs? Because if you are, I want some."

A young reporter stuck her head into Hank's office and knocked on the already-open glass door. "Mr. Steel, your appointment is here."

"Thank you. Tell them I'll be right there." Hank turned to Smith and Wynn, handing them the postcard. "I have a meeting. I hope you guys aren't conspiring to pull one over on ol' Hank. I'm too pretty to be messed with. Keep me in the loop, yes?" He giggled and placed his hand over his mouth. "How captivating!"

"Will do," Smith said, straightening his red tie and readjusting his revolver in the shoulder holster.

"Great. Until next time: toodles!" Hank said and kissed Smith and Wynn on their cheeks before exiting his office.

They could hear the *clarp-clarp-clarp* of his cowboy boots long after he had disappeared from their sight.

"Hank hasn't changed, huh?" Wynn asked as they drove past the Golden Mirage Casino.

"Hank will never change. He proved he was the only one I could trust when all that brouhaha went down with the sheriff's office. He was the only one who stood behind me and didn't try to backstab me. He didn't let the county officials' corruption compromise his integrity to do the right thing."

Smith's black 1937 Chevrolet bumped and rattled along the

potholes and divots in the roadway. He pulled the vehicle to the curb and parked in front of a sidewalk parcel box. When Wynn closed the passenger door, the window slid down slightly and jammed.

"When are you getting rid of this jalopy?"

Smith patted the faded paint of the Chevy's roof. "I happen to like this jalopy. She's given me ten good years."

"So what's your plan? To ask around if anyone has seen Maggie's husband? It's pretty apparent we can't show them the Polaroid for obvious reasons."

Smith walked around the front of the Chevy and stepped onto the sidewalk. "I can't imagine we're the *only* two people who can see the photograph. Odds tell me that the more people we show it to, eventually someone *has* to see what we see."

"Yeah, or lock us up in the looney bin."

Smith put his arm around Wynn's waist and guided her down Las Vegas Strip toward the alleyways.

"I really doubt anyone who can help us will be out in broad daylight," Wynn protested, now backtracking on her earlier statement after surveying the sordid state of the downtown area.

"You'd be surprised. I know some *charming* areas."

"I'm sure you do."

They turned right, between two monolithic buildings, down an alleyway so narrow that the sunlight didn't penetrate past the first few yards. As they passed a large trash receptacle, Smith punched its side. A cat squawked inside from fright and jumped out, scampering deeper into the shadows.

"What was that for?" Wynn asked.

"Never know where they'll be sleeping."

"Where *who* will be sleeping?"

"*Them*. Any of them."

"You do know that they are people too?"

"Doll, when you've been doing this as long as me, you'll realize that these *things* down here are not like real people but dirty, low-life garbage."

"Hey, Smith," a female called from farther down the alleyway.

Wynn and Smith stopped walking as two figures approached them. Smith stuck his hand inside his trench coat and gripped the handle of his revolver.

"You find out anything else about that cat you're looking for?" the female asked.

"Who?" Smith asked, relaxing his hold on his firearm.

"Last night you were down here, crazy to find some job's husband. Asking everyone if we'd seen him."

"What time was that?" Smith asked, stealing a glance at Wynn.

"I dunno, man. You were gettin' all frosted with us though. Screaming how worthless we are."

"Sounds like you," Wynn whispered.

The female's companion chuckled and wrung his hands together. "You were actin' strung out, man."

"Lola, can you get your hypodermic boyfriend under control, please?" Smith said.

"Hey, detective, private eye, sir. I don't mean anything by it." The man took a step closer and smoothed Smith's lapel. "Don't flip your wig. We're all friends here."

Smith took an exaggerated step backward and vigorously wiped the spot on his coat where he had been touched, as if the man's hand had caused a spontaneous infestation of filth. Then he removed a handkerchief from his trench coat pocket to clean his fingers. "Don't ever touch me again."

The man raised his hands into the air, like he was surrendering. "C'mon. Let's get out of here," he said to Lola.

"Wait," Smith said, only addressing Lola. "Did I say anything else?"

"You weren't like yourself, that's for sure. Kept going on about some postcard."

"Did I show anyone the Pola—um, postcard?"

"No. You said you couldn't find it. You looked like a clown, all in a panic searching your pockets. You were a trip."

Smith put his hand in his pocket to feel the Polaroid. "Did I ever find it?"

"I dunno. Business picked up, and it was time to go to work."

"Have you seen anyone here lately you don't recognize?"

"C'mon, baby. Strangers make up half my business, and repeat customers make up the other half," Lola said.

"Aren't you scared, with the recent murders?" Wynn asked.

"I don't remember this job ever being safe, sugar lips," Lola replied.

"So, I was down here, acting weird, looking for a postcard. How long did I stay?" Smith asked.

"Like I said, business picked up, so I was back and forth quite a lot last night. Plus it wasn't my turn to babysit you. Although you know? I could get into taking care of you, the right way, if you ever wanna take this for a ride. I'll even give you the Lola Special—half off."

"Let's go," Smith said to Wynn. "Lola, as always, it's been a pleasure."

"Don't be a stranger," the man said and burped.

Smith and Wynn sidestepped around Lola and her friend and continued deeper into the alley. After passing a handful of entrances, they stopped in front of a brightly painted red door. Smith knocked and took a step backward.

"Who lives here?" Wynn asked.

"Someone I've known for a long time."

"You have a friend down *here*?"

"I didn't say he was a friend. I said I've known him for a long time."

The door swung open, and a man with hair resembling a cotton ball stood in the archway. He wore a black suit and black patent-leather shoes. The red undershirt looked like crimson goo had emerged from the depths of a black hole.

"Smith, I get to see your ugly mug twice in the same day?

What've I done to deserve this privilege?" the man asked, extending a hand.

Smith looked at the man's hand in disgust and refused to shake it. "I gotta ask you about last night, H."

Horvat wiped his hand on his pants, shrugging off how Smith had blatantly ignored his attempt at a friendly handshake. It made him look like a chump in front of the fresh meat Smith had on his arm.

"Come in. Come in," Horvat said and moved aside. His gaze followed Wynn's bottom as she passed him in the doorjamb. "*Woo-wee*. I bet that's an ass that just doesn't quit! You gonna pimp her out, Smith? That what you're really doing on my turf?"

In one fluid motion, Smith unholstered his revolver and pressed the muzzle firmly against Horvat's forehead.

Wynn grabbed Smith's forearm. "Is that really necessary? I'm a big girl. I can handle myself. Put it away."

Smith didn't move for a few moments. Horvat stayed motionless with both hands in the air, like he was being robbed. Finally Smith exhaled loudly and secured the weapon under his coat.

"Simmer down, hotshot," Horvat said and grabbed the lapels of his red undershirt and fluffed his clothes, as if everything was copasetic.

"Apologize."

"Oh, I don't think that's necessary," Wynn said to Smith.

"I don't care what you think right now. I care about my man here showing you some respect."

"This is ridiculous," Wynn said. "Mr. H? Nice to meet you. I'm Smith's assistant. We're trying to find out what Smith did or may have said last night while he was downtown. He's having a bout of short-term memory loss."

Smith shot her a disapproving look.

"Yeah, man. You were hanging on Lola's corner. Thought maybe you were finally giving in to temptation. But you were acting all crazy. You left right around the same time a john picked up one of my newer girls. In fact, she hasn't come back yet."

"The recent rash of dead prostitutes doesn't concern you?" Wynn asked.

"What do you want them to do? Have a buddy system? Lady, as soon as I lose one, another dame is always in line lookin' for steady work."

"So you have a missing girl right now?" Smith asked to confirm what he had heard.

"I'm sure Pum'kin is fine. She'll probably be on her corner tonight."

"My client's grandson seems to have a taste for the girls. And she's convinced he's the one snuffing out your employees—"

"What? You think you're tracking the Boulevard Killer? C'mon, man. Even when we patrolled together, coincidences didn't just fall into our laps like that. How many cases did we have that were *that* easy to solve? Zero. Your client is probably just looking for some fame and attention, trying to weasel her mug onto the front cover of the *Gazette* or something. Taking you for a chump!"

Smith could see Wynn glaring at him. "We do know that he's married."

"Well, there ya go! How could a married man have that many opportunities to snatch hookers, in the dead of night, off the streets, without a nagging wife becoming suspicious?" Horvat questioned, further driving his point home.

"Depends on what he does for work," Wynn interjected.

"I never asked what he did," Smith muttered. "If we knew where he worked, we could stake him out there and get a better idea if a pattern correlates with the days he works and the days he has off. Then we might lock down some semblance of a timetable when he'll strike next."

"Well, call the old lady back. That sounds like the most logical solution."

"I told her that I wasn't taking the case. She wouldn't play along with my rules."

"He won't call her," Wynn added, rolling her eyes. "Pride."

"Oh, I know that side of Smith better than anyone."

"Birth certificates," Wynn blurted out.

Smith shot her a quizzical look.

"If he has any kids, his occupation will be listed on their birth certificates. How many Covingtons do you think live in the city? It's the first time *I've* ever heard that name. I can't image it'd be like sifting through files and files of someone with the last name of, well, Smith, for instance."

Horvat chuckled and tried to wave off exploding into full-blown hysterics.

Smith snapped his fingers and pointed at her. "Bingo!"

"You've lost your step, Smith," Horvat interjected. "That would've been one of my first courses of action. Instead of running around downtown like a chicken with its head cut off. I never thought I'd see the day when you weren't the one being all forward-thinking."

Smith rubbed his forehead. "I can't believe I didn't think of that already."

"You're getting old. You're slipping."

"Piss off," Smith replied and grabbed Wynn's hand. "I hope your girl shows up for work tonight."

"I'm sure you do. Here. Let me show you out," Horvat said in mock sarcasm.

The red door slammed shut behind them when they entered the alleyway.

"He used to be a deputy?" Wynn asked.

"He was my partner for almost five years. He realized that sometimes crime *does* pay, quit the department, and set up shop out here. Probably makes more money than I'll ever see. I was hoping he might have had his thumb on some kind of pulse that could help us, but, for him, it's just business as usual. Even with the rash of girls getting killed."

They returned to the Chevy, and Smith opened the passenger door for her.

"And who says chivalry is dying?" Wynn said. "I always knew you were a gentleman."

"You tell anyone, and I'll kill you," Smith replied, laughing.

They pulled away from the curb and merged with the midday traffic. The Chevy was bumper to bumper with Buicks, Bentleys, Fords, and Packards.

"How difficult do you think it'll be to get someone to let us scour through the birth certificates?"

"Depends on who's working the desk," Smith answered. "This might be one of the few times where being associated with the sheriff works in my favor."

"And we have to cross our fingers that Mr. Covington even *has* children."

Smith veered the Chevy down a side street toward Las Vegas City Hall.

Smith steered the vehicle into a parking spot near city hall's entrance. They passed the mayor's office, unoccupied, as they walked down the long marble corridor on the way to the city clerk's desk.

"Not surprising," Smith said, motioning to the dark office. "He's probably too hungover to come to work again. What a waste of space. No wonder this city went down the toilet. You know what they say. The fish rots from the head back."

"Mr. Smith!"

"Good afternoon, Margo. It's always a pleasure to see you."

"What brings you here?"

Smith propped his body weight against the city clerk's desk, plopped his fedora on the top, and turned on the charm. "You know I miss seeing you. I thought I heard it was your birthday this week. What're you this year, twenty-nine?"

Margo blushed and lightly patted the gray hair behind her ears.

"I told them that I don't believe it. Margo can't be twenty-nine! She doesn't look a day over twenty-four."

She giggled. "Oh, you! I bet you say that to all the girls."

"Only the pretty ones," he replied and *boop*ed her in the chin with his index finger.

"Isn't he just terrible?" Margo asked Wynn, with a huge smile spread across her face.

"Yep. He's the worst."

"Enough with the foreplay," Smith said. "I was hoping, my dearest Margo, if there is any way we could look at some birth certificates."

"Oh, I don't know, Mr. Smith. Those are, you know"—she nervously rubbed the back of her neck—"confidential. You'd need a power of attorney or court order to see any of those."

Smith leaned in closer. "No one has to know. I won't tell if you don't."

"Well, um . . . er . . . is it at least for a case?"

"It is."

"A good case?"

"What's your definition of good?"

"Are you investigating someone bad?"

"Oh, very bad, Margo. The worst."

She leaned across her desk. "How bad?"

Smith looked left and right, exaggerating the secrecy of what he was about to say. "Let's say, downtown-killer bad."

Margo flung backward and clasped a hand over her mouth. "Really?" she squeaked.

"I wouldn't lie to you. And you'd be doing this fine city of ours a great service if you'd let us take a quick peek at the birth certificates. Might even be the final clue we need to catch the monster."

"Jeez," Margo said, her gaze flitting back and forth between

Smith and Wynn. "You really think you're that close to catching him?"

Wynn, following Smith's lead, shrugged her shoulders, as if to say, *Anything is possible, if you let us see those certificates.*

"What a monster, preying on those girls."

"You're right, Margo. What a monster," Smith repeated, winking at Wynn.

"Mayor Freeman isn't in today. He had some personal issues to deal with."

"Yeah, I'm sure," Smith retorted sarcastically and rolled his eyes at Wynn.

"So I think it's safe for the rest of the day," Margo finished and placed a BE BACK IN 15 MINUTES placard on her desk. "Follow me."

Smith gave Wynn the pistol sign with his thumb and index finger before falling in behind Margo. The three of them wove down a metal spiral staircase into the bowels of city hall. After turning on the overhead lights of the hallway, she removed a set of keys from her pocket and unlocked a door.

"They are all filed by the father's surname. The boxes are alphabetical. Do you know the name you're looking for?"

"Covington," Smith answered.

"*C . . . C . . . C . . .*" Margo repeated as she ran her finger along the outside of the cardboard boxes. "Ah! Here we go."

She yanked a box from the shelf and placed it on the long folding table situated in the center of the room. She removed the cover and flipped through the files. "Covington . . ." She removed two rectangular pieces of paper and held them up. "These are the only two with that last name. Rose and Raymond."

"Yes. That'd be them," Wynn replied, noticing Maggie's name as the mother. "It *is* common practice for the fathers to list their occupation on their children's birth certificates, right?"

Margo handed the certificates to Smith. "Nevada state law requires that field to have *something* printed in it before the birth certificate can be notarized. Dads use that block as a badge of honor to brag about whatever posh job they have when their kids are born. Especially children born during the Depression. Even shady characters will write *Businessman*, and some unemployed fathers will write *Entrepreneur* in that spot—you know, to save face."

"How long have you worked here, Margo?" Wynn asked, making small talk to settle the city clerk's nerves. Wynn thought Margo looked on edge, like they would all be caught with their hands in the cookie jar.

"Oh, dear. Almost thirty years."

"I'm sure you've seen some pretty crazy occupations listed before."

"Yes, dearie," Margo answered and placed a motherly hand on Wynn's forearm. "One gentleman tried to convince us that his occupation was *Martian*, because he believed he had come from the red planet."

Smith cleared his throat as a signal for Wynn to stop the chitchat. "Does anyone know what a *hydroelectric power technician* is? That's what's listed."

"Golly, no," Margo answered. "I'm pretty astonished this was even filed in this manner. Mayor Freeman notarizes all these himself, and he's pretty diligent with making the fathers use the most basic occupation titles as possible. Preferably one word. I can't even question him about it because there's no good reason why I should've been looking through these files in the first place."

"Well, Margo, you're a peach," Smith said, jotting down Covington's occupation title in his handy-dandy sleuth notepad. Then to Wynn he said, "And we wouldn't want to get you in trouble with Freeman the Drunk, would we?"

"Of course not."

"And even though the answer seems to just add another layer of mystery to this supposed killer, I believe you've shed *some* light on the investigation. You know I always appreciate your time."

Margo replaced the lid on the box, slid the box onto the shelf marked *B – D*, and escorted them from the room.

"I owe you a lunch," he said. "You still fancy Monks' Seafood, right?"

"Oh, you!" she said and playfully punched him in the arm. "You don't owe me anything."

"I remember. You like the scallops plate with onion rings. Every good deed, Margo, every good deed. I'll bring you some Monks' next week."

"What a catch he is, huh?" Margo asked, looking at Wynn. "Too bad Wendy never recognized it."

"Okay, Margo. That's enough now," Smith said, retrieving his fedora from the desk and flipping it end over end numerous times on his fingertips before landing it square on top of his head.

"I think he was too much man for her, and that's why she left," Margo whispered.

"It was a pleasure to meet you," Wynn said, derailing the personal banter when she noticed Smith shifting back and forth uncomfortably.

As she followed him from city hall to his Chevy, Wynn teased, "Margo has a sweet spot for you."

"And I'll exploit that all day long if it'll help us solve this—" Smith pressed both hands to the sides of his head and grunted loudly, leaning forward over the steering wheel.

"Smith? What's going on?" Wynn asked frantically as she placed a hand on his shoulder.

He waved her off and clasped his eyelids shut, waiting for the pain to dissipate. He rubbed his temples with his fingers and slowly leaned back in his seat. "I'm okay. It felt like someone driving a spear through my head. It came out of nowhere."

She rubbed his back. "Are you sure you're okay? You want me to drive?"

"Nah, it's going away," he answered as he pressed his thumb into his temple to alleviate some of the pressure. "Plus I wanna see if Hank is available to talk now."

Smith navigated the Chevy into the city traffic and headed toward the *Henderson Gazette* headquarters.

Smith and Wynn almost collided with Hank as they entered the newspaper's vestibule.

"Perfect timing, guys," Hank said. "You're coming with me."

"What's going on?" Smith asked as they turned and followed Hank down the front steps.

"They found a high heel in the desert," he answered, opening the passenger door for Smith and Wynn. "They only found one shoe, but"—he closed the door and walked around the car to get in—"they found a set of footprints leading to what looks like some kind of grave."

"Did they find a body?" Smith asked from the backseat.

"Not sure yet. I think they're still digging. Your buddies have the area taped off, but I think we can get close enough to see what's going on."

"Your pimp friend told us about one of his girls not coming back," Wynn said to Smith.

"What's this?" Hank asked as he took a right onto Interstate 15 toward the desert.

"Horvat said he had a girl still unaccounted for."

"You guys went to see *him*? I'm sorry you had to endure that," Hank said to Wynn. "How was he?"

"Charming," Wynn answered.

"Who found the shoe?"

"An anonymous tip to the sheriff. Said they saw a man in a Rolls drive off the road and then appeared to have some kind of altercation with a female."

"And they didn't think to do anything to stop it?"

"I don't know. That's all we got so far. I'm sure the fuzz knows more."

Hank sped along the highway, and they could see a plethora of emergency vehicles ahead.

"All this over a single shoe?"

"Do you blame them? With the Boulevard Killer still on the loose, any oddity that could involve any kind of hooker sends the authorities into panic mode."

Hank eased the vehicle off the blacktop and onto the desert sand. He kept the car moving forward at a slow pace to maintain momentum and to not get stuck in the loose sand. "Even if this has nothing to do with the killer, I'll have Dougie tag this story with a headline linking him to it. Nothing sells papers better than injecting fear into the readers. The scarier this serial-killer degenerate appears, the more the masses will want to know about him."

"Business as usual," Smith said.

"You got it, love. It's the name of the game."

"Right over there," Wynn said. "Looks like you can get closer to the site if you park by that cactus."

Hank steered the vehicle to the right. "I didn't have a chance to ask you earlier today, and, if you don't want to talk about it you don't have to, but any updates on Wendy?"

Wynn craned her neck to look at Smith for a reaction and then focused her attention out the passenger window.

"Nah. It's like she flew the coop. I confronted her after I caught them having lunch at the Monk's Seafood and never heard from her again."

"Are you even *trying* to track her down?"

"You know, Hank, at first I did because I was more scared for her well-being than anything. But now, screw her. Good riddance, is what I say."

"Has anyone heard from her at all?"

"Her parents have called me, asking me to do my gumshoe magic to find her, but I'm at the point now where she can just go to Hell. I sleep easier at night pretending she doesn't even exist anymore."

"It's a shame. All those years wasted."

"Yeah, but now I have more time to do what I really love. Hunt down lowlifes and scumbags, and hang out with your beautiful tush in the desert heat."

"Oh, stop it!" Hank said and snorted on a giggle. "You're making me feel funny in my loins."

Wynn bit on her fist to stifle a chuckle that had escaped through her nostrils.

Smith grabbed the back of the front bench and scooted himself forward. "I think that's the same exact spot where we found another dead hooker, about ten years ago. I was a rookie on the department. She had been buried, and the investigation even leaned toward her possibly being buried alive."

"How would they know that?"

"Her fingertips were all worn down, like she had been scratching at something solid above her." Smith snapped his fingers in quick succession. "Her name was . . . um . . . Anita."

"I remember that!" Hank said. "I covered that story. And her name was Cyana, not Anita. Well, her street name was Cyana. I'm not sure we ever positively identified her. I know you guys never located a next of kin."

"Did they ever catch who did it?" Wynn asked.

"No. Well, not as of when I quit," Smith answered.

"As far as I know, they haven't," Hank added. "I just added her murder to the Boulevard Killer's repertoire in the article. You know, sells papers and all that jazz."

"Hey, there's Sheriff Wilcox. Cop scum."

"You should go say hi," Wynn joked.

"I think I might just do that," Smith said, exiting the car. "I'll see how far I can get before I'm tackled or arrested."

"I was only kidding," Wynn yelled as Smith walked toward the designated crime-scene perimeter.

"Well, phooey. Looks like we should follow him before he gets himself killed," Hank said. "And you'd think these boots would be ideal for sand."

Wynn glanced at his cowboy-style footwear and laughed. "Don't ever change, Hank."

"Never, darlin'. C'mon."

They followed behind Smith, who had accelerated his pace toward the row of patrol vehicles.

A young deputy stepped from behind the trunk of one of the black-and-whites and placed a palm on Smith's chest. "Excuse me, sir. No one is allowed past this point."

"It's okay, Olli. He's with me," Hank called, trying to catch up.

"Still, I can't let you guys through. This is a working crime scene. You know the rules, Hank. Media has to stay on the other side of the tape until given the all-clear."

Hank got between Smith and Deputy Olli, his front side rubbing against Olli's chest. "Not even for little ol' me? C'mon, love. It's me: Hanky-Panky-poo."

Smith noticed Deputy Olli swallow hard and turn white when Hank placed his hand over his crotch.

"I'll make it worth your while after you get off shift tonight. Scout's promise."

Olli slapped Hank's hand and quickly regained his composure, clearing his throat. "None of that here. The sheriff is right behind me. And, no, I can't let anyone in."

"Jesus H. Christ," Smith said and stepped sideways to get a clear view of the sheriff. "Sheriff Wilcox! Hey!"

Sheriff Wilcox glanced at Smith and stormed toward them.

"Olli, you tell that man to leave immediately, or he will be arrested . . . or worse."

"Oh, now you're threatening me? You are such a son of a bitch."

Olli stood motionless, both apprehensive and flabbergasted at how the situation had escalated this quickly.

"Deputy Olli, I am not dicking around."

"I assume you're new? Deputy Olli?" Smith asked, smoothing his red tie. "The best advice I can give you is to jump ship as quickly as possible before your soul gets sucked from your body working for that chump."

"C'mon, love. Let's beat feet," Hank said to Smith, pulling him backward.

"Is that Hank Steel?" Sheriff Wilcox yelled. "I see all the fine, upstanding marks of society are present and accounted for. That's a party I wouldn't want to miss."

"I think you guys should leave now," Olli whispered to Hank. "But call me later?"

"*Hrm.* I'll think about it. In fact, why don't you swing by my office when you get off, so we can chat about all this," Hank said, swirling his finger toward the crime scene. "And, Olli, sometimes you need to grow a pair of balls and do the right thing. Especially around tyrants like your boss."

"You're lucky I don't bring you in for questioning, Smith! Don't think I wouldn't rule you out as a prime suspect," Sheriff Wilcox yelled.

Smith kicked a mound of sand in frustration on the way back to Hank's car. "I truly despise that man."

"Looks like I'll be writing another article about another dead or missing call girl."

"And what's wrong with that?" Smith asked. "I long for a world free of these varmints. I silently applaud this man with each dead whore or pusher they find rotting out here. Lowlifes of society."

"You mean, job security," Wynn said.

"*Pah-leez*! They can have this job. I'm done with it. For real this time. As soon as we find Mr. Covington, I'm gonna hang up my fedora."

"And then what'll you do?" Hank asked.

"Retire. Buy a little cottage on a lake somewhere and maybe write the great American crime novel."

"I'll believe that when I see it. Did you guys find out anything more today about your new case?"

"We went to city hall to pull his children's birth certificates so we could get a good lead on his occupation," Wynn answered as they reached the car.

"Oh yeah? And what's he do?"

"Some kind of technician of power thingamabobs or something," Smith answered. "Hold on. I have it written down."

Hank stopped and looked at them over the roof of his car, raising one eyebrow. "Well, now that's just something to tickle our thinking caps. Was Margo working today?

"She's the one who helped us. It's a hydroelectric power technician," he said, reading from his notepad.

"Had she ever heard of it before?"

"She was bewildered as well. Said she couldn't help any further because she was doing us a favor that could get her fired in the first place."

"Sounds like something to do with the dam. Get in."

"It's just another oddball cog in this wheel, like the Polaroid no one can see but me and Wynn."

"You mean the postcard," Hank said, laughing.

"Tomato, *toe-mahto*. Polaroid, postcard," Wynn said.

"She's funny, Smith. Don't let her get away again. She's a keeper."

Smith reached into his back pocket and retrieved the photograph. The car jumped and jostled as Hank merged onto the empty highway, and the Polaroid fell from Smith's hands. He reached down and picked it up from the floorboard.

"You okay back there?" Hank asked.

Smith didn't answer. His gaze was locked on the picture, his mouth unable to obey any instruction his brain sent.

"Smith?" Wynn asked, turning around from the front bench. "What's wrong?"

He handed her the Polaroid. She gasped and clasped her hand over her mouth.

"What? What?" Hank asked, peeking at the postcard while keeping the vehicle in its lane.

"Mr. Covington is completely missing. All that's left in the photo now is the desert."

"Show me."

Wynn held up the picture so Hank could see it.

"You guys are killing me. It's still just a postcard."

"It's not just a postcard. It never was *just* a postcard," Smith exploded from the backseat. "It's a Polaroid of the Vertigo Motel and Eva's grandson standing in front of it. Now, somehow, over the past day and a half, the motel and our target have vanished from the picture. Like they were erased, leaving just the desert sand and the horizon in the photo."

Hank spun the steering wheel with such force that Wynn and Smith were thrown against the car's passenger side as he made the U-turn.

"What're you doing?"

"We're going to the Desert Palms, love. That's what was built there after the Vertigo burned down. Before your collective hallucination of this so-called Polaroid disappears, maybe we should see if there are any clues in whatever picture you think you see."

Hank mashed the gas pedal, and they accelerated past the crime scene visible in the distant horizon.

After an hour of traveling at the vehicle's top speed, the Desert

Palms Motel came into view. Finding a spot in the parking lot, Hank shut off the car.

"Hold up the postcard and try to find the exact spot where your client took the picture," Hank said after they had exited the vehicle.

Smith held the Polaroid straight out in front of him, moving it around while walking sideways like a crab.

"Hold it up a little higher," Wynn suggested from behind him. "Almost. Not perfect, but we're close."

Hank kicked a broken piece of concrete across the parking lot with his snakeskin boots.

"A few small steps to the left again," Wynn instructed. "Stop! Right there. Look. It's perfect."

Smith bounced his gaze from the Polaroid to the landscape in front of him. Back and forth. Back and forth. The photograph appeared more like a window into the past now, held up against the backdrop of where it had been taken.

"So what do you see, love?" Hank asked.

"The terrain hasn't changed at all. The Vertigo was slightly smaller than the Desert Palms. Wynn, can we maybe find where Covington had been standing in the photo?"

"It was about . . . here," she said, moving into position in front of Smith.

"Okay," Hank said, "so you've simulated the photo, but using a different building and a different person. Does anything look, I dunno, cluelike?"

Smith looked from the photo to Wynn, from the photo to Wynn, from the photo to—

"Sonofabitch," Smith blurted out.

"What? What!" Wynn said, looking all around her.

"Was that Rolls here when we arrived?"

Wynn spun around and looked toward the entrance of the motel. A black Rolls Royce Phantom was parked between her and the front doors.

"I don't want to jump to conclusions, but I don't remember seeing it when we pulled in. And I think one of us would have noticed an automobile like that in a place like this," she said.

"Smith, I told you the anonymous tip to the sheriff stated they saw the girl get into an argument with someone in a Rolls."

"You think that's the Boulevard Killer's car?" Wynn asked.

"Stay here," Smith said, handing her the Polaroid.

He approached the car, scanning the area for signs of anyone watching. He touched the driver-side door handle and pulled. The door released from the frame and swung open. He bent down and leaned inside the car, looking at the front floorboard.

"Sand," he whispered. "And lots of it."

Smith closed the car door and headed for the motel lobby. He could hear the sound of Hank's cowboy boots grow louder as the reporter trotted to catch up. Smith jogged through the front entrance and made a beeline for the reception desk.

"May I help you, sir?"

"Yes. I was wondering if the owner of the Rolls Royce outside is a customer here."

"I'm sorry. We can't release information on our guests."

"You just answered my question. Thank you."

Wynn and Hank entered the lobby.

"Whoever it is, stays here," Smith said.

"What do you want to do?"

"I don't wanna talk in here," Smith said, giving the receptionist a cold stare.

They exited the motel and followed Smith to Hank's car. He opened the passenger door and slid into the backseat.

"I need to sit on that car, but I don't want to do it in your car. If it moves, I need to follow it. Hank, can you take Wynn back to my place so she can drive the Chevy out here? I'll stay here and keep an eye on it."

"Aye-aye, Captain," Hank said and saluted.

Smith tossed Wynn his keys. "I'll be over there at that picnic table. Try to make it snappy. I don't want it leaving without any way to tail it."

He watched Hank's car leave the parking lot and enter Interstate 15. He sat at the wooden picnic table adjacent to the building and removed his fedora. He could feel a small semblance of another headache manifesting behind his eyes as he rubbed his temples to keep it at bay.

Then pain consumed him, like a Houdini punch right in the gut, and dark spots invaded his peripheral vision. The world spun as he panicked, feeling his consciousness sink like stones in a river.

Smith came to, swaying in place on a sidewalk while pedestrians ignored him as they bustled past. He blinked a few times to clear the cobwebs from his head and realized his fingers were in a ball, clutching what felt like crumpled pieces of paper. He slowly opened his hand, and two photographs automatically unwrinkled, making small popping sounds as they reverted to their natural and original states. The first image stared at him: a woman, standing on a street corner underneath what must have been a neon sign—the pink glow from behind her illuminated the top of her blond hair and an obnoxiously large white bow. He thought, *Such a large bow looks absurd on such a petite girl,* and then realized someone had taken the photo from inside his car because the top of his Chevy's door panel was visible in the bottom of the picture. The second picture was of the same woman, naked and standing on a bed, blowing the photographer a kiss.

He crumpled the photos, grunted, tossed them into the street, and fell backward.

"Smith? Holy mackerel, Smith! Are you okay?" Hank scooped his hands underneath Smith's armpits and propped him against the

Henderson Gazette building. "We looked *everywhere* for you last night."

Smith stared lazily at Hank. "Huh? What happened?"

"Wynn and I spent all night trying to find you. When we got back to the motel, you were gone. And so was the Rolls. We searched the entire surrounding desert. Then we went to your house. Then we checked your office. Wynn hasn't slept yet. She's downtown right now, looking for you."

"I don't . . . I don't know how I got here. Where . . . where am I anyway?" Smith asked, looking upward at the building.

"You're at the newspaper. I have to head in to work. C'mon. I'll help you inside. You can rest in my office."

Smith struggled to his feet and tried to whet his palate with saliva. "My mouth is so dry. I think I had another blackout."

Hank helped him climb the front steps. "Are you hurt anywhere, love?"

"I don't think so."

"Have these been happening frequently?"

"Lately, yes. Oh, damn. My hat. Where's my hat?" Smith frantically looked back at the sidewalk for his fedora.

"Don't worry about that now. If we can't find it, you can always buy a new one."

Smith reached into his trench coat. "At least my gun's still here."

Hank escorted him to the back office.

"Hey, Mr. Steel," Doug yelled. "I got some woman named Wynn on the line for you."

"Tell her that I found Detective Smith, and she should come here as soon as possible."

Smith crawled onto Hank's black vinyl couch, laid his arm across his forehead, and moaned.

"Can I get you anything?"

"Water would be fantastic. I was holding photographs. Ones I took apparently. But have no recollection," Smith slurred. "A lady

. . . a whore. Standing on a corner downtown. Naked on a bed, blowing . . . was it, *me* a kiss?"

"Hold that thought. I want to hear everything. Let me get you some water first. You look like a ragamuffin."

When Hank returned with a paper cup filled with water, Smith was fast asleep on the reporter's couch. Hank placed the drink on the small side table next to the couch and touched Smith's forehead to check for a fever.

Satisfied that Smith was not running hot, Hank left Smith sleeping and approached Doug's desk. "When Wynn arrives, tell her to go ahead into my office to take care of Detective Smith. I have to follow up with a deputy about that high heel they found yesterday."

"Sure thing, boss."

Hank left the *Henderson Gazette* building and headed toward Deputy Olli's apartment complex to get some answers on the mysterious lone high heel.

"You sure you want the gory details?" Olli asked Hank, handing him a freshly brewed cup of jasmine tea.

"I'm a journalist. The gore is what excites me, love."

"Her body was all . . . pecked."

Hank choked on his tea. "*Pecked*? As in, like a bird?"

"Sheriff Wilcox doesn't know. Or at least won't tell me."

"No offense, but it's probably the latter. Your beauty doesn't match your brains."

"What does that mean?"

"Exactly," Hank replied, laughing. "Go on, love."

Olli walked around his living room couch, sat down, and crossed his legs. "She had chunks taken from her flesh. Like something was hungry."

Hank sat next to him and placed his hand on Olli's thigh. "Do they think it's another Boulevard Killer victim?"

"It looks that way unless something glaring about her death leads them to think otherwise. I heard the sheriff tell a detective that they're logging her into the same case file."

"Any idea who she is?"

"Prostitute. I'm sure all we'll get from anyone downtown is her street name—*if* anyone downtown will talk to us at all."

"Smith can get them to talk, love."

"What do you even see in that wretched man?" Olli asked and sipped the tea, furiously waving his hand in front of his open mouth to stop the sudden burning.

"Transparency. Honesty. Someone whose ship is one crest away from falling off the edge of the earth. And I think he's one of the only men I've ever met who tries to do the right thing, no matter the consequence."

"He seems so sad and angry all the time."

"Well, his wife's been missing for a bit now. And I'm sure he's frustrated that his livelihood relies on finding *other* people's loved ones when he can't even seem to find his own wife."

"I had no idea. Has he reported it yet?" Olli asked.

"You really think Smith, who was strong-armed out of the force and left to lick his wounds, would actually go to the law? He'd probably rather *not* find her than crawl back to the department— the department *you* work for—and ask for help with something he couldn't figure out himself."

"We're not *all* bad."

"No, no you're not," Hank replied and leaned in to give Olli a peck on the lips.

"What about his sidekick? His lady friend?"

"Wynn? I don't know too much about her personal life. Sweet as apple pie though. She used to work for him, and they had a falling out, and now they've reconciled. Or something like that. I haven't gotten the whole story of what happened yet. I'll have to ask . . ." Hank fell silent, staring into his teacup and swirling around the liquid.

"There's something else," Olli pried. "Something else bothering you."

"Huh? No. It's just these killings."

Olli dipped his tea bag up and down and studied Hank from the corner of his eye. "Liar."

"Beg your pardon?"

"You're lying to me. Hank Steel is a big fat liar!"

"Am not," he retorted and went in to tickle Olli's side.

"Don't. I'm serious, Hank. What else is it? I can tell by the crow's feet around your eyes. They tell me more than your mouth is ever willing to."

"I think Smith is having some kind of psychotic episode. I know it's unhealthy to indulge him, but that's what I've been doing. And I think he's influencing Wynn too."

"I don't follow."

"He's convinced he has a Polaroid, given to him by the Boulevard Killer's grandmother, of the killer standing in front of the Vertigo Motel."

"That's that new instant-picture camera, right?"

"Right. Keep up, love."

"I'm trying. Technology is just so *fast* nowadays. What's so odd about the Vertigo?"

"You really are adorable sometimes. The Vertigo burned down ten years ago. Were there such things as Polaroids ten years ago?"

Olli pursed his lips and took a sip of tea. "I guess . . . no?"

"Is that a statement or a question?"

"No," Olli said definitively.

"But here's the play. I can't see the Polaroid. When I look at it, it's just a postcard with a Norman Rockwell painting."

"Wait. What the hell do you mean?" Olli asked, readjusting himself and sitting upright on the couch.

"I don't know if it's some sort of stress-related hallucination or—"

"Something supernatural!"

Hank closed his eyes and shook his head in disappointment. "Just when I thought your brain was matching your brawn. No, love. I don't believe in the supernatural or witchcraft or ghouls or things that go bump in the night. I think he's slowly falling off sanity's deep end and taking Wynn with him."

Olli stayed silent, contemplating the more realistic explanation. "How long have you known Smith?"

"Since he was a rookie at the sheriff's department. I was an intern at the *Gazette*, and he was the only deputy who cared about me when I wanted to report that I had been assaulted. Not only did he not care that I was queer but I always felt he cared about catching the perps more *because* I was queer."

"So, under all that gruffness, Smith's a good guy."

"The best. I trust him to always do the right thing," Hank confirmed and used the heel of his right foot to peel off his snakeskin cowboy boot from his left foot and curled his toes until the knuckles cracked. "Enough about the mysteries of Clark County. Tonight I just want to fall down the rabbit hole with you."

Olli snuggled up to Hank. "Sounds perfect. But, Hank?"

"*Hrm?*"

"I know he seems to have your undivided devotion, but, for the record, I don't trust him."

Hank chuckled. "Everyone's entitled to their opinion."

"Thank you."

"Even if their opinion is wrong."

"He's in there," Doug said, directing Wynn to Hank's office.

"What in the hell?" she said, cupping Smith's head in her hands.

He grumbled something unintelligible as he woke up.

"Another blackout?"

Smith lovingly grabbed her forearm and pulled her down to him. Opening his eyes and focusing on her delicate features, he placed his other hand behind her neck and brought his lips to hers. This time she didn't recoil. Wynn closed her eyes and let his lips graze hers; his tongue lightly flicked the inside of her open mouth. She groaned and placed a hand on his chest, pushing deeper into his kiss.

Smith pulled back slowly and opened his eyes. Both his mouth and his eyes were smiling. "I swear you're the only good thing sometimes in this rotting world."

She sighed and leaned in for a hug, placing her cheek on his as he squeezed her. "What do you remember this time?"

"Nothing. When I came to, I was here, outside the *Gazette*. I have no idea where I've been, what I've done, or how long I've been out. I'm lucky I didn't get run over or mugged."

"I think you need to get evaluated. By a professional. A doctor. At a real hospital."

"I've said it before, and I'll say it a million more times if I have to. Hospitals are for two types of people—the dying and the birthing. And I'm certainly not dying."

"That you know of," she retorted. "Have you been drinking again?"

"No."

"I doubt that."

Smith scooched into a sitting position. "Why are you acting like Wendy? So what if I drank last night, this morning, tonight? I've earned that right."

Wynn pushed herself away from him, creating an obvious distance between their bodies. "I can't do this anymore."

Smith ran his fingers through his hair. "Can't do what?"

"This. Us. Or not us. I dunno. I mean, you're still married even if Wendy *has* skedaddled. I think you're the smartest and most intuitive person I've ever known. You are brilliant at your job. But your demons control your life. They're not my demons. They are yours. And they seem to speak louder than I ever could." She stood up. "I knew coming back was a bad idea. Both professionally and . . ."

Smith gave her a few moments of silence before speaking. "And what?"

"Emotionally."

"What's that supposed to mean?"

"For being so smart, Detective, you sure are dense."

Wynn stepped out of Hank's office and stopped in the doorway. "If you can't tell by now how much I love you, then it's pointless to have to verbalize it. Hope you catch your killer."

Smith didn't breathe until she had disappeared from his sight among the rows of desks with ringing telephones and busy-bee reporters.

5: Siddhis

"Have a good weekend."

"You do the same," he answered as he stormed past the motel's reception desk.

"Oh, Mr. Covington . . ."

He slowed his pace and stopped with his hand on the door handle leading to the parking lot.

"I forgot to tell you. A man was here, asking about your Rolls."

He released the door and took a step closer to Cheryl's counter. "Oh yeah?"

"He seemed almost frantic. Like he had been looking for your automobile for a while."

Covington smirked. "Good," he whispered. Then out loud he said, "Did you tell him anything?"

"Heavens no, sir. We pride ourselves in keeping our guests' comings and goings private. You know, because of the nature of your stays."

"I appreciate that, Cheryl. I'll see you later."

"Have any plans for the weekend?" she asked, stalling the tall, handsome man from leaving.

"Going to the in-laws'. It's my boy's birthday. Might take him fishing afterward."

She licked her lips, hoping he would notice the seductive gesture. "Sounds wonderful."

"Thanks for always looking out for me," he said and pushed through the glass doors.

Cheryl rubbed her ankles together to create some friction to redirect the tingling sensation she felt all over her body as she watched him exit the motel's vestibule.

Standing next to his car, Covington rested his hand on the raised wheel well of the Rolls and closed his eyes. "You're closer than I gave you credit for. At least within such a short amount of time."

"Rose, dear, you can go into Mommy and Daddy's closet and pick a pretty bracelet, if you want to wear one today."

Rose excitedly galloped through the Covington house, her stocking feet pitter-pattering on the hardwood floors. She flipped the light switch and looked in a low drawer for the jewelry box where her mother kept the costume jewelry. When she couldn't locate it, she looked higher where her mother stored the more lavish jewelry. Scanning the other items on the shelf, Rose tilted her head in curiosity and reached for the maroon-bound book. The cover felt grainy, and the insignia engraved into the front felt metallic when she ran her fingers over the design.

"Rose? Did you find one you want?"

"Almost," she called back to her mother. "Just need one intsy-teensy sec!"

Rose opened the book—the weathered and yellow-discolored pages flopped to and fro—and flipped to the blank first page. The pages' sturdiness had long ago been manhandled out of them, and the edges were crinkled, like they had been submerged in water more than once and left to wind dry. Rose lightly clasped the top corner of the first page and lifted it, hoping the next page would have some cartoons or drawings—those were her favorite to look at.

A decrepit and decaying hand reached through the work clothes hanging in the closet and grabbed Rose's wrist. When Rose screamed, the hand yanked her in, her father's coveralls colliding with her cheek and nose. She pushed the clothes from her face with her free hand but froze when a pale face, partially visible behind a black lace veil, emerged from the darkness behind the rows of garments. Rose couldn't see any other part of the witch—for she assumed it *was* a witch because of the fairy tales her mother would read to her from all the books in her bedroom; the books with the cartoons and drawings—except the white hand and the floating face were suspended in the darkness.

"Drop the book, bitch. That's *mine!*"

"I—I—I can't. You're holding my wrist too tight," she stuttered between terrified sobs.

Anya leaned forward, and her veil touched Rose's nose. "Drop my book now."

The witch's breath reminded Rose of the fish market where her father would sometimes take her on Saturdays. He would let her pick the fish for the family's dinner that night, if she promised not to tease her brother about this carte blanche award. Disappearing into those memories soothed her enough to relax her fingers and to let the book drop to the ground.

"Rose? Do you need help finding the box?" Her mother's voice grew louder with each word—closer with each step.

"Touch my book again, wench, and I'll kill you. And you won't even see me coming." The old woman released Rose's wrist, and her dad's work clothes swayed slightly as the levitating head disappeared into the confines of the closet's shadows.

Maggie entered the bedroom. "What is taking you so long, girl? What are you *doing* in here?"

Rose turned and sprinted toward her mother—a rotting hand reached out and collected the book, sliding it into the safety of the shadows—and wrapped her arms and legs around Maggie's thighs. "There's a witch! A witch, Mommy! Hiding in your closet!"

"Oh, fiddlesticks. You know witches and monsters aren't real. I think I know a little girl who needs a break from *Hansel and Gretel.*"

Rose tried to get her sniffles under control. "No, no, Mommy. I found Daddy's purple pyramid book, and she grabbed me from behind the clothes and said she'd kill me."

"That's *enough*! I don't like to hear you say nasty things like that. Do I have to wash your mouth out with soap, young lady?"

"No, Mommy. I swear. The book is on the floor. Come look," Rose said, pulling her mother into the closet, like a tug boat hauling a freighter into harbor.

Maggie planted her weight and tapped her foot. "I don't have time for these shenanigans, Rose. See? No book! Now I'll pick out the prettiest bracelet, and you and Ray wait outside. Daddy should be home any minute, and we're leaving right away."

Rose fled from the house, impatient to tell her brother about the witch in the closet. Maggie chose a sparkling Bakelite-plastic bangle and shut off the light as she exited.

Anya huddled in the corner with the book clenched tight against her chest until she heard the front door close. Then she returned it to its shelf high above anyone's prying eyes before disappearing back into the nothingness.

The Rolls hadn't even come to a complete stop on Maggie's parents' dirt driveway before Rose and Raymond opened the vehicle's doors.

"Grandma!" Rose yelled, running toward the house.

"There are my precious buttons," the woman called from the porch.

Maggie collected a luggage bag from the trunk and headed for the house.

"What did you pack?" Covington asked. "You know we're not staying over. I have to be back at work tomorrow night."

"All of Ray's presents are in this bag."

"*All* of? How many did you get?"

"Well, I got him the electric train he's been asking for since Christmas, the erector set he saw inside Ensminger's Basement at the mall, and a model airplane."

"Can we even afford that much stuff?"

"You're the one who told me that you're definitely getting a bonus this summer," she replied as the bag slipped from her grasp and collided with the dirt.

"Yeah, but things can change. Just because I told you that I was getting one doesn't mean something won't happen between now and then. The dam could decide to cut the bonuses from the budget. You are spending money we don't have yet."

"You're right, but I just wanted this birthday to be special. He's been shortchanged on every birthday so far, and I guess I let guilt get the better of me."

Maggie's father stepped from the porch steps and reached out to assist with the bag. "Here, let me help you with that."

"Hiya, Dad," she said and kissed her father on the cheek.

"Glad to see you guys. We've missed the wee ones. Mom keeps saying we need to spend more time with them." He extended his free hand to Mr. Covington. "Nice to see you."

"Nice to see you too, sir. Thank you for hosting Ray's party."

"Our pleasure. It'll be nice to have the babies here for the day."

"Where did the kids go?" Maggie asked, stepping into the house.

"Oh, they've already targeted Grandma . . . *and* her chocolate chip cookies," he whispered, like it was some dirty secret.

"And birthday cake," Maggie's mother said, entering the room. "Come. I have tea and coffee brewing."

They followed Grandma into the kitchen where the two children were already covered in gooey chocolate chip cookie dough.

"Isn't Grandma the best?" Maggie asked her children.

"The bestest best!" Rose answered. Melted chocolate created strings, connecting her upper teeth to her lower row as she talked. "They tastes so sweet!"

Maggie's father turned to Mr. Covington. "How's work?"

"Still there."

"Heard the dam is having some issues and might be shutting down for a while."

Maggie shot her husband a quick accusing glare. Then she furrowed her eyebrows in confusion.

"I haven't heard anything about that," Covington replied, more to answer his wife's silent inquiry than to answer his father-in-law's question.

"Well, the end of the war certainly has guaranteed job security for the factories now making more than just tools and machinery parts. You ever think about considering factory work?"

"With all due respect, I enjoy working at the Hoover Dam. I'm proud to be a technician there."

"*Aah*, that's right—the *Hoover* Dam now. I don't know if I'll ever get used to calling it anything but the Boulder Dam. Well, I heard the Lechner factory is excelling in producing gun barrels and catapult tubes for aircraft carriers. Might be an automatic pay increase, and you'd be part of a good cause, something that matters—assuring the country remains safe from another evil empire regime."

Covington was borderline insulted by his father-in-law's implication that making war machinery—mundane hooey was how he thought of it—in a factory was more important than monitoring a colossal construct that prevents floods, regulates irrigation, and provides hydroelectric power.

"The war changed everything for the best, don'chya think?"

"Something like that," Covington muttered.

Maggie steered her husband from the conversation before the two men could escalate a political conversation into fisticuffs and ruin Raymond's birthday weekend. She wouldn't let that happen. Not this time. Not again.

"Wow, RayRay! You gots a *traaaaaiiin!*" Rose said, reaching for the box.

"You can build two different tracks," Maggie said, adding to the excitement.

Raymond squealed and jumped to his feet. "Can I build it now, Mommy?"

"Don't you want to open your other gifts, champ?"

"There's *more*, Daddy?"

"There sure is."

Maggie gave her husband's hand a loving thanks-for-understanding squeeze before removing the next wrapped gift from the luggage bag. After all three presents had been revealed, and the children were happily indulging in harmonizing play, the four adults sat at the kitchen table with coffee and tea. The dirty plates, covered in half-eaten birthday cake and smeared frosting, sat stacked in the sink.

Covington took a sip of coffee and put down his mug. "Excuse me. I need to use the lavatory."

"Do you want a refill?" Maggie's mother asked, reaching for the percolator.

"No thank you, ma'am," he answered as he stood, pushed in his chair, and headed for the bathroom.

After relieving himself, he collected water from the sink into his cupped hands. When he had pooled enough water, he splashed it on his face and stretched his cheeks downward with his fingertips. He looked into the mirror; a pale graying figure stood behind him.

"Hot nuts!" he squeaked and clutched his chest. "You scared the bejesus out of me. You can't do that to me, Anya."

She placed a decayed and pallid hand on his shoulder. He made eye contact with her reflection in the mirror instead of turning to face her.

"I heard you tell Maggie that you work tomorrow night," she said. "That you had to be back home in time. I hope you weren't talking about the dam, and, by *work*, you really meant—"

"I really wish you wouldn't eavesdrop."

"Oh, sir. We *all* do it. Not just me. Pum'kin is the most interested in what you have to say, being a new cult bantling and all. I'm just the only one who's always suspicious about what you tell people when it comes to the mission."

"Makes me glad they're not all like you."

"Me too. You know what they say, *too many chiefs and not enough Indians*."

"Is that what happened to your husband?" he spat. "Did you off him? Too many chiefs and not enough—"

Anya grabbed Covington by the collar of his shirt; the ever-present black veil covering her pale face flailed outward with the inertia of her sudden movement. Her eyes turned from gray to red. "You little shit. I know this is a love/hate relationship between us, but don't you *ever* talk about him again. He died because I couldn't get to him in time. I was too weak to free myself from their grasps as he burned. I had to watch him *burn*. Have you ever had to watch a loved one burn to death for something they didn't do? For lies? For everyone else's ignorance? He's the only one I've ever loved, and I make sure every dark shadow and blemish I cast on your pathetic version of society are always carried out in his name. The vile and despicable shall never stop feeling my wrath. Monsters and hypocrites are disguised as salvageable knuckleheads. All just pathetic, little sheep-children following the herd. Somedays I have a hard time stomaching the necessity of partnering with the likes of mere mortals; your kind haven't always been the ideal consorts. I shouldn't have to handle you with kid gloves or boss you around, but sometimes I feel like if I don't, you'd be good for nothing. Plus all the offerings you bring me are all so damn *stupid*," the pale widow added. "Why can't we collect the . . . somewhat bright ones?"

He slapped her hand off his shirt. "Because if they had any sense at all, they wouldn't be out there staining the very fabric of society, would they? Smart people don't drain and feed off the public's morals and well-being. So I'm sorry your servants, the cult I'm helping to build for *you*, aren't all rocket scientists and highly learned. We are cleansing. We are exorcising. We are doing society a service. And, in turn, you get your ghouls, or whatever you're collecting. This tandem agreement of ours"—he waved his index finger quickly back and forth between their chests—"is a perfect symbiosis for cleaning up the streets."

Anya grabbed his waving finger. "He'll see the postcard soon, you know? The picture is fading, one item at a time. We're running out of time, and you're *here*, playing Daddy."

Covington pinched the bottom of her veil and attempted to lift it off her face.

She smacked his hand and growled like wolf. "You touch that again, and I'll bite off your hand and feed it to the vultures." Then she smiled to show him her perfectly squared teeth, like a double row of dice, to send the message of how much it would hurt without any sharp points.

Covington turned as the doorknob jiggled, and then someone knocked on the bathroom door.

Rose's muffled voice wafted from the other side of the door. "Daddy? I gots to go pee!"

"Okay, Rose. I'm coming out," he answered, glaring at Anya as a cue to leave.

"Don't fail me, or I'll have to find someone else who's more well-suited for the job."

"Don't worry, Anya. We're a good team. You'll get your girls. And I'll get satisfaction that I'm making this world a cleaner place for my kids."

"DADDY! I'm going to pee right *here!*"

"Okay, sweet pea. I'm coming."

He opened the door, and his daughter barreled past him toward the toilet.

"Who were you talking to?"

"Nobody, sweetie."

He almost added, *I was talking to myself,* but decided against it. He wasn't so sure what kind of demon he spoke to anymore.

6: Private Eye

Smith spit out another peanut shell onto his Chevy's floorboard as his gaze stayed trained on the Desert Palms Motel's front entrance. His fingers instinctively found the opened bag in the complete darkness and pinched another nut. He squeezed his eyes closed to ward off the simmering residual headache from the most recent blackout. The sound of the rain pelting the windshield was soothing.

"Come on. Where are you? You took the last two nights off. I can't imagine you being on vacation."

Headlights turning into the parking lot diverted his attention from the motel's front door. He squinted to decipher the make and model of the vehicle through the downpour. A Bentley. He sighed and returned his focus to the motel as he fingered the brim of his newly purchased replacement fedora and then tossed it next to him in frustration.

Smith removed his revolver from his shoulder holster and checked that all six chambers were loaded for the umpteenth time. He secured the weapon and grabbed the small notebook from underneath his discarded fedora, lying on the passenger seat, where Wynn should be sitting. But she had maintained radio silence throughout the past two days since storming from Hank's office. He shook his head in disgust for letting Wynn's drama distract him from the job at hand.

He swiped the Chevy's dashboard with his palm to clean off the thick layer of dust that had collected from months of neglect. He wiped his hands on his pants, leaving a graying smear across the fabric covering his thighs. He reached into his trench coat's inner pocket and removed a silver flask. He opened the top and looked at the engraved insignia on the front. His index finger traced the shining eyeball hanging freely in the cut-out middle of a pyramid. Taking a swig from the decorated flask, he grimaced as the brown liquid hit the back of his throat.

Smith retrieved the Polaroid from the dashboard and cleared his throat. "Let's see what tricks you're playing on me now." He flicked the corner of the photograph as he sighed deeply in expected disappointment.

The picture had dissolved half of the desert sand and one-fourth of the sky into a white smear. He thought to himself how it appeared like the images on the photo were slowly evaporating—eroding almost—into nothingness, leaving no signs that an image of Eva's grandson or the Vertigo had existed at all on the photo. And now the sand and sky were following suit and going by the wayside as well.

Smith took another swig from the flask but didn't stop when the alcohol hit his tongue. He closed his eyes and kept them shut until the whiskey's flow slowed to only a drip from the flask's mouth, like a leaky faucet. He tossed the empty container onto the passenger floorboard and watched two giggling teenage girls exit from the backseat of the Bentley. A man dressed in a business suit closed their door and quickly escorted them into the Desert Palms to get out of the rain, his hands pressing firmly on their lower backs as they entered the motel. *Double the fun for that guy tonight*, Smith thought.

Smith reached to the left side of his waistline and let his fingers dance along his belt until he found the chain to his pocket watch. Trying not to take his focus off the motel's parking lot for too long, he stole a quick glance at the time—11:11 p.m.

Even though it was still on the early side of night for the Boulevard Killer, Smith thought it felt really late. Later than his watch said, at least. Maybe it was the diverging headache; maybe it was the alcohol; maybe it was . . . Wynn.

Thunder boomed overhead.

Smith arched his back over the front bench of the Chevy and strained to reach the attaché case in the backseat. His fingers wrapped around the handle, and he dragged the briefcase into the front seat with him. He unsnapped the latches and opened the cover, grinning when he saw he hadn't drank this bottle yet. He unscrewed the bottle of scotch and flung his head back. Flask be damned. Tonight called for something more than a slow trickle from a tiny canteen. Tonight the gods demanded the floodgates be opened and the liquid be poured freely.

Another pair of headlights. A Rolls Royce Phantom.

Scotch dribbled from Smith's mouth as he pulled the glass from his lips. He wiped his chin and replaced the cap on the bottle. He remained motionless—only his gaze trailed the vehicle as it slowly approached his camouflaged Chevy. He slumped in the bench when the headlights illuminated his front bumper. When the Rolls had passed, he scrambled for his Kodak and fumbled with the camera, knocking the cap off the bottle of scotch. The alcohol spilled on the floorboard with the *glug-glug-glug* of a stopper being pulled in a sink full of water. He cursed as he uprighted the bottle to save more alcohol from escaping while not dropping his recently purchased Kodak 35 in the expanding pool beneath his feet.

The Rolls stopped between two parking spots around the near corner of the front of the motel. Smith brought the Kodak to his right eye and observed the vehicle through the camera lens. The buckets of rain coating the windshield made it difficult to see, so Smith removed his face from the camera's eyepiece and tried to get a better look at his subject. Even just being on the outskirts of the lamppost's splashes of light, Smith could unequivocally tell this man matched the one from the disappearing Polaroid. Smith brought the Kodak back in line with his eye and noticed an unknown female accompanied the man. He pushed the shutter release.

SNAP!

The man walked around the front of the Rolls and touched the passenger door handle. The rain let up and turned to a slow drizzle.

SNAP!

The man reached into the vehicle's cabin and offered a splayed hand, as if they had just arrived at a red-carpet event.

SNAP!

The man guided the female from the passenger seat. Smith could make out her short flapperlike dress, red lipstick, and messy cropped hair.

SNAP!

Smith watched them embrace through the camera's eye before—

SNAP! SNAP!

—the man closed her door with his foot. The rain finally stopped altogether, but the sounds of rolling thunder could still be heard in the distance as the storm headed east toward the Grand Canyon.

"What'd you say your name was again, doll?" Smith heard the man ask.

"Candy," the unknown female replied, their voices intertwining with the sound of the wind blowing across the desert behind them.

"Heh, I'm sure you are," the man said, chuckling as they headed arm in arm toward the Desert Palms Motel's entrance.

SNAP! SNAP! SNAP!

Smith stealthily exited his Chevy and ran hunched over toward cover. The man and woman entered the motel and disappeared into the lobby. Smith realized he couldn't chance going into the motel just yet; the receptionist from the other day might recognize him as the lunatic who had made a scene about the Rolls. He would have to lurk in the shadows and hope he'd notice which room they were in by watching for a light turning on in the next minute or two. He backed up so he had a more widened scope of the motel, allowing him to see more rooms from the outside.

He checked his pocket watch—11:18 p.m. Three rooms with their lights on already. The rest, twentysomething rooms, were all dark.

Smith nervously shifted back and forth, his gaze darting down one length of the motel's exterior and back again.

He checked his pocket watch.

Still 11:18 p.m. Three rooms with their lights on. The rest all dark.

Smith coughed into the crook of his elbow to stifle the sound as another set of headlights swept across the parking lot. He stepped backward to prevent as much of his body from being illuminated as possible when the vehicle turned into an available parking spot. The car stopped, and the driver killed the engine.

He checked his pocket watch—11:19 p.m. Only two rooms had their lights on now. The rest still all dark.

Smith watched two men exit the vehicle and stumble toward the doors, using each other as crutches to stabilize their balance. Smith couldn't bring himself to avert his gaze from them until the two men had disappeared into the motel.

Back to three rooms with their lights on, and the third was not the same room that had turned off its light a few moments earlier.

"Bingo!" he whispered. "I have you now."

He crouched down and ran alongside the motel underneath the other guests' windows toward the Boulevard Killer's room. As he ran by a bush, a black blur jumped from underneath it and scurried up ahead. He gasped loudly. "Damn stray cats."

Smith reached the window of the newly illuminated room and peeked over the outside sill. The window was closed, but the white curtains were sheer—enough to see through. He placed both wrists on the sill for support so he wouldn't fall backward while taking more pictures.

Eva's grandson sat on the bed, leaning on his elbows like kickstands. His shoes were removed, and his bare feet were planted level on the carpet. Smith snapped a handful of photos and stopped just as Candy exited the bathroom on the far side of the room, wearing nothing but a frilly bra and high heels. She sashayed across the carpet, exaggerating the movements of her hips and long bare legs. Smith captured more snapshots of their actions before she sat next to the man, tracing a single long fingernail delicately along the outline of his upper body.

"So what turns you on?" Candy asked, her voice muffled through the closed window.

Smith had to strain to hear their words. Between the barrier of the glass panes and the wind coming off the desert, their voices sounded like they were broadcast from a radio speaker somewhere in the distance.

"Pretend you're dead. That'll turn me on."

She stretched out her body on the bed next to him, crisscrossed her wrists to mimic being tied up, and closed her eyes. "Sick little fuck, aren't ya?"

"I just get what I want. Even if it's by force."

Candy opened her eyes and propped herself up on one elbow. "You don't have to rape the willing."

That's probably not *a turn-on for this guy*, Smith thought. *He only gets off if there* is *a struggle. You may have just pissed him off, stupid dame.*

The man didn't indicate he had a more-than-half-naked semiattractive woman coaxing him into sex. He sat expressionless, like the Tin Man in *The Wizard of Oz* before he gets oiled. Smith thought he felt Candy's growing frustration by the way she slapped her thigh before standing again.

"Got anything to drink?" Candy asked, placing her hands on her hip and tapping her foot. "Maybe in your car?"

"I'm not paying you to sit around and drink," he retorted with a hint of anger showing through his voice, like a parent reaching the end of their fuse with a toddler.

"Well then, shut up. I'll punch the clock, and you can fuck me 'til the blood scares you."

Candy bit her bottom lip and tossed her bra on the carpet. She jumped on the bed, giggling as their bodies collided, and almost bounced off his chest. The man wrapped his arms around her back and spun Candy underneath him, pressing his weight against her chest. His fingers played on her privy parts, and she moaned loudly, arching her back.

Smith continued taking pictures and rolled his eyes, thinking how fake and exaggerated her so-called pleasure looked. *What an actress*, he thought. *But it's probably good for repeat business.*

The man was fully inside her now while his mouth completely consumed one nipple, and his right hand clamped down around her neck.

"My God, is he . . . strangling her?" Smith whispered, then heard a rustle in a bush to his left and looked quickly to see if someone approached. "Cat's gonna be the death of me out here."

Smith peered into the room again, and the man groaned loudly as he jackhammered in and out of Candy. She continued the same Academy Award–worthy moaning, raising her volume so her screams were always louder than the man's, even through the pressure on her neck from his clenched hand. Then Smith noticed the man make an unusual movement. Without removing his hand from Candy's neck, or releasing her nipple from his teeth, or even slowing the thrusts from his hips, he reached down below the top of the mattress with his left hand, fishing for something.

Smith took one more photo and then the Kodak made a whirring noise, indicating the roll of film had reached its end.

"Sonofabitch. Really? *Now?*" he said, flipping over the camera.

He looked through the sheer curtains again and saw the man holding a Colt .38 revolver over her face. Smith knew, without a doubt, the make of the weapon; it was what he had carried on duty for years. Candy's eyes were closed, and she was too busy writhing in fake pleasure as the man thrust harder inside her to notice the barrel of the gun inching slowly toward her open mouth.

The man groaned louder—Smith was convinced this moan was purposefully obnoxious to keep Candy focused on moving in sync so she wouldn't open her eyes prematurely—and finally released her nipple from his mouth.

He's really going to kill her. And I'm really going to witness it, Smith thought as he placed a hand on the windowpane and held his breath. *Yes, yes!*

The man put the Colt beside her head and covered her open mouth with his.

"No, no! Shoot the whore!" Smith whispered, his breath fogging the glass. "What are you waiting for?"

The killer took his right hand and placed it underneath Candy's buttocks, gripping her ass cheek tightly and accelerating the force of his thrusts as he spoke through sporadic bursts of breath. "Take it all, whore."

"That's it. Drill the floozie good and proper first," Smith whispered. "Wham, bam, thank you, ma'am."

Their gyrating bodies bounced the bed so hard that Smith thought the headboard would crash through the wall into the next room. He didn't realize he had been running his finger up and down a bulge in his pants until a rustling in the bushes distracted him.

"That sonofabitch cat," Smith muttered and returned his attention to the inside of the motel room, watching as he was convinced the man *had* to be close to finishing.

"Dirty little bitch," the man mumbled just loud enough for Smith to decipher the words.

Smith wondered if the man would whack her before or after

the killer ejaculated. Then Smith wondered if the man would come before or after he snuffed her out.

He couldn't be that *sick*, Smith thought, never contemplating necrophilia into the killer's bag of surprises. *Could he?*

Candy's screams grew louder, and Smith saw the man raise the .38 again.

"Good little girl," the killer said and closed his eyes, expelling a loud, long grunt as he released inside her.

"Don't stop, baby. I'm almost there too!" she replied, scrunching her eyes tighter and scratching his back as all her muscles contracted.

"Do it now," Smith whispered.

The killer pulled out quickly, right in the crest of Candy's last wave of pleasure. When she opened her eyes, he jammed the muzzle of the .38 into her mouth.

"Say good night, bitch!" he said through clenched teeth.

Smith was sure the gun was so far down her throat that it touched her tonsils.

Candy screamed in a mix of terror and pleasure, and the Boulevard Killer pulled the trigger. One shot. One dead hooker. One scream silenced. One sheet covered in blood. One Peeping Tom private eye applauding outside the window.

The killer turned abruptly and looked through the curtains. Smith slid down the side of the motel underneath the window, his back pressed firmly against the stucco. He frantically collected the Kodak and scooted away on his hands and buttocks. When he had safely cleared the window, he stood up and collected himself.

"He didn't see you," Smith whispered to himself. "He might have looked directly out the window, but he didn't see you."

The window opened, and Smith gasped, taking a step sideways. The killer tossed Candy's lifeless body through the open window, and she landed in the bush—her body slid until her neck, bent in an unnatural angle, hit the ground and stopped her from moving any farther. Her legs were draped up and over the top of the bush, and her open dead eyes looked directly at Smith.

A leg appeared out of the window, then another, as the killer ducked underneath the bottom of the window. He jumped down onto the dirt and grabbed Candy under her armpits.

Someone knocked on the other side of the motel room door.

"Mr. Covington?" The female's voice was distant and faint. *KNOCK! KNOCK! KNOCK!* "Everything okay in there, sir?"

The killer stuck his head back into the room through the open window. "Yes, Cheryl. Everything's fine! Thank you for checking on me. Did you hear that noise?"

"I did. It sounded like a gunshot," Cheryl replied from the hallway on the other side of the door.

"Really? It sounded like someone's jalopy backfiring," he called back.

Smith was an arm's length from the killer and on the verge of hyperventilating. He knew he couldn't move, or he'd be discovered. He also knew, as soon as the killer stopped chitchatting with the night desk girl, Smith would be discovered. Either way it was a lose/lose situation for him.

"You'd know more about those things than me, Mr. Covington."

"Yes, I should say I would. Good night, Cheryl."

"Good night, sir. Sorry to have bothered you," she said and walked away from the closed door toward her reception desk in the lobby.

The killer backed his head through the window and turned to carry his slayed harlot through the shadows to his Rolls when he found himself eye to eye with the detective. Smith stood silent, his back pressed against the motel's wall. He had inhaled deeply but had yet to release the breath. The killer, with Candy's body—blood draining from the back of her head and painting the bushes, and brain matter falling like crumbs onto the front of the killer's pants—stood silent. Unwavering. Eyes boring into Smith's soul.

Smith swallowed hard and nodded once. A single head bob. A silent affirmation and understanding they were on the same page with the killer's choice of victims. Smith opened his mouth to finally speak to the man who had been so elusive to law enforcement over the years but—

The sound of a bush rustling to the killer's left distracted him, and he redirected his attention to the ground. Two small paws and a black feline face peered from the shrubbery and proceeded to step forward into the pathway between the motel and the bushes.

"Fucking cat," the Boulevard Killer said and kicked the cat as hard as he could.

He readjusted Candy's body on his shoulder and walked away with his prize, leaving Smith standing rigid, like a Queen's Guard at Buckingham Palace, while the cat scurried through the parking lot to lick its wounds.

As soon as the killer had pulled from his parking spot with the dead hooker, Smith sprinted across the parking lot toward his Chevy, using the shadows as cover—he certainly didn't want anyone to think *he* had killed someone, had anyone heard the gunshot and come out to investigate. The Rolls's headlights swept across the other parked vehicles and headed straight for the highway.

Smith slid into the front bench of his car and, without turning on his headlights, sped to catch up. The Rolls took a left toward the wide-open area of the desert between the motel and the start of civilization, sand spitting from its rear tires, and Smith followed. The Rolls's headlamps illuminated the cacti and scattered skulls of long-ago-deceased animals.

Smith gripped the steering wheel tightly as it violently spun from right to left as the vehicle bounced and smacked into small dunes of sand. His Chevy launched upward and slammed downward over the divots and knolls. Smith was convinced the killer knew he was behind him by now.

"Playing a little cat-and-mouse game, are we?" he said as his voice hiccupped over the rough terrain. "Or are you bringing me somewhere specific?"

The Rolls stopped abruptly, and Smith slammed on his brakes and spun the wheel hard right to avoid ramming the rear of the killer's car. The Chevy slid sideways through the sand, resting against a small cactus—the spines scratching the black paint. The Rolls sat motionless and gently idling, its headlights traveling into the vast nothingness of the desert ahead.

Smith couldn't hear anything except the two motors. He couldn't see any movement in the car ahead of him. The driver—the *killer*—sat perfectly still. And Smith found no visual signs of Candy. He assumed she was laid out on the back bench and became concerned as the seconds ticked by without the killer moving his head. No signs of life or movement came from inside the Rolls at all.

Then he heard the unmistakable sound of flapping wings. And lots of them.

Smith leaned forward and peered through the windshield for a better view. A gaggle of black figures dotted the sky, circling above the two cars and slowly descending with each cycle of their sky-whirlpool. As they approached, he made out grunting noises coming from the sky that sounded like dogs barking in the distance. But Smith knew the sounds weren't coming from any kind of canine; they came from whatever winged creatures were descending upon the vehicles. The swarm circled lower and lower, and Smith could now decipher their featherless faces and sharply hooked beaks.

He swallowed hard. "Vultures."

As if they had heard him identifying their presence, they flung downward with one powerful swoop of their wings, gliding in a single-file line straight for the killer's Rolls. Smith gripped his steering wheel in fright and anticipation. The vultures didn't seem to care or acknowledge Smith or his Chevy as they bombarded the

Rolls. One by one, they nose-dived into the open windows of the killer's car. Smith gasped and clasped one hand over his mouth to stifle any further screams that might escape.

Vultures, dozen after dozen in a continuous line, kamikazied into the back open window and disappeared, never exiting the other side.

"How the hell are they all fitting in there?" Smith mumbled.

He could see the silhouette of the killer's head. Unmoving. Motionless. Staring forward without flinching. Catatonic. Like a mannequin. Or someone possessed. When the last vulture entered the vehicle, Smith couldn't see the birds anymore.

Where the heck did they all go? No way they all fit inside that car, and, if they could, they would fill the automobile to the roof.

The desert returned to hosting only the sounds of the two car engines. Nothing moved, not even Smith. The smell of the spilled alcohol on his floorboard wafted to his nostrils and turned his stomach. He gathered a small pool of spittle and swallowed to keep the urge to vomit at bay.

The killer's Rolls rocked back and forth, like someone thrashed around inside. Smith's knuckles turned white from gripping his steering wheel. But he still couldn't see anything through the Rolls's rear window except the killer's inert head. Then new sounds grew louder, overtaking the engines' rumbles. Raspy, drawn-out hissing sounds. Demonic feeding sounds. Inhuman sounds of pleasure.

The birds of prey left the Rolls through its open windows, rising into the night sky—chunks of Candy's flesh and limbs secured inside their beaks. Smith watched, paralyzed, as the flock of vultures carried away the prostitute until disappearing into the cloud covering. Then he jumped when the Rolls lunged forward and made a U-turn around the skull of a longhorn steer partially buried in the sand.

Unable to move or process anything he had just witnessed, Smith watched the taillights of the Rolls fade in his rearview mirror.

"Wynn!" Smith yelled, knocking continuously as hard as he could on her door. "I'm not leaving until you open up!" He stopped his banging when he heard movement from inside.

"Knock it off!" she called from inside her apartment. "You're gonna wake up the whole floor!" She flung her door open. "Go home and sober up," she said, rubbing the sleep from her eyes.

Smith pushed her out of the way and barged into her living room.

"Or . . . come in."

"I gotta tell you what I just saw."

"What time is it?" she asked.

Smith looked at the clock above her couch, and it read 11:18. "I dunno. Your clock's dead."

"I should call the police. You barging in here like this. I'm sure they'd *love* to get a call on you like that, huh? Trespassing. Or better yet, unlawful entry."

"Just shut up for a moment," he ordered as he realized the time on the clock. "Your clock stopped at eleven-eighteen."

"Yeah, so what?"

Smith stood on the back of her couch and reached for the clock.

"Your shoes better be clean, or you're gonna shampoo my couch."

He tossed his fedora on one of the couch cushions and grabbed the circular clock. "This was the exact time the killer embraced Candy in the parking lot, in essence, signing her death warrant."

"Wait. You saw the Boulevard Killer tonight? And with a prostitute? In action?"

He stepped down from the couch and removed the clock's backing. "Thought you wanted me to leave?"

She playfully punched him in the shoulder. "Oh, you're such a dolt."

They locked gazes for a moment, and he leaned in. Wynn allowed him to steal a quick kiss before pulling back.

"I'm still angry," she said. "One kiss won't fix that."

"But it's a start, right?" he asked, laughing and inspecting the exposed back of the clock. "I don't get it. It's wound."

"Of course it's wound. I don't neglect my responsibilities."

"Why do I feel like that's more of a personal shot at me than about you keeping your clock wound?"

"If you think that, then you must be guilty," she said, smirking.

"More is going on here than meets the eye. I remember this exact time specifically because I kept looking at my watch while I was staking him out. And wait until I tell you about the vultures."

"Sit down, and start from the beginning," she said, running sink water into the teakettle. "Don't skip a single detail."

Smith hadn't realized how bizarre the entire ordeal had been until he rehashed his whole experience to Wynn over a cup of tea, ending his night's adventures with her clock stuck on 11:18.

"Now that we've found the Boulevard Killer, I take it we're not going to the police?" Wynn asked.

"So now it's *we* again?" he asked, laughing. "I do all the hard work, and you want back in, just like that?"

"Obviously we can't trust the fuzz with all that bizarro stuff about the birds," she continued, ignoring his jab.

"No. We are definitely *not* going to the sheriff's office. Sheriff Wilcox wouldn't know how to handle something this intricate. Nor would I trust him with any of what I've collected. Also I don't know if I *want* to do anything about it yet."

"Excuse me?"

Smith took Wynn by her hands and guided her to sit on the couch with him. "Look. This guy, he's . . . he kind of . . . I mean, he . . ."

"He *what*, Smith? Spit it out."

"I would never admit this to anyone else but you."

"And I'll never repeat it."

"He's doing what the law has never been able to do. Not even when *I* was on the force. And certainly not after."

"You're not saying you admire him?" she asked, slightly horrified.

"He's cleansing the streets. He's getting the filth off the streets. Filth that continues to devalue this city. Do *you* want your future children to grow up with these scumbags crawling through the streets? Don't you want a safe, wholesome environment for the future generations? I certainly do for mine."

She chuckled. "*You?* You want kids?"

"Is that so far-fetched?"

She cleared her throat and realized maybe it wasn't. Maybe he was a better man than she sometimes gave him credit for. Maybe he *was* husband and father material . . .

Stop it! she thought, chasing away any chance of traveling down that fantasy road. "Sorry. Go on."

"I want to tail him a little more. To figure out what the hell the deal was with those vultures, where they took Candy's remains, and dig up some background on our killer. I also would like to see if I can catch him from the moment he comes in contact with his next victim and follow him through the whole process. That might shed some light on all these odd occurrences."

"Like the disappearing Polaroid?"

"Exactly. And that reminds me. I need to develop these photographs."

"Just so I'm clear. You don't want to blow the whistle on a Jack-the-Ripper-style serial killer who has been stalking our city, because you *agree* with his choice of victims?"

"Something like that."

All of a sudden, it was a lot easier for Wynn to *not* fantasize about a marital and parental relationship with this man. "For the record, I do not condone investigating him any further until the authorities are notified. Just because the sheriff and municipal police are a bunch of corrupt Keystone Kops doesn't mean we can't go over their heads with this."

"Like, to the FBI?"

Wynn nodded.

"You do realize the moment we turn this over to *anyone*, we'll get treated like civilians and won't have any access to any progress in the case. That means probably never discovering what in Sam Hell is going on with that Vertigo Motel Polaroid or those vultures. Isn't a piece of you itching to know those answers?"

"Don't play me, Smith. You're just using my curiosity to manipulate me into agreeing to go along with you, to buy the killer more time to do what he's been doing to the streets. Because that's what you want him to continue doing. *Cleansing*, as you said yourself. You could care less about the Polaroid or the birds. You applaud his intentions and execution." She pushed a stiffened finger into Smith's chest. "You're just jealous that this sicko has more balls than you, to do what you could never do yourself."

Smith remained silent and stood from the couch.

"Maybe you should, at a minimum, contact Eva and tell her you found her grandson, and she should know some interesting factoids about him. That might put the squeeze on her to come clean with the Polaroid. Don't give her any actual info unless she gives up the story behind the vanishing photograph."

"Maybe putting a little pressure on her will work in our favor. I have her number at the office," he said, reaching for his fedora. He stopped at Wynn's door and turned to face her. "Well, are you coming?"

"You're calling her at *this* hour?"

"I'll be waking her from hopefully a dead sleep and disorienting her. Confused people tend to be more honest. They don't have the faculties to concoct fibs."

She located her shoes. "You don't mind I'm in my pajamas?"

"I don't mind if it doesn't bother you."

"Vegas won't know what hit 'em when they get a load of Wynn in her floral-pattern sleepwear!" she announced as they exited her apartment into the hallway.

Smith dialed the final digit of Eva Covington's phone number. The tone pulsed in his ear; then he heard a series of clicks as the lines connected. "I love not having to go through a party line anymore," he said, covering the receiver with his hand. "I really can't afford the private line, but it was getting harder to maintain confidentiality when I called clients about their cases."

Wynn nodded and tightened the outside layer of her pajamas by pulling the small drawstring around her waist.

Smith held up his index finger to her, in case she would reply, and spoke into the phone. "Mrs. Covington? Sorry to wake you in the middle of the night, but there's some new developments about your grandson that you might find interesting."

Smith winked at Wynn, and she smiled, her eyes sparkling.

"Excuse me? . . . Oh, I'm terribly sorry. This isn't HO7-5309? . . . Oh, really? Well, forgive me, ma'am."

Wynn shot him a quizzical look as he replaced the receiver on the cradle.

"Wrong number. Lady said she's had that same number for years. And the number is correct."

Wynn slid the notepad that contained the phone number closer to her. "Your handwriting sure is sloppy, but you clearly wrote HO7-5309. Are you sure you copied it correctly?"

"Almost positive."

"We should develop those pictures you took tonight. But first, can you drive me back home so I can get some things and change?"

"Get what kind of things?" he asked, egging her on.

"Oh, you know. Stuff. Just in case we're in the middle of some grand discovery and I need to stay over."

"I feel like I'm being set up . . . and I'm not complaining."

Wynn giggled. "Do you have the Polaroid on you?"

Smith reached into his trench coat pocket. "Never leave home without it."

"Let me see."

He handed her the photograph. It was finally completely blank.

7: Ad Nauseam

The morning sun stabbed through Smith's living room windows when Wynn and Smith exited his small makeshift darkroom in his house. Wynn carried the stack of photographs to the kitchen table and spread them out.

"Want a drink?" Smith asked from the kitchen.

"Water would be good."

He chuckled. "No, I mean, a *drink*."

"Isn't it too early for a nightcap?" she asked, giggling.

"Not for yours truly. It's never too early. Anything of interest in those photos yet?"

"Everything you described to me."

"So nothing odd?" he asked, approaching the table.

"Some of the shots of him and Candy outside the motel are blurry, but I think it's just because of the rain on the windshield, not because anything supernatural is happening. And all your shots of them inside the motel room are crystal clear, except the curtain conceals some of their naughty bits."

Smith picked up a few of the snapshots, reliving the previous night through the images. "I wish I had been able to get pictures of the vultures."

"And you didn't think to pack another roll of film?"

"I didn't have you there to remind me," he teased and planted a quick peck on her lips.

"*Hrm.* Such a goof," she said while studying an image of the Boulevard Killer and Candy lying on the bed. "Should we bring these to Hank? See what his take is?"

"Are you trying to trick me into exposing this guy? You *know* what my plan is. Nobody is to know about these. So maybe it's best if we stay away from everyone else for a bit."

"Because you think he's doing the city such a *great* service."

Smith remained silent.

"I need some time to process this. We're treading dangerous water here by not going to the police. And every night we hoard this information is another night he has the ability to kill another girl. Another *girl*, Smith. Someone's daughter. Someone's sister. They're just *girls*. Have you thought of that yet?"

Smith didn't react; he continued to stare at the array of pictures on his kitchen table.

"Fine. Enjoy your day," she said and headed for his front door.

"Aren't you taking your overnight bag?"

She stopped with one hand on the doorknob and, without turning around, said, "It might be the only thing that'll get me to come back here."

Smith smiled as she slammed the door behind her.

"She can't resist me," he mumbled to himself.

A loud rapping on Smith's front door awoke him. Startled from sleep, he rolled off the couch and wiped the drool from his mouth. The sun had already set, and long shadows of his furniture formed across his living room floor. He flipped on a light to see his pathway through the room. He wasn't surprised to see Wynn when he opened the door, but he was perplexed to see a brown wicker picnic basket draped from her forearm.

"Thought you might need dinner."

He nodded and stepped aside to let her enter.

"You cleaned up the photographs?" she asked as she placed the picnic basket on the table.

"I organized them. In here," he said and motioned for her to follow him.

Attached to the wall above his headboard hung two clotheslines perfectly parallel to each other. All the photographs he had taken with the Kodak were clothespinned to the lines. The top line held the pictures of the killer and Candy at the Rolls Royce in the parking lot, and the second line held the pictures from inside the motel room.

"They're in chronological order," he commented.

Wynn stepped farther into the room, and her focus grazed over the framed portraits on the dresser, depicting Smith and Wendy during happier times; one black-and-white photo of the married couple laughing on the beach, Wendy wearing a respectable one-piece bathing suit and Smith splashing water at her from the surf. Wynn let her fingers glide over a jewelry box with a painted dragon donning the cover. She opened the cover, and *"Für Elise"* gently escaped from underneath the tray that held Wendy's bracelets and earrings.

"I'm so sorry, Smith. I'm sorry if I was the catalyst for whatever went wrong between you two."

"Don't be sorry. I don't blame you. Or *us*."

"I'd like to believe that. I'd like to know where she is too. Just to confirm she's safe. Don't you care about that also? You guys were married for almost twenty years."

"I'm sure she's fine. Probably just ran off with that boy toy of hers. My memory is vague about what happened directly after catching them at Monks' Seafood, but I remember her getting hot under the collar when I demanded that she stop seeing him. She used walking in on us in my office against me, as a defense for her own actions. Threw *that* right in my face without hesitation. That's why I'm not killing myself to find her. If she wants to be found, she'll reach out."

"I know you had to fire me to save face with your wife even though the marriage had passed the point of reconciliation, but it just feels so *cold* when you talk about her disappearance like that."

Smith shrugged.

"I feel like I shouldn't be in here. Like I'm invading her personal space."

"Well, *I* don't feel like that. And it's my house."

"Fair enough," she said, sneaking a peek through the open closet door at Wendy's evening gowns. "Doesn't it seem odd she didn't take any of her clothes or jewelry with her?"

"When you make an escape in the middle of the night, I think you're more concerned about just getting away unnoticed. I'm sure she has bought a whole brand-new wardrobe by now. Can we drop it, please?"

Wynn noticed an empty bottle of wine and a drugstore bag sitting next to each other on his nightstand. She walked to his side of the bed and picked up the prescription.

"Antihistamines," he said before she could inquire. "To help me get some shut-eye."

"And wash them down with a bottle of wine?"

"I do whatever it takes."

She returned the bag to its place beside the empty wine bottle. "So has anything popped out at you from looking at the photos like this?"

"Not a single damned thing. At least nothing more than we already know."

"But it's worth it, just having these images," she added.

Smith stood with his arms folded, staring at the double lines of hanging pictures. "Yes. For now."

"You're contemplating going out there again tonight, aren't you?"

He turned to face her. "And you're not? We're *this* close to maybe getting some answers to—"

"You mean, this close to watching him snuff out another girl's life while we sit idly by without intervening."

Smith sighed and changed the subject. "So, what'd you bring us for dinner?"

"I packed the prettiest-looking stuff I could find to help brighten this drab interior," she said as she emptied the picnic basket.

"Thanks? I guess?"

Wynn spread out the bright red-and-white-checkered tablecloth and placed the pastel-yellow plates across from each other. Two pink glasses and orange napkins were added to the setup.

"Obnoxious is more like it," he said. "What did you bring for actual food? Or are we just going to sit around and throw up from the color scheme?"

"I cooked some salmon and rice pilaf."

"And you know what goes best with fish?" he asked, already heading toward the refrigerator.

"I can only imagine."

He reached inside and removed an unopened bottle. "White wine!"

She rolled her eyes and sighed. "Okay, I'll take a glass."

Smith stopped in his tracks. "You mean, I won't be drinking alone tonight? Wynn the Prude is going to drink with me?"

"All right, all right. That's quite enough. You're about to make me rethink my decision. Where do you keep your candles?"

"In the armoire," he answered as he grabbed two wine glasses and popped the cork.

Wynn opened the cabinet's double doors and found a candelabra with two half-burned candlesticks. She lit the two wicks with a match and placed the candelabra in the center of the table.

Smith handed her a glass of wine. "A toast. To you and me, and wherever this crazy investigation may lead us."

"Cheers," Wynn replied and clinked her glass against his. "*Ooo,* I almost forgot," she said and rummaged through the picnic basket, placing the prepared fish dinners on the table.

"What else do you have in there?"

"More decorations."

Smith rolled his eyes as she littered the table with brightly colored beads and trinkets.

"Pretty things," he mumbled.

"Don't be such a grouch. Now sit down, and eat with me."

They took their seats at the kitchen table. Smith had already finished his first glass of wine before Wynn placed her napkin on her lap. He poured himself another glass instead of taking his first bite of food.

"Do you recognize what that is on your plate?" she asked after swallowing a heaping forkful of rice.

"Beg your pardon?"

"It's called food. I'm not sure you even know what it's for. You *eat* it. You can't survive on alcohol alone."

"Do you *even know* what's in your glass?" he countered.

"Oh, here we go," she said and leaned backward in the chair, folding her arms. "This should be rich."

"It's called wine. I'm not sure you *even know* what it's for. You *drink* it. You can't survive the throes of normal life without it."

"You are hopeless, Mr. Smith."

He winked and pointed his clean fork at her. "Right back at'chya, doll."

"Try the fish."

"Try the wine."

Wynn giggled and took a sip. "This is pretty good."

"Same here," he said, letting pieces of salmon and rice fall exaggeratedly from his mouth when he spoke.

Wynn tossed her head backward and finished the wine in her glass.

"Now that's not very ladylike," he said.

"Pour me another, and I'll show you ladylike."

"Intrigued," he said as he filled her glass. "They say alcohol consumption lowers inhibitions."

"What are you? The surgeon general now?" she asked, her words already slurring.

He poured the remainder of the bottle into his glass and got up to open a second one.

"*Another* bottle? What are you doing to me, Mr. Smith?"

He sat down at the table and shoveled in a few more mouthfuls of dinner. "This salmon is really tasty. I didn't realize you were such a good cook."

"There's a lot about me you don't know," she said, taking another gulp of wine.

The flames from the candles bounced their shadows off the walls, and Smith topped off her glass with the newly opened bottle. "Well, enlighten me."

Wynn wiped a dribble of wine off her bottom lip. "With what?"

"Tell me one thing I don't know about you."

She put down her glass and dabbed the corner of her mouth with the napkin. "My daddy drank too much. Then he'd beat me up."

Smith was taken aback by the straightforward confession. Paralyzed, he couldn't even reach for his drink.

"Sorry, was that too forthcoming? I didn't mean to damper—"

"No, no. I'm really sorry. I—I had no idea. I would never have teased you about drinking if I had known."

"Prohibition was the catalyst of his downfall, if you can believe the irony. The one law put into place to curb alcoholism and violence became the vehicle for many beatings and a deadbeat father. A few blocks from our apartment was a speakeasy—passcodes at the door, secret knocks, the whole nine yards. Like hiding the drinking and it being a dirty, illegal secret gave him permission to drink *more*."

Smith consumed his current glass of wine and pointed at hers. "Finish that."

Wynn sighed, and he thought a glimmer of a tear formed in the corner of her eye. He stood from the table, and she emptied her glass in four solid gulps. Reaching for her hand, he felt the wine warm his insides and watched the soft candlelight play on her features: her button nose, her baby-blue eyes, her small mouth. He decided to take a gamble on whether or not she was in the right frame of mind to submit to him. It was always touch-and-go with Wynn. And she could change her mind in a flash, like a yo-yo jerked up and down. He thought she was giving him silent permission to woo her. But he knew his window of opportunity could close in a jiffy—it almost always did.

Smith leaned down and forced her lips open with his. She reached behind his neck, and he guided her to her feet. She walked backward toward the couch, pulling him down with her. They crashed onto the cushions, stripping as many articles of clothing off each other as fast as they could. Smith pressed his tongue deep inside her mouth and tasted the wine on her breath, exciting him even more. He slid his hand along the curves of her hips and found her waistband. She moaned as he yanked off her pants.

"God, I want you," he whispered as his fingers and hands went into automatic pilot, fondling creases and caressing her smooth inner thighs. "You're the sugar that makes the medicine taste so sweet."

She used her fingernails to slowly draw ten visible lines up his naked back. She arched her back in pleasure when he entered her and gripped the back cushion with one hand and the bottom of the couch with the other. Smith's thrusts grew faster and harder until he pushed in . . . and didn't immediately pull out. He gasped loudly, and she knew he had finished. Inside her. He collapsed onto her naked body, allowing all his weight to relax on her.

Wynn wrapped her arms around his torso and closed her eyes. "Stay with me tonight. Here. We can just lie here and not worry about the Boulevard—"

"You sneaky dame!" he said and quickly pushed himself up

onto the palms of his hands so he stared directly down into her eyes. "This was all just a ruse to stall me from following the killer tonight!"

"Absolutely not," she said and shimmied her body from underneath his, nervous of his temper. His couch's upholstery chaffed her bare skin.

"Don't jive me. I can see right through you, bringing your picnic and asking for *wine* and talking about your dad and luring me into shacking up with you again with those bedroom eyes of yours!"

Wynn pushed his chest to get his body off her. "What are you talking about? Everything here has been sincere! I thought we were having a nice night—connecting even—maybe leaving our past behind for the first time and starting fresh. But obviously you just do what you always do. You turned this into someone sabotaging what *you* want to do. Jeepers, Smith. I'm thinking maybe the sheriff and his deputies weren't the shady ones, and Wendy was smarter than I gave her credit for by leaving."

Smith punched the wall above the back of the couch as hard as he could, sending thread-like cracks outward from the point of impact. "Damn you, woman. Damn you for making me fall for you again. Damn you for getting in the way of my work. And damn you for—"

"No, Smith. Damn you for making me think I was something more important than a bunch of dead hookers. Go find your friend and jerk off while he kills another girl."

"You know what?" he yelled, stepping aside so she could stand up from the couch. "This conversation's over. Pack up your . . . pretty things there and get the fuck out!"

Wynn wiped the snot dripping from her nose and frantically tossed everything she had brought into the brown wicker picnic basket. She accented her anger by slamming the decorations with as much force as she could muster into the basket. She hoped the sound would add to his regret and haunt his dreams.

"You know what my problem is? Every single time when it comes to you and me?" she asked, closing the top of the picnic basket. "I always give myself just enough rope to hang myself."

Smith chuckled sarcastically as she stormed toward the door.

"And I'm terrified I'll never learn," she spat before slamming the door behind her, leaving Smith alone to do whatever he pleased with the remainder of his night.

And the night was young. Very young, indeed.

8: Sin Under the Covers,
Blood Between Lovers

The sign above Rippetoe's flashed and buzzed, casting incandescent shadows into the puddles forming in the potholes of the sidewalk. Smith, not paying attention to his footing, accidentally stepped in one; water splashed up his leg, and the fabric of his pants around his ankle absorbed the liquid like a sponge. His socks became damp, too, as his shoes weren't the best barrier for stepping in three inches of rainwater. He cursed, lifting his wet leg so he could wring out some of the excess water.

Music emanated through the walls of Rippetoe's, and lights flashed inside. Smith ran a quick calculation through his head of what night it was—Jazz Night. That might be exactly what he needed. A little smooth jazz while he knocked back a few glasses before trekking downtown.

He entered the lounge and headed toward the long bar that lined the far back wall. He sat down on a dark gray stool and drummed on the counter with his open palms, waiting for Matt to notice him. He swiveled in his stool to face the band. A small banner hung above the drummer's head, announcing their name: Anacostia Trio.

"Evening, Smith. Didn't see ya come in," Matt said, wiping the area in front of him with a damp white dishtowel. "What's your poison tonight? Same as usual?"

"Nothing but the best."

"So house whiskey?"

"Like I said, nothing but the best."

Matt laughed and turned toward the multiple rows of liquor bottles in front of the lengthy mirror across from the counter. Smith directed his attention to the Anacostia Trio and tapped his foot as the stand-up bass player straddled his bass, almost riding it like a bull, and played a diminished scale over the boogie-woogie of the piano player. Smith glanced around the half-full room of patrons— mostly young couples—sitting at small circular tables with their drinks, watching the jazz band. A single candle was lit in the center of all the tables, throwing flickering glows against the front half of the lounge.

Smith was the only patron sitting at the bar, and his gaze fell on the jukebox.

"You got ol' Loella fixed up?" he called, projecting his voice over the crescendo of the Anacostia Trio's current ditty.

Matt turned around with Smith's whiskey and placed it on the bar in front of him. "No, but it's same exact model. Strangest thing. The other jukebox, the one I got from that bar Sneakers, just stopped working midsong right after you left a few nights ago."

"Really? I thought you said it had been refurbished."

"That's what I had been told too. Smack-dab in the middle of Benny Goodman's rendition of 'Puttin' on the Ritz'—and you *know* how much his version just tickles me to pieces. Cockamamie thing flickered out, like someone had unplugged it. And talk about coincidences. I get a phone call the very next morning from Wurlitzer about Loella, and they tell me there was no reason it should have quit working like that. And to keep me as a loyal customer, they sent this one—Loella II—free of charge. Yes siree. Came yesterday morning on a big swanky truck with Wurlitzer in big silver letters on the side. *Wooo-wee*, it sure was *purdy*."

"That's great, Matt. Glad to have *any* model Loella in the joint. Nice band you have tonight."

"*Thems* boys from DC. Call themselves the Anacostia Trio."

"I can see that from their banner."

"Any further development with that there postcard?"

Smith wasn't ready to open *that* can of worms and have to explain how now the Polaroid—the Polaroid Matt couldn't even see in the first place—was slowly vanishing.

"Nah, you were right, Matt. Turns out, it *was* a postcard all along. I must've been hallucinating or something."

"*Or something* is right, man. I gotta do my rounds to the people up front. I'll be back in a jiffy."

Smith watched Matt approach the hep cats sitting at the tables to take their drink orders. The Anacostia Trio finished their song, and the crowd clapped softly. Wisps of smoke floated from many of the females' long cigarette holders, clouding the area in front of the stage as the band played the opening notes of Louis Armstrong's "Basin Street Blues."

Smith lifted his glass and went to take his first sip when a hand was placed firmly on his shoulder. He craned his head backward and looked up, right into the smiling eyes of the Boulevard Killer.

"Would you like to get a table with me, or can I sit with you at the bar?" the killer asked.

Smith gripped his glass, the condensation making his fingers slippery. He glanced at Matt returning to the bar area. "A table would be safer."

"Does your friend want a drink, Detective?" Matt called.

Smith slid off the stool and looked at Covington. "Do you want a drink?"

"I'll pass, thank you."

"Order a damn drink," Smith whispered. "It'll look less suspicious."

"On second thought," Covington said, glaring at Smith but speaking to Matt, "I'll have whatever the barkeep suggests."

"House special it is," Matt said and turned toward the liquor.

Smith couldn't take his gaze off the killer towering over him. Covington played with a wedding ring, spinning it around and around with his thumb and middle finger. Smith couldn't tell if it was a nervous habit or a subconscious tell. Matt returned with the man's concoction, and they headed for a table in the back of the pub, away from the jazz band and the other patrons.

"How did you find me?" Smith asked, pulling out a chair.

"You're not the only one who's been tailing their subject."

"You've been following me?"

Covington unbuttoned his coat, letting it drape about his thighs, and sat down across from Smith. "I chose you."

"Beg'a pardon? What do you mean, *you chose me?*"

The killer stretched out his right arm, laying it across the back of the chair next to him, and rested his right ankle on his left knee. "Can you imagine what it's like to want to hire someone for a job, but you're not allowed to accept résumés, and the applicants don't even know they're applying?"

"I'm not sure I follow."

Covington quickly placed both feet on the ground and leaned forward across the table. "I've been looking for you for years. But I didn't know it was *you* that I was looking for." He leaned backward in his seat again. "I didn't know *who* it was supposed to be. And it's been a long and arduous process, whittling down and weeding through all the failures and just all the wrong people for the job."

"What job are you talking about?"

"My job, Detective Smith. My job."

"We couldn't figure out what your title meant."

"Not *that* job. That's easy. I'm a hydroelectric power technician at the Hoover Dam—night shift. I sit around and stare at dials and gauges all night, assessing water flow. Boring. I could care less about that job. I'm talking about my job that makes a difference. Makes an impact on the neighborhoods. An immediate cause and effect. Do I have to say it out loud, or are you tracking?"

Smith nodded.

"Trust me. We've been watching and studying you. You and a whole slew of your gumshoe cohorts."

"*We?*"

"Myself and the Mushroom Cult. My . . . people, if you will."

"So you don't work alone?"

"Strength in numbers, dear friend. Strength in numbers. You've proven to be the most exquisite subject, exceeding my expectations."

"Could you just speak English please, Mr. Covington?"

The killer slammed his hands on the table. The two perspiring glasses bounced from the impact. Smith jumped backward in his chair.

"Because you want to *be* me!" Covington almost yelled, then lowered his voice. "Your disgust for the lowlifes that slither and feed off the streets consumes you too. You just never knew you could do anything about it. You joined the illustrious Clark County Sheriff's Office as a young man, thinking that was your ticket to round up the scum and purge the filth from the streets. But that backfired on you when you realized the department was worse than the bottom-feeders you were hired to arrest. It's frustrating, I know. The one entity we expect to protect us turns out to be just another black stain on the white fabric of society."

Smith shifted uncomfortably in his seat. He was uneasy at how much this man knew, not only about Smith's work history but his own internal thoughts and feelings. Like the man was some kind of witch.

Covington stroked his brown mustache. "Then you became a statistic. A cliché. A typical can't-keep-his-wife, disgruntled, down-

and-out, alcoholic private eye. So tragic. So damn predictable. Except for that one thing that makes you special—makes you very special to me."

Smith coughed, and the Anacostia Trio finished their current tune.

Covington waited for the next song to begin before he spoke again. "You've always had this tiny egg inside you. An egg you never would've admitted to anyone else existed. Would never admit to even yourself. An egg that sat and just waited to hatch. You knew it was there, but you were afraid of what was inside the egg. I hatched that egg for you, and now you can see its contents. And you realize it wasn't as bad as you thought. What you believed might make you a terrible person, a criminal even, has now blossomed into something you actually like."

"You're saying I've always harbored these feelings toward the degenerates of society?"

"And allowing you to come along for the ride with me has opened up a whole new attitude for you, a free pass to justify my . . . *our* . . . actions."

"*Our* actions?"

"Have you blown the whistle on me yet? Ratted me out yet? I'm sure you've conversed with your sidekick, but I can't imagine you've told anyone else. So you are now vicariously involved—guilty by association. We're in this together. And I think that makes you happier than you're willing to admit to yourself."

"Everything okay over here?" Matt asked, approaching the table.

"Everything's peachy, Matt. We're fine. Thank you."

As the barkeep returned to serving drinks to the young couples enjoying the live music, Smith fished inside his trench coat pocket and removed the Polaroid. He gasped when he realized he was holding a postcard—a postcard with a well-known Norman Rockwell painting adorning the front side. All remnants of the original image had finally been replaced.

He handed the postcard to Covington. "Can we start with this? It's been driving me mad. At first I thought everyone was insane because Wynn and I could see a photograph, but everybody else only saw a postcard. But now I think I'm the one who's slightly deranged. Because it *is* only a postcard."

The Boulevard Killer took the postcard from Smith and tapped it against his knuckles. "I see a picture of me in front of the old Vertigo Motel. That shouldn't be hard to see for such a seasoned detective as yourself," he answered indulgently. "Fun fact about the Vertigo—about forty years ago, the locals exposed a serial killer who had drowned all his victims in a well. The citizens banded together and killed the guy in the Vertigo Motel while he slept in his room."

"Don't patronize me. You know there's something off with that Polaroid or postcard or whatever it is."

Covington handed the Polaroid/postcard back to Smith, who pocketed it. "Maybe they're suffering from postcard amnesia," he said and laughed uncontrollably.

"I don't even know what that means! I don't even know what any of what you're saying means."

Covington stopped laughing abruptly, and his gaze bore into Smith's eyes.

Smith swallowed hard and grabbed his glass without looking for it. He felt the man's stare burn through his soul.

"I couldn't let anyone else but you see who I was or what I looked like, or I'd certainly be sitting on death row right now, waiting for my turn to ride the lightning. No, I needed someone who saw the beauty in what I do, someone who'd be willing to partner up with me. I needed *you* to find me, and you only. I'm only one guy, and the filth multiplies like rabbits out there. I'm losing the fight. The Mushroom Cult helps, but, as servants, they can't independently hunt. They can only spay whoever I've offered to them."

"Spay. That's an interesting way to put it. I still don't know what this Mushroom Cult is. You have other people helping you?"

"*People* is a very loose term. But, yes, something like that.

They're the true definition of yin and yang. Vaudeville assassins and porcelain angels, all wrapped into one. I like to think of them as born-again apostles. Their godless selves have been exorcised, and they're resurrected as pure servants."

"Where do they come from?"

"They've been recycled. From the streets."

"Are you saying they're your victims? That you bring them back to life?"

"They certainly aren't victims, Smith. How could someone be a defiler *and* a victim at the same time? Society is the victim. And I don't bring them back. The vultures do."

A cold shiver snaked its way down Smith's spine. He hadn't been entertaining any of what the man had said so far, but, when the mention of the black birds of prey matched with what he had witnessed with his own two eyes in the desert, it seemed nothing should be discredited as a possibility now.

"Are we talking . . . ?" Smith paused. He had a harder time saying the word aloud than he thought.

"Say what you're thinking."

"Witchcraft?"

The Boulevard Killer laughed heartily, reminding Smith of a jolly Santa Claus. "That word has such negative connotations, don't you think? I'd like to think it's more than witchcraft and sorcery. I like to think it's closer to the dark arts. A little shake here, a pinch of something there. That's how you saw what I needed you and Wynn to see in the Polaroid. She's the only one who's proven to be completely loyal to you, and the only other one I could trust also. I spent a long time deciding on how to get your attention. How to get you to take the case. I knew I had one shot, but, if it was good enough, you'd be smitten to the point where you couldn't rest unless you solved the mystery."

"This postcard"—Smith pointed to it in his pocket—"was just a catapult to get me intrigued enough to follow you, so I could see what you were doing downtown, hoping I'd join you? You took a big chance revealing yourself to me like that. You really couldn't have known I wouldn't have turned you in."

"Oh, I knew. I know you better than you know yourself."

Smith folded his arms. "And pray tell, how can you make such a claim? You've never met me."

"Because, at the end of the day, we might have different names and lead different lives, but you *are* me. We're the same in what we want and how we think, and we share the same mindset to push aside what society says is immoral, even if acting in illegal ways to do so."

Smith was stunned and remained silent. He didn't dare utter another word. Every time he countered anything Covington said, Smith had been shown an alternate side of what he considered reality. Instead he tapped a cigarette from his metal container and lit the end.

"You weren't my first choice. I've been weeding through many inspectors over the years, searching for the one who *gets* me. It's been a delicate and tedious process, and, after many failed attempts to find the right guy for the job, you were the only one to bite as hard as I needed someone to bite to know they're the one. The others failed my audition process, if you will. But you proved to be a stellar candidate, hands down."

Smith took another drag of his Smolens. "What happened to the ones who failed?"

"They were forced into, let's say, early retirement," Covington answered and winked. "But not before your name came up multiple times as the real go-to guy."

"That's what Eva, your grandmother, said to me too."

"You told her that you wouldn't take the case, but I knew you would at least try. And that's all I really needed. The doctored Polaroid was the ticket. All I did was set the ball into motion. I never expected you to pick it up and run so fast with it."

Smith retrieved the postcard and fondled it. "So this is the result of some curse or spell you put over a generic postcard?"

"Simmer down there, hotshot. No reason for you to get the burning stakes ready," Covington said and chuckled. "Let's finish our drinks while you decide on the most important conundrum of your life."

"Which is?"

"Do you turn me in right now, or do you go for a ride with me? Downtown."

Smith placed the postcard on the table and pressed on the young boy's face in the Rockwell painting with his middle finger so hard that his knuckle turned white. He snuffed out his cigarette in the ashtray and finished his whiskey in two gulps. The small crowd behind him clapped and cheered as the Anacostia Trio bowed at the edge of the stage.

Smith snatched the postcard off the table, ripped it in half, then ripped it in half again, and let the four pieces flutter to the table. "Let's roll!"

The Boulevard Killer smiled and stood from the table. "Yes, let's roll."

Sitting in the passenger seat of the Rolls, Smith glanced out the side window. The moon was full and high enough to illuminate the entire city.

"Can I ask about the vultures? I saw them dispose of Candy. And it was frightening."

"Yes, they can be terrifying. They need to be treated with the upmost respect at all times. They do not do my biding, however. They're Anya's pets. I can just give the green light for them to be called. And thankfully they'd never be used against us. That'd be treason. But they don't listen to me. Only members of the Mushroom Cult underneath Anya's control."

"Anya?"

"You'll recognize her when you meet her. All in good time, all in good time. Just sit back and enjoy the ride."

Covington turned the Rolls onto Fremont Street and slowed the vehicle to a crawl. Smith could see the city was alive again tonight. Druggies, hookers, pimps, pushers, faggots, and addicts crept along the downtown area with him in the passenger seat of the vigilante's car, a vigilante dedicated to exterminating the zombies walking the streets. The adult shops' neon lights blinked, splashing the inside of the car with pink and purple hues.

"Right there. See that one who sticks out the most? The one who *looks* like she's trying too hard?"

Smith scanned the sidewalk and then saw the tall brunette standing next to a postal box. "The one who thinks she's Rita Hayworth?"

"Bingo! She's our mark. Look how pathetic she is. Out here, dressed like one of them dames in the picture shows. Who does she think she is? She's just a cheap whore."

"She certainly doesn't look like any of the other working girls I've ever seen downtown."

"And *that* is why she won a free ride tonight."

"Because she's different from the rest?"

"Because all work makes a dull man, Smith. Variety is the spice of life, and profiling a certain look down here starts to make it feel like work. Plus, who's to say she isn't dolled up like that because she thinks the Boulevard Killer is after a certain type? And, by looking like that—by looking completely different from my normal *modus operandi*—she believes she's taking herself off my radar? Quite the opposite, sweetheart, quite the opposite."

Smith glanced at Covington and swallowed hard as the Rolls eased to the side of the road in front of the girl. Hearing the man refer to himself with the same nickname the newspapers and police had given him was slightly unsettling.

Covington rolled down his window. "Hey, baby. You got time for two customers tonight?"

The Rita Hayworth lookalike stepped to the Rolls and leaned on the window frame. "I got the time, if you have twice the clams."

"We have the money. Get in the back."

Smith opened the passenger door and leaned forward so she could squeeze into the backseat. She fluffed the bottom of her manicured hairdo with the palm of her hand as she sat down.

"What's your name, doll?" Covington asked.

"Greta. Greta White. Well, that'll be my stage name, so I'm trying it out before I go to Hollywood."

"You're an aspiring actress?" Covington asked, making a left onto Interstate 15 toward Mesquite, Nevada.

"Sure am. Took me almost a month just to get to Vegas. My parents are probably still looking for me back home. I didn't even leave a note. I'm hoping to make it the rest of the way after I've saved enough money to get my own apartment. Heard Vegas was the best place to make some extra moolah, so this is just a quick stopover for a few weeks to pad my pockets. My dream is for the world to see me dancing as smooth as a cobra on the silver screen," she said and sighed, as if entering the daydream and visibly *seeing* herself on the theater screen. "Aren't you two the lucky ones tonight! You'll always look at me, larger than life, and think about how you had your way with the sexy superstar Greta White!"

"Where did you come from?" Smith asked, stifling a chuckle at Greta's benighted delusions.

"Salem, Massachusetts."

Smith and Covington remained silent in the front seat, the Rolls shaking and rattling over the uneven roadway.

"You know? Where they burned all those witches," she added.

"Are you a witch?" Covington asked drily, without any humor in his voice.

"What? No, silly! I'll be a famous Hollywood star! I'll take the world by storm and razzle-dazzle them. They'll write headlines about me in the papers, and my name will be surrounded in lights on every marquee."

Smith glanced back at Greta, and she wore a childlike smile as she stared out the window at the passing desert landscape. He tried to pinpoint her age. Nineteen? Definitely not more than nineteen. Seventeen? *Fifteen?* Definitely not less than fifteen, yet he failed to convince himself. She certainly looked the part of a Hollywood star, down to the blouse and skirt. Covington was wrong about her looking like this to hide from being the next victim. She was just naive and already method acting. Maybe she wasn't the right mark for them. Maybe there should be some discretion about who gets taken. Maybe they should throw her back into the mix and hope she stays true to her Hollywood aspirations. Maybe he should say these things to Covington. Smith looked at the driver and saw Covington's brows furrowed, his lips pursed, his body rigid, and his knuckles white from gripping the steering wheel——or maybe not.

"Oh, good. We're going to the Desert Palms," Greta said from the backseat when they passed the first distance-marker sign for Mesquite almost an hour later. "They've told me about this place. This is where married men take girls when they want to really get down and dirty all night long, since it's so far away from the city. Is it true sometimes you'll take a girl here for a few days and have your way with her? It certainly sounds like a good hideout if you're planning on having one of those marathon drills and need to hide her away. Is that why you're taking me here? Want to keep spicy Greta White all to yourselves for a few days?" Greta leaned forward and playfully tugged on Smith's ear. "The girls tell me the beds are just so *comfy!*"

Smith rolled his eyes, convinced Covington hadn't blinked once since they had entered the highway.

"Greta, maybe it's best if you don't speak until we get there, okay?" Smith suggested.

"Oh, sure thing. Whatever you want. You're the boss," Greta

said and finished by making a catlike *rawr*ing noise and flexing her hands in front of her, as if she had claws instead of fingers.

A few miles later, Covington pulled the Rolls into the parking lot and found his normal spot around the front of the building. He grabbed a briefcase from beside Greta in the backseat before exiting the vehicle. Being gentlemanly, he held the door open for Greta, and the three of them entered the lobby of the Desert Palms.

"Hey, Cheryl."

"Good evening, Mr. Covington. Hey, that's the man I told you about. The one who asked all those questions about your automobile."

"I know. Thank you. He's an old friend and recognized the Rolls and didn't know how else to get in touch with me."

Cheryl smiled. "That's nice that he found you. Your regular room?"

Covington grabbed a handful of matches donning the Desert Palms Motel logo from a large candy bowl to the right of a box of tissues. "Yes, please."

Cheryl handed him a large red key with the room number handwritten in gold ink as he slipped the matches into his pants pocket, and Smith and Greta followed him down the hallway. Greta reached across and gently grabbed Smith's hand, intertwining their fingers. He snatched his hand backward in surprise.

"I'm sorry, mister. You just seem like a nice fella, and I thought we could hold hands. Make it more intimate."

Smith's heart felt like it would explode in his chest. Every moment Greta acted childlike was another moment that he didn't think this was such a good idea. At least not with *her*.

"Here we are," Covington said and unlocked the door. He held out his hand to welcome his two guests into the room.

"Oh, wow. What a fabulous room! Is this a suite? You must be well-to-do to afford this room!"

Smith shook his head and wondered how anyone, even the

most innocent, could ever think a tiny rat's nest like this room could be a suite.

Covington placed the briefcase on the dresser and opened it. "Do you like wine, Greta?"

She straightened her skirt and tugged on her blouse. "I've never tried it. But who wouldn't like wine, silly?"

Smith tried to get Covington's attention to shoot him a disapproving look, but the killer never took his gaze off Greta. He watched her enter the bathroom and gently touch her lipstick line with her pinkie finger. Covington removed a bottle of wine and a single glass, along with two white unidentifiable pills. He filled the glass three quarters with red wine and dropped in the two pills. They sunk halfway, then floated to the top, swimming in the crimson-colored liquid. Greta exited the bathroom and looked at the two men as Covington handed her the glass.

"Aren't you gentlemen joining me?"

"We will, after we have our fun with you."

"*Ooo*, I like the sound of that," Greta said and took her first sip. Then she poked one of the pills with her painted fingernail and watched it bob back to the surface. "What's in here?"

"Just something to help you relax and have more . . . fun."

"Swell. I *love* fun! Now, are you taking turns or doing me at the same time?"

Smith looked nervously at Covington. He hadn't prepared for this part of the killer's process. Would he have to engage with the girls too?

"I like to watch," Smith blurted out.

"You dirty bird," Greta said and grabbed his tie, letting it slowly slither through her fingers. Then to Covington she said, "Where do you want me?"

"Finish the drink first. All of it."

Greta swallowed the rest of the glass's contents, as well as the two pills, and choked on the last gulp. She placed her fingertips to her mouth and excused herself.

Covington took the empty glass from her and placed one hand on her hip and the other around the back of her neck.

Smith sat down on the chair next to the window—the same window he had peered into just last night.

Covington and Greta fell on the bed, with her giggling as he kissed her neck and opened her blouse to expose her bra and cleavage. Then he pulled back the covers and adjusted her shoulder to strip the blanket past their waists.

"Under the covers? But I thought your friend wanted to watch," she said.

"Oh, he'll get a show all right."

Smith used his teeth to tear the fingernail from his thumb and couldn't help but think the killer was doing his deed under the covers purely for Smith's benefit. Maybe he wasn't confident that Smith was ready for the whole process yet.

Covington tossed a pair of undergarments from under the covers onto the shaggy carpet and pushed himself inside her. Greta wailed and sobbed when he pumped faster.

"Are you okay?" he asked, for the first time ever and slowed his thrusts.

She nodded and got control of her cries. Smith thought the sounds coming from Greta's mouth were closer to an animal in pain than a woman in pleasure.

"Wow," she said, panting. "That wine is going straight to my head. I'm feeling a little funny." She moaned and closed her eyes. This time she didn't open them.

Covington propped himself up on his palms and stared at her face. "She's asleep."

Smith stood from the chair. "What are you going to do?"

"I decided during the drive that this one would go peacefully. She didn't seem to deserve the normal treatment."

"Normal treatment?"

"Fear. Fear just before death. Fear during the violence. It's such a rush. The look in their eyes is the only vindication and payback I need."

"So now what?"

"Well, the vultures still have to have their way. I'll hand her over to the cult."

Smith watched in fascination when the killer kneeled upright—the covers falling around his upper body—and straddled Greta's hips, wrapping his hands around her neck. He pressed his thumbs into her trachea, and she arched her back in a reflexive protest. But her eyes never opened. She was too far down, sedated in a medicated slumber. After a few moments, her back relaxed, and she remained motionless on the bed.

Covington felt for a pulse and placed his ear over her nose. "She's gone," he said and swung his leg over her body to get out of bed, accidentally dragging the sheets with him.

Smith stood, pointed with one hand, and covered his mouth with the other. "What the hell did you do to her?"

The sheets were already absorbing the puddle of blood that had pooled underneath Greta's groin.

"Damn it! That was her first time."

"She was a *virgin*?" Smith yelled.

"Looks like it. Must've been her first night on the streets. Her first customer. Just trying to get to Hollywood, man."

"Are you sure it wasn't just her period? How can you be so sure that's the cause of the bleeding?"

Covington studied the darkened stain. "I can't be sure. It's either her period or I broke her hymen. I'm not really hip to how much tissue bleeds during a dame's first time."

Smith thought he would be sick. "What do we do now?"

"This doesn't change anything. She was still selling herself, still defiling society. If it wasn't us, it would've been someone else. And then someone else tomorrow. And the next day. And so on. We just caught it before it could spread. Before she could spread her legs, like a disease."

Smith sat down on the chair.

"No! No resting. We got to get her to the desert so she can be recycled."

A gray and bony hand slithered over Smith's left shoulder from behind him, and a gruff voice spoke. "Is he ours now?"

Smith yelled and leaped from the chair, scurrying to the other side of the motel room, passing Greta and her bloody sheets. "It's . . . you!"

Anya stepped forward from behind the chair, her black veil masking all her features sans her gray eyes.

"You're Eva! How the hell did you get in here?"

"Detective Smith, let me formally introduce you to Anya."

"But that's your grandmother."

"Funny. For being so smart, you sure believe most everything you're told. She certainly *looks* like a grandmother, but Anya is far older than anyone's grandmother, I can assure you."

"Let's get the broad out of here before she becomes cold and stiff," Anya ordered.

"Ya know, Anya. I don't appreciate being bossed around. This partnership is such a messed-up piece of work, and your directives are really fraying my tolerance."

Anya glowered at the Boulevard Killer, giving him the evil eye. "Chop-chop!" she spat, clapping twice to punctuate each syllable.

"Smith, help me," Covington said, shaking his head in defeated disgust. "We'll go through the window."

"I remember that part."

Smith peered over Covington's shoulder and gestured for the killer to turn around. Anya was on the bed on all fours, her nose inches from Greta's crotch. She sniffed deep and long and closed her eyes to savor and analyze the scent.

"Well, gentlemen, it's definitely not menstrual blood. What we have here is a tramp who was a bona fide virgin when she woke up this morning. Good going, chump. Now get her out of here before I lose my temper on you again."

Smith inquisitively eyed Covington as the two of them grabbed a leg and an arm posthaste and lifted Greta.

"What about the bloodstains?" Smith asked.

"I'll take care of those," Anya answered. "You just worry about getting her to the motorcar."

Smith didn't want to find out what Anya meant by *taking care* of the sheets. None of this was what he had signed up for.

The Rolls bounced and bounded over the small sand dunes as they headed farther into the void of the desert. The moon was brighter than the previous night, so they killed the headlights and could still navigate without hitting a cactus or bull skull. In the backseat, Greta's lifeless body flailed and jolted around with each bump.

Covington stopped the car in a clearing and leaned into the backseat to prepare Greta. Smith stepped out onto the sand and spun in a circle, surveying the landscape around him. Even with the moonlight, the darkness consumed the car from all directions. Smith placed his back against the front of the Rolls as the darkness seemed to eat the light, like a fog rolling in. Then it stopped, holding its position just a few yards from the vehicle. Smith looked into the invading darkness but couldn't see anything past the frontline. He thought it looked like nothingness. Not just darkness but *nothingness*.

Then he saw movement in the nothingness. A lot of movement. Creatures, resembling females, crept from the nothingness and into the moonlight surrounding the car. Smith bent backward over the Rolls hood, creating as much space between himself and the shuffling brood. He looked behind him and saw the same number of creatures saunter from the nothingness there too, like an incoming high tide toward the car.

"Um . . . Covington?"

The Boulevard Killer looked up from working on the dead prostitute and noticed the arriving disciples. "Smith, meet the Mushroom Cult. They won't hurt you. They might be a little overcurious, but they won't harm you." He returned to preparing Greta in the backseat as if the scene outside the vehicle was as normal as hot dogs at a baseball game.

"Are they all . . . girls?"

"Yeah," Covington said, sticking his head out of the vehicle again to answer Smith. "They're all stains of society who've been purified over the years. I inherited them when the previous guy . . . I dunno, retired? Not really sure. Anya is kind of their immortal queen, but whoever possesses the book holds ownership of the flock. That is, until she can one day locate the specified prized possession that'll dismiss her limitations and then she won't have any use for us mortals anymore. We'll be tossed out with yesterday's bath water and her exclusory reign will begin. But until then, she needs us just as much as we need her. That's what the book alludes to, at least."

"The book?"

"It dictates and decodes all her mysticism. Don't get me wrong, Anya will serve you well, if you continue to add to her ranks. That's really the only reason she keeps us—the generations of caretakers—around. She relies on us to deliver the polluted offerings."

"You mean, like sacrifices."

"Wouldn't you like to think of it as more of a cleansing? She gets what she wants and—"

"An army."

"Sure. And we get to help our community."

The front rows of the flock stopped walking, and their decayed and paper-thin fingers fondled Smith's lapel. His eyes grew larger when he recognized Candy reaching for his fedora, like an infant reaching for a toy. A gunshot wound had blown out the back of her neck.

"I saw Candy get taken away in pieces. But here she is, all intact."

"These aren't their original bodies. That's why the law keeps finding girls buried in the desert graves. Baby vultures probably ate Candy's real body. The birds need to eat sometimes too, you know. What you're seeing are residual apparitions but solid manifestations. That's why they're all the same color and why the trauma of how they died is still visible."

"Have you ever wondered what she might be building this army for?" Smith asked, taking a step sideways, distancing himself from the zombielike movements of the cult.

"I'm saving their souls, Mr. Smith," Anya said, stepping from the shadows and flipping her veil over the top of her head so he could see her face clearly for the first time since that initial meeting in his office. "Without me intervening, they'd all be damned to Hell for an eternity of brimstone and gnashing teeth. This way they're saved, both in life from their heinous crimes against your kind and from the atrocities of down there."

"If you're referring to me as 'your kind,' then what *kind* are you?"

Covington stopped yanking Greta from the car and looked at Anya with tremendous concern.

"You've found a bold one, Covington. Even you've never been so brash to ask me that question."

"Did I do something wrong?" Smith asked, rubbing his hands together.

"I don't know. Did you?" Anya asked, her nose almost touching his. "You tell me. How's Wendy these days?"

"I don't know what my wife has to do with any of this."

"You asked if you had done something wrong. We can only answer that question when we slow down our thoughts and really *dig* into our souls. Introspection. Don't you think so, Covington?"

"I do," he answered and dragged Greta's body from the backseat and through a few feet of sand.

"Let's get this over with. This one doesn't sit well with me," Smith said.

"Why? Because she was a virgin?"

"That, and I'm not sure she was even old enough to be in high school yet."

Anya bent down beside Greta's body, flipped her veil like a curtain over her face, closed her eyes, and placed her decrepit hand on the girl's forehead. When she opened her eyes, she said, "You can sleep easily tonight, Mr. Smith. This sapling was of consensual age. If a little bit of blood makes you that nervous, maybe you're in the wrong business."

Covington realized he needed to direct the focus back to the ceremony, or Anya and Smith would come to blows. "Pum'kin, would you like to do tonight's honors and welcome a new sister to the clan?"

Pum'kin stepped forward with a grin splayed across her face. Smith thought, if she smiled any wider, her ears might fall off. The cult clapped and gurgled unintelligible noises, congratulating her for being the chosen one tonight. The inhuman guttural sounds that invaded the quiet desert night sent goose bumps down Smith's arms and chest.

Pum'kin sat with her legs crisscrossed next to Greta on the sand and rocked back and forth. She hummed a tune Smith did not recognize but did not *feel* was foreign either. The melody wasn't in the correct tempo, nor even in the correct notes, but, as soon as she reached the end of the first bar, he realized she was humming "*Für Elise.*"

Just as he turned to mention the odd coincidence between Pum'kin's choice of song to summons the vultures and Wendy's musical box, the flapping of wings overpowered the murmurs from the Mushroom Cult. Smith looked to the sky, and the moonlight was blacked out, shrouded in a kettle of vultures. He took a step backward away from Greta's body, knowing what they were after and unsure if they ever got confused and missed their target. He didn't want to find out tonight.

Smith ran his fingertips along the Rolls to guide him, never taking his gaze from the approaching swarm. He collided with somebody—something—and turned to apologize, then realized an apology was futile when he saw the female he had bumped into; her head flopped from side to side, and she had a permanent stare fixated on the sky. She had no idea she had been struck.

The vultures descended so quickly on Greta's body that Smith yelped in fright, and a plume of loose feathers rose into the air. The thunderous sound of the Mushroom Cult clapping was the last thing he remembered before waking up in the passenger seat of Covington's Rolls as it traveled down the highway back to civilization.

Even all the years on the force and all the despicable things he had seen had not been able to drop the curtain from his eyes like it had been dropped tonight. Smith believed, after witnessing tonight's events, the only truths he would ever see of his city were the miles of neon lights and shallow graves kept hidden from the loving, law-abiding families tucked snug and safe in their houses.

9: Antiquity's Small Rewards

The sun crested over the Mesquite horizon, and a blast of light woke up Smith in the backseat. He rubbed his eyes and sat upright, noticing Covington was still fast asleep in the front bench.

"Hey," he said, shaking Covington's shoulder. "Wake up."

The Boulevard Killer stirred and stretched. "What time is it?"

Smith looked at his pocket watch. "Almost six thirty. Is it safe for you to go home yet?"

"Yeah. My shift ends at six o'clock, so I would be driving home right about now. Do you wanna come back to the house and meet the family? I could introduce you as a new guy at the dam who just recently moved to Boulder City."

"Nah. I wouldn't want to intrude."

"Oh, hogwash. The wife would love to see I'm mingling with coworkers. She's always on me, saying it's unhealthy I work so much."

"If she only knew, huh?" Smith said. "So how long does it take to get one of the girls back?"

"Back?"

"Yeah. How long for the vultures to do their thing before the girl is part of the group?"

"Sometimes it's the very next night, and sometimes it takes weeks. There doesn't seem to be any rhyme or reason behind the time. We can only summon them; we don't have any influence on their methods."

"I saw Candy tonight. She tried to play with my fedora."

"Yeah, about that. It might behoove you to lose the hat, trench coat, and gun. My wife is pretty, but she's not stupid."

Smith removed his outer layers in the backseat as Covington pulled the Rolls onto the roadway.

"Is there anything I should know? You know, about myself? So I don't blow the cover with the missus?"

"What's your name?"

"*Uhhhh* . . . how's Todd Arbuckle sound?"

"Nice. And where are you from, how long have you been in Clark County, and what brought you here?"

"I'm from Florida. Let's say, Sarasota County. I've been here three months. And I'm just a free spirit chasing the American dream."

"Touché! I love it, Todd."

"Honey, I'm home!"

"Daddy, Daddy!"

"Hey, sweet pea. I want you to meet Daddy's friend from work. This is Mr. Arbuckle."

"Nice to meet you, kind sir," Rose said and curtsied.

"Nice to meet you too, young lady."

"George!" Maggie called from upstairs. "Is someone with you?"

Smith looked at Covington and mouthed, *George?*

"Yes, dear. A new guy at work," George Covington answered,

ignoring Smith's silent inquiry of his first name. "Thought he could use some friendly hospitality. He won't stay too long."

"I wish I had known, or I would've been more decent."

"I'm sure you're fine, honey. There's no rush." Then to Smith he asked, "Do you want a cup of coffee or anything?"

"Something harder maybe?"

"Is scotch okay?"

Smith nodded and scanned the Covingtons' home. "Nice place you got here."

"Yeah, it does the job. We got the two wee ones. Rose and Ray. Speaking of which . . . Rose? Is your brother up yet?"

"No, Daddy."

"We just had his birthday last weekend."

Maggie appeared in the doorway. "I'm terribly sorry for the mess."

"No need to apologize, ma'am."

"Can I make you two something to eat? Eggs and bacon?"

"I want eggs, Mommy!"

"That would be just fine, ma'am. Thank you."

"Name's Maggie," she said, extending a hand.

"Todd, ma'am. Todd Arbuckle."

"You stop calling me ma'am, and I'll make those eggs!"

"Fair enough, Maggie. Thank you."

Smith and Covington sat at the kitchen table while Rose played with the radio. She turned the tuner until the static gave way to a clear reception. The melody of Benny Goodman's clarinet filtered from the single speaker, implying unvoiced descriptions of high hats and arrowed collars and where Rockefellers walk with sticks. Smith froze and directed his attention to the radio.

"Everything okay there?" Covington asked, noticing the change in Smith's demeanor.

"It's . . . it's nothing. Just that song reminded me of something, is all. No worries."

"How long have you been working with George?" Maggie asked as she cracked an egg into the frying pan.

"A few . . . weeks now?"

"Has it been that long? Wow, time flies," Covington said. "We'll go on the porch and smoke a morning cigar while breakfast cooks. Send Rose out to get us when it's ready."

He tapped Smith on the elbow, and Smith followed Covington into the parlor, where he opened a desk drawer and removed two Cuban cigars. Smith stole a glance at Covington's wife as he exited the house with his new "coworker." George offered him a cigar when Smith closed the door and then lit the end of it for him. Both men puffed on their Cubans in silence as the sun exploded the sky into hues of oranges and reds.

"Thanks for having me over. And thanks for the cigar."

"You're very welcome. We still have to get you back to Rippetoe's so you can get your car. But we'll worry about that later."

"You have a very nice family."

"Thank you. But you haven't met Ray yet."

"I'm sure he's just as respectful." Smith puffed on his cigar and contemplated his next question. "Do you feel like you're living two separate lives?"

"Of course. You try sitting around and eating birthday cake and watching your son open presents, knowing just twenty-four hours ago you were stabbing some bimbo you had just drilled."

"And then throw in the Mushroom Cult and a handful of vultures."

"Then it's a party!" George said, laughing. He collected himself and continued. "It's been nice getting to know you a little bit. I've forgotten what it's felt like to have a friend."

"Is that what we are? Friends? Gotta be the most dysfunctional friendship—"

"Boys, breakfast is ready," Maggie said, opening the front door. "I'm gonna go powder up, if you'll excuse me. Rose is already eating, and Ray just woke up."

"We'll be in, in a minute," George said.

Smith took a strong puff of his cigar and gripped his head, grimacing.

"Jeez, you okay?" George asked, taking a step forward.

Smith waved him off. "Yeah, yeah. I just get these migraines. They come on suddenly."

"How bad do they get?"

"Sometimes pretty bad. Sometimes they lead to black—"

"Daddy!" Raymond squealed as the door opened.

"Hey there, slugger. You ready for some breakfast?"

The three males entered the house, and Smith joined the Covingtons for a seemingly normal family breakfast.

"Thank you so much, Maggie. The breakfast was delicious. And you have a fine family. Very lucky," Smith said, dabbing his mouth with a napkin and finishing his coffee.

"Any friend of George's is a friend of the family. We enjoyed your company, and you are welcome here anytime for breakfast. Or any other meal for that matter."

Smith stood from the table. "Where's the toilet?"

"Down the hall, outside our bedroom."

Smith pushed in his chair and headed down the hallway. He reached the bathroom and peered into the Covingtons' darkened bedroom. He leaned backward to catch a glimpse of the family, still conversing and eating. Confident he had a few spare moments to explore and investigate George's private space, Smith bypassed the lavatory and entered the bedroom.

Everything appeared copasetic: unmade double-size bed, white dresser, throw rug on the wooden floor, rocking chair with an ottoman near a writing desk, and the open, private bathroom door leading to an open closet door. Smith took a step toward the entrance of the closet. Squinting—not wanting to turn on any lights—he deciphered the closet's contents in the darkness. Smith took a deep breath and strained his ears to ensure no one had gotten up from the table to check on him yet. So far the coast was clear. He decided just a little snooping into George's everyday lifestyle wouldn't harm anyone, and, if anyone caught him, he would wing it. After all, that's what he was best at: opening his mouth and letting unrehearsed words fly out.

He stepped into the closet and quickly surveyed the small space. Work overalls, dresses, suit coats, and a slew of other attire hung neatly from hangers. Smith's focus grazed across the few shelves cluttered with shoes, jewelry boxes, and a hardbound maroon-colored book with weathered page edges. The book looked out of place and like a relic from a long-forgotten era. Knowing he was pressing his luck with time, he slid the book off the shelf to quickly inspect the odd artifact. He stumbled backward a step when he saw that the engraved insignia of the book's cover closely resembled the design on his flask: the shining eye inside the golden pyramid.

"I'm gonna check on Todd," Smith heard George say from the kitchen, followed by the sound of chair legs dragging along the hardwood flooring.

Instinctively Smith jammed the book inside his blazer and underneath his armpit, trapping it against his body with his elbow. Successfully scurrying out of the closet, out of the en suite bath, out of the bedroom, and into the hall bath before George could make it to the hallway didn't seem to help Smith's heart rate. He delicately closed the door and ran the water in the sink.

"Everything okay?" Covington said from the other side of the door.

Smith wiped the sweat from his forehead and repositioned the book under his elbow so the bulge wasn't so obvious and opened the door. "Everything's hunky-dory. But I think I'd like that ride to Rippetoe's for my Chevy now. My headache is getting worse."

"Sure thing. Let me grab my keys."

Smith followed George to the living room, keeping the book

jammed against his body in an elbow death grip. Maggie stood to shake his hand after George explained he needed to give Smith a ride to his car, which was parked at their place of employment: the Hoover Dam.

Watching the Rolls drive out of Rippetoe's parking lot, Smith finally removed the maroon-bound book from underneath his blazer and placed it on the passenger seat of his Chevy. He flipped to the first page and found no title or author name listed. Was it a work of fiction? A textbook? A manual? A book of—

A bird landed on the front of the car and perched, looking like a hood ornament, and cawed loudly. Smith jumped and placed his hand over his heart. After collecting himself, he slapped the windshield to shoo away the bird. With his heart still racing, he reached for his pack of Smolens and lit one before flipping farther through the book.

His fingertips tried to regulate the speed and amount of pages that flipped, but the age and ratty texture of the paper made it impossible to control. Frustrated, he let the pages flop open wherever they may. His eyes grew wide after a bundle of floppy stuck-together pages came to rest. The cigarette dangled from his open mouth, hanging on only by the thin layer of saliva on his bottom lip as he stared awestruck at the subject matter of this particular chapter of the book.

He used his finger to scan the paragraphs in the chapter aptly titled "Mushroom Cult." Instructions and explanations on how to build an "army of unholy ghosts" who will "march in morbid rhythm, chanting mantras of the dead" filled an entire page of very fine print. He flipped the next few pages and found potions and methods on reincarnation. The chapter ended with what appeared to be an amendment to the original print. Whereas the typeset looked like it had been formed by an old printing press, the added section was scrawled in meticulous calligraphy. The graceful swirls of the capital letters complemented the subtle brushstrokes of the lowercase ones.

Smith whispered aloud the few handwritten cursive words as his finger traced the exquisite sinuosities of the faded writing. "Collecting Impures translates to Longevity. Collecting Virgins is noxious; however, the Book shall appoint a single Chosen Virgin. One attains nonpareil Divinity through the sacrifice of said appointed Chosen Virgin. Absolute assistance of a Caretaker is mandatory at all times to exterminate all Targets, unless probable cause exists that a Target may be the Chosen Virgin."

He looked up from the book and stared blankly through the windshield at the closed lounge. A thousand questions ran through his head: *Was that why Anya collected the dead hookers? Each one adds to the length of her existence? She can't kill on her own and relies on a Caretaker's hand? And the Chosen Virgin is the Holy Grail for her, not having to rely on a mortal Caretaker of the book anymore, freeing her from a need for a partner? How does the book pick the Chosen Virgin? Did George ruin Greta from possibly being the Chosen Virgin by deflowering her? And how dangerous is Anya really?*

Opening to the next segment, his gaze caught the word VULTURES printed numerous times. A grocery list of chants and procedures appeared before his eyes. Commentaries on why and how and who the vultures can be controlled by filled the next three pages—all typeset, no further postscript calligraphy. He continued to a smaller section, toward the end of the book, and stopped immediately. His hands shook as he removed the dangling cigarette from his bottom lip and tossed it out the Chevy's window.

Smith slammed the book closed and sped from Rippetoe's parking lot, anxious to share his newfound comprehension.

With the maroon-bound book tucked underneath one arm, he

exhaled deeply to build his courage. He closed his eyes and rapped hard on the door. A moment later, he heard someone move around in the apartment and then pause on the other side of the door, probably peering through the keyhole.

"Go away, Smith."

"Wynn, you need to see this."

"Baloney! I've seen enough. I've heard enough. I've . . . cared enough to last me two lifetimes. I'm not giving you any more of *me*, Smith. Please, go away."

He sighed and tapped the edges of the book's discolored pages with his index finger. "I know how the Polaroid trick works."

Silence reigned on the other side of the door.

Silence . . .

Silence.

CLICK! The lock unbolted, and the door crept open.

"Don't presume, just because I'm letting you in, that I want to see you."

"Of course not. No," he affirmed and stormed past her to the dining room table. He set down the book and tapped the cover. "I . . . commandeered this from the Boulevard Killer's house."

"You mean you *stole* it?" she exclaimed. "How did you get inside his house? What's he like? Does he have a family? Are they normal? Does he have the skin of dead hookers hanging in his garage?"

"Whoa, slow down there, doll. Me and him had some conversations together, and he invited me to his house for breakfast. Nothing more, nothing less. His wife and two lovely children were home, and we broke bread together. I asked to use the toilet and detective-ed around—"

"You snooped."

"Yeah, that's what I said. *Detective-ed*. And found this book in his closet." He took his hand off the cover so Wynn could inspect it. "Look here." He flipped to the segment on suggestive hallucination. "Read that. The Polaroid was just an illusion for only you and me—a catered mirage, if you will."

Wynn read the chapter in earnest, only remembering to breathe when she consumed the final word on the matter. "So, he's a wizard or something?"

"He says he's in cahoots with a group of ghouls—although I think they seem closer to a herd of mummies without the wraps than zombies—who materialize in physical form of their earthly bodies. They're called the Mushroom Cult and are led by what I believe is a witch. Here." He opened the book to the chapters about the cult and their leader's immortality.

"Do you believe him, or do you think he's just deranged?"

"He certainly believes it. I haven't witnessed anything out of the ordinary yet though," Smith said, nervously scratching the back of his neck and hoping Wynn couldn't tell he was fibbing.

"But you have. We both have. The Polaroid."

"I've already thought of that. And, while you're correct, I'll sleep better at night believing he's only mastered the art of that particular spell."

"I thought he was the love of your life," she teased.

"I think you know who that is."

"Yeah, too bad she's still missing."

Smith gritted his teeth to keep from lashing out and slapping the condescending retort right from her mouth. But, he came here to reconcile. To use the book and the specific entry that explains the hallucinations as a catalyst to engage in normal, civil conversation again. He knew he had already wasted his last concrete chance with her; he was just running on fumes now.

"Are you going to turn him in now?" she asked.

"I'm shocked! I would think this revelation would steer you *further* away from wanting him incarcerated. You're not curious to find out what makes this guy tick?"

"You *know* what curiosity did to the kitten. And I can't believe you, Smith. Why do I feel like this is all a ploy so you can justify continuing to admire this sicko from afar and to somehow recruit me for it too. Gosh, I just never learn!"

"Look. I don't want to keep going down this path with you. I'm sick of how, every time one of us flies off the handle, it escalates the other one, and we both wind up angry. That's not productive for anyone. We're a good team. Both professionally and . . . outside of work. I'd hate to lose that."

Wynn remained silent and nodded. Smith was afraid to continue talking and say something to muck up any headway he may have made this afternoon, so he collected the book, tucked it under his arm, tipped the brim of his fedora with two fingers, and headed toward the door.

"Three days," she said when he reached for the doorknob. He stopped without turning around. "Three days, Smith. I'll give myself three days to decide whether or not you ever hear from me again."

He nodded, keeping his back to her, then opened the door and disappeared down the hallway with the book cradled safely under his arm.

10: Dead Virgins Don't Sing

The percolator hadn't even finished brewing the morning coffee when someone knocked on Smith's office door. To keep some shred of dignity in case it was a potential new client—although he knew, deep in his heart, there probably would never be another *new* client after this fiasco—he quickly collected the half-drunk liquor bottles from the top of his desk and crammed them into the bottom drawer.

He heard a second knock—this one more impatient than the first.

"Coming! Hold your horses!"

Smith opened his office door, and George barged in, flustered. He stormed to the middle of the room and spun to face Smith.

Oh, damn, he knows I took the book. Just do what you do best: open your mouth, and some half-believable excuse should just fly out like it always does.

Smith opened his mouth to explain the mystery of the missing book when a waterfall of agitated words exploded from George's lips. "Stupid broad doesn't know her place. Doesn't think she needs to fall in line. Doesn't think she needs to enter the ranks." George paced from Smith's desk to the small bathroom—narrowly avoiding the stacks of newspapers each time—and back again, like a caged tiger. "Thinks the rules of the cult don't apply to her. Well, we'll show her, won't we, Smith? We're gonna run her through good when we find her."

"Stop for a minute and calm down. Who has done what?"

"Greta has gone rogue. She was returned to the Mushroom Cult and, before we knew it, *poof!* She beat feet and fled. I've never seen one of them move like that—so nimbly—other than Anya. It was like she wasn't fully converted."

"You mean, dead? Do you think it had anything to do with her losing her virginity during the process?"

"I don't know, man. I've never recycled a dame before who didn't have more notches in their bedpost than I own socks. I'm not sure how it works with a recently spoiled virgin. I'm not really sure how *any* of this works, to be honest. The mechanics behind it, I mean. But she took off, like a tumbleweed in the wind. Anya has the whole flock searching for her."

"Then why did you come here? What do you need from me?"

"You're the only human who understands me, who knows what's going on. Anya and her army of ghouls are like a single-minded blob. Plus, if you haven't noticed yet, she's not the most pleasant business partner. You're really all I have when it comes to the human side of our endeavors. I can't talk to her like I can talk to you. A part of her wouldn't understand the intricacies of the situation. All she cares about is stockpiling her coven. But *we*—me and you—we see the bigger picture. We see the endgame. We *get* the ultimate goal."

"Cleansing the streets," Smith mumbled.

"Exactly! Doing what you and your ex-cohorts couldn't do for years. But we, we are *doing* it. We can't allow Greta to go far. I don't know what kind of state she's in, and, with her only being converted two days ago, she's like an infant right now. A *bantling*, as Anya would call her."

"But you don't know that. You said yourself how she's been

acting different from the get-go because of the uniqueness of her situation."

"Right. That's why we need to find her."

Smith nodded, grabbed his fedora off the coatrack, checked that his revolver was snuggled in the holster, and extended his arm toward the doorway in a lead-the-way gesture.

"They don't like to come out during daylight," George stated as he veered the Rolls off the highway onto the desert sand.

The sun had reached a blinding eye level, and the two men had to squint to see without it being painful. Scattered cacti and small dunes—Smith wondered how many of the lumps in the sand were yet-to-be-discovered converted cult members—dotted the landscape. The highway grew farther and farther behind them as the vehicle swerved and wove around the obstacles. Smith noticed a convoy of clumsy footprints in the sand, leading in the same direction as the car.

"This is where she ran, and they started tracking her. We'll follow the footprints until we meet up with them." George cupped his hand over his eyes to shield the sun. "I think that's them in the distance."

As the vehicle rolled closer toward the horizon, Smith saw what looked like an army of ants in the distance. The car's tracks flattened some of the cult's shuffling footprints, and he wondered what kind of chaos and panic would ensue if the Mushroom Cult ever took a stroll through Suburbia, USA, while looking for their rogue comrade. Then he contemplated what actual state of mind Greta could be in. If she had the ability to think outside the group's hive mentality, she could be anywhere, doing anything. And what would Citizen Q. Public think about *that*? The closer he and George traveled toward the cult, the more Smith realized how dire the situation was.

"Can you imagine the field day the fuzz would have with Greta if they lifted her walking around downtown? All undead and reanimated? They wouldn't know *what* to do with her."

Smith chuckled, thinking of Sheriff Wilcox's face when he didn't get any response from the ghoul while using his "diplomatic" interrogation skills. "Yeah. That might make not finding her worth it."

The Rolls eventually caught up with the shambling pack, and George rolled down his window, calling for Anya's attention. She turned and stopped walking, letting the car roll to her.

"We found her footprints," Anya said. "Thankfully bantlings don't immediately know how to teleport or vanish. That usually comes after the third or fourth day."

"Well, girls," George yelled while speeding forward, "let's pick up the pace and find the bitch!"

The disciples moved out of his way as the car took the lead position. Smith noticed the sole trail of Greta's footprints once they cleared the pack. Then they heard the low, guttural hissing from above. The men leaned forward to peer through the windshield and spotted a kettle of vultures circling in the distance. George mashed the gas pedal, and sand flung skyward as the tires fought for traction, lunging the vehicle toward the minitornado of black-winged birds of prey.

"I think they did our job for us . . . again," George sneered. "Anya talks a big talk, but, when push comes to shove, it's always those flying vermin who bail us out."

"What's to keep the vultures from eating us?"

Covington shot Smith a hard glare. "The book formulated their decree. It is written as such, so it is abided. Like the cult, the vultures don't have freewill."

As they got closer, Smith could make out a female figure straggling deeper into the desert. He pointed, and George nodded, aligning the car directly behind Greta. Her messy footprints disappeared underneath the center of the car; the vehicle's tire tracks formed perfect bookends on either side of her prints. Then Smith's head whiplashed backward as George pushed the gas pedal as far as it could go against the floorboard.

"What are you doing?"

George remained silent, smirking. Smith glanced through the windshield as Greta rapidly grew closer.

"Are you going to run her over?"

George's smirk morphed into a full-blown smile. Greta never looked back. Smith didn't know if she couldn't hear the approaching vehicle or if she still had enough sense about her—still had enough *Greta* inside her—that she welcomed an end to her new, cursed existence. Either way, Smith realized they would never know the answer as the Rolls clobbered her, slicing her completely into two. George slammed the brakes, and the car fishtailed in the sand and came to rest sideways a dozen or so yards ahead of the carnage.

Smith used his elbow to prop himself over the front bench and look through the rear window. "Sonofabitch! You cut her in half!"

George shifted the vehicle into reverse. "Is she moving?"

"I don't think so. And the vultures are leaving."

"Good. That means she's been permanently incapacitated."

The car slowly inched backward toward the two lifeless heaps on the sand.

"But this isn't her *real* body, right? I thought you said the Mushroom Cult's bodies were just . . . I dunno, like a replica shell or something?"

"Right. Their real bodies are wherever I—*us*—leave them. When the vultures come do their thing, a mirror image is created."

"But why? Or how?"

"I'm still figuring out how it all works too. But, to be honest, I gave up quite a while ago. I mean, it works, right? Who cares about its logistics or mechanics? All we really need to know is that we take the scum off the street, and Anya keeps them for herself. I stopped worrying about the *how*."

George stopped the Rolls, and they exited the vehicle.

"Huh. I've never seen a dead one before," George said and kicked Greta's body.

Smith slapped his thighs in laughter. "Could you imagine if they find Greta's real body and then find this one here too? Oh, if I could be a fly on the wall when Clark County's *finest* start scratching their heads with *this* investigation. And Hank would be giddier than a kid with a sucker-pop, spinning up yarns of conspiracy headlines. I can see it now. *Call-Girl Doppelgangers Invade Las Vegas.* The city would go berserk."

"The city would call *bushwa*. And your reporter friend would be laughed out of journalism. I think we should dispose of this . . . secondary Greta and pretend this never happened."

Smith regained his composure. "You're no fun!"

George glared at him while he raised himself onto the back fender of the Rolls and waved to the oncoming flock.

"What are you doing?"

"I want them to bury their own. I want to use Greta as an example. As a deterrence. I want Anya to take control of her sheep, once and for all."

George never stepped down from the rear fender the entire time it took the cult to mosey to the car. Anya reached the Rolls first, and George extended a hand, like a gentleman courtly assisting a lady from a carriage. He helped her step onto the fender with him, where every present member of her flock was visible.

"Greta wasn't ready," Anya whispered to George. "She hadn't gotten her hands dirty enough yet. It was her first night as a defiler, with no previous blemishes in her past. Plus she was a virgin, and dead virgins can't sing our songs. The process seemed to have sautéed her essence. I blame—" She fell silent.

George looked at her, concerned. "What's wrong?"

She pursed her lips. "More are missing."

Smith scanned the crowd to investigate but realized he couldn't tell if one ghoul was missing or a dozen. "How do you know?"

"I *know* my servants, Mr. Smith," she answered through angry and clenched teeth. "I *know* when they aren't all accounted for."

Smith raised his hands in front of his chest, palms facing outward, in an exaggerated forfeiting motion.

"I don't think they are too far though," she added, then inhaled deeply and cupped her hands around her mouth. "Anyone within the sound of my voice, listen to my every word!"

Smith startled backward from her voice's booming bass register. He had not expected that sound to come from her mouth. His teeth seemed to rattle when she yelled.

"This is, indeed, a threat! I will not tolerate anything but your complete and utter devotion to me!" Anya's eyes transmogrified from gray to red. "I need to know that, if necessary, you will die for me! Now tell me, will you die for me?"

Her flock cheered in agreement and pumped their exanimated hands into the air, like the home crowd at a high-school football game during the roster announcement. Smith noticed a few of them even hugged each other, gleefully jumping up and down in unison.

"My guidance doesn't come at a cheap price, and my words shouldn't be taken lightly."

The Mushroom Cult simmered down and returned their undivided attention to their chieftain.

"I am the air you take into your lungs and the reality of your existence. And, for those of you who stray, you will be hunted down like dogs."

This stirred a murmur among the ranks. Smith noticed how they didn't use actual words, but they seemed to communicate verbally with each other through intricate grunts and croaking noises.

"Those who obey find paradise in a place we can all call home."

The murmur evolved into an anticipatory rumble.

"In a place we can all someday die in!"

The rumble erupted into thunderous applause. Smith glanced

at George and noticed him roll his eyes. Then George stepped down from the fender, leaving Anya standing in front of her servants.

"Get in," George commanded Smith.

They entered the vehicle and closed their doors, muffling the whoops and hollers from the excited clan outside.

"I can't stand it when she gets like that. Makes me want to terminate the whole deal and just fly solo. Who does she think she is? Some kind of deity? Not yet, anyway!"

"I don't understand why you need her or this partnership in the first place."

"How do you think I've been cleansing the streets for this long without getting caught? The fuzz aren't even *close* to suspecting me of being the Boulevard Killer. They don't have any leads. That's all Anya's doing. She keeps me under a protective shroud of secrecy, and I deliver her new inductees, bantlings. And that protection is now yours too, should you choose to follow this path and join our team."

Anya ripped the driver's side door open. "Where do you think you're going? We have missing girls out there! Girls who could lay a pathway directly to *your* front door."

George grabbed the inside handle of his door. "Don't worry, honeybunches. The vultures will round up your missing ghouls for you. I have no doubt about that." Then he slammed it shut.

The Rolls spewed sand into Anya's face as George pointed the vehicle toward the direction of the Las Vegas skyline, leaving the Mushroom Cult in the desert with their mouths agape and stupefied expressions plastered on their faces.

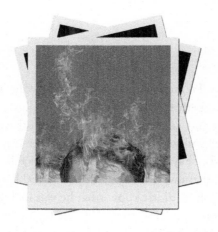

11: Sweet Insanity

The sun was an orange fireball in the sky, slowly elongating the shadows of the pedestrians below as it set behind the tall buildings that obstructed the view of the desert from Smith's office window. With dusk came the sound of loud chitter-chatter and an increase in motorcars on the roadways, indicative of the city coming alive. And with the unavoidable city's wake from its daytime slumber comes the inevitable prowling of the lowlifes and bottom-feeders that gorge themselves on the fragilities of the streets.

Smith took a long drag of his cigarette and exhaled. He brought his flask, now filled to the brim with whiskey, to his lips and gulped almost half of the contents. He released an exaggerated *Ahhhhhhhh!* and filled the flask to the top again from the recently purchased bottle sitting on his desk. He secured the flask in the inside pocket of his trench coat while it still hung on the rack. Then he placed his fedora on his head before donning the coat.

He left his office with the intention to test himself, to see if he really had it in him, to see if he could be a contributing factor to his new alliance.

Cruising down Fremont Street, he slowed his Chevy to a crawl and scoped for the perfect mark. The girls were slowly emerging onto the sidewalks and corners, preparing for another lucrative night with the eager and willing. A few girls, gathered in a clump, blew him kisses and sashayed their hips as their gazes followed the car. He knew none of them were his target tonight; he'd know when he saw her, even though he didn't know what he was looking for.

Horvat stood underneath the ADULT ONLY sign on the corner and waved to him. Smith waved back and then returned both hands to the steering wheel. Horvat continued to talk with a girl Smith had never seen before—a new hire, he assumed—while Horvat stealthily placed his hand on the girl's bottom. Smith assumed she didn't mind the friendly gesture since she didn't flinch when Horvat touched her. The Chevy rolled on, and they drifted out of sight.

Smith turned the corner and immediately noticed Lola standing with a girl he thought he recognized. He stopped the Chevy and leaned across the bench to roll down the window. Neither girl had noticed him yet so he had a moment to study her. She didn't look *average*, so it wasn't a case of mistaken identity. He definitely believed he had communicated with her before. Her profile reminded him of, who? The way her shoulder-length hair was tucked behind her ear and the point of her nose—

He had seen her in a photograph. He was sure of it. He ran through all the possibilities: a client's missing daughter? A runaway teen? A cheating girlfriend?

Lola noticed the Chevy idling a few yards away and ran to the car. She stuck her head inside the open passenger window. "Hey ya, handsome. I think tonight's the night when you should finally take me on that date you've been promising me."

Smith scoffed. "I have *never* promised anything of the kind. You've been soliciting me for months! Who's your friend?"

"*Oooohh*, I see how it is. Turn me away, your buddy pal Lola, for some fresh meat. Okay, okay. I get it." She put her arms around the other girl's shoulder and nudged her toward the open window. "Introducing . . . Luna!"

"Hey again," Luna said.

Smith snorted. "Lola and Luna? Don't bust my chops. And what do you mean, *again*?"

"What's wrong with her name?" Lola asked in a sticky-sweet tone, ignoring his secondary question. "Horvat gave her that name since she's been assigned to me. We're a team. I think it's cute."

Smith realized his mission was to now get the new girl in the car to see what she meant by *again*. "How much?"

"I assume you mean for the Lola-and-Luna team, the both of us."

"No, Lola. Just for her. Just for Luna," Smith answered and then whispered under his breath, "I can't believe those names just came out of my mouth. Like Tweedledee and Tweedledum."

"You're breaking my heart, Smith."

"I'll break something else if you don't answer my question. How much for the new dame? Or do you *want* a knuckle sandwich right in the *kissah*?"

"Jeez, Louise! No need to get your panties in a wad. Last time she was on the house, so tonight you'll get the repeat-customer special."

Last time? Smith thought. "Okay, just . . . get in. Whatever it is, we'll discuss it."

Luna opened the door and slid into the bench. Smith noticed she tried to act seductive as she entered the Chevy but looked clumsy and uncoordinated at best. She closed the door, and Smith saw Lola waving in his rearview mirror as he pulled into traffic and headed toward the motel that lay deep beyond the outskirts of civilization.

The Chevy glided into the parking spot George favored next to the motel's front door. Smith walked around his car and opened the passenger door for Luna. Extending his hand, she reached for it, and he guided her from the vehicle. He amused himself by wondering if there might be another sleuth on the other side of the parking lot taking snapshots of him with a Kodak. *Oh, how the tables have turned in such a short amount of time,* he thought.

Smith escorted Luna into the Desert Palms, and Cheryl merrily greeted them. "Please take some complimentary matches. Your friend, Mr. Covington, takes a handful every time he stays with us."

Smith politely declined and then requested any available room, making it clear he was not sentimental about any particular room. She handed him the keys to Room 242, and Luna bounded and giggled the whole way down the corridor. Smith unlocked the door, and Luna ran in, like an excited child at the entrance to a carnival, and jumped on the bed. He lazily tossed his trench coat and fedora over the chair sitting in the corner next to the window.

"So?" she said, slithering onto her stomach and placing her hands underneath her chin to prop up her head. "Are you going to take photographs of me again? That was a gas."

Images of the girl in the photographs Smith had found crumpled in his hand when he had awoken from his blackout in front of the *Gazette* rushed like an avalanche through his memory. Now he remembered why Luna looked so familiar.

"Not tonight, doll face. I left the camera at home."

"Oh, applesauce! Well then, what else would you like to do? We have all night!"

Smith couldn't answer her. He was too distracted, wondering what had happened during his blackout that night. Was taking pictures of Luna the only thing they had done together, or had they partaken of other indulgences?

"Well, why don't we do what we did last time, just minus the photoshoot."

"Aww, that's no fun! And scary, to be honest."

Smith gulped. "Scary?"

"After you took all those sexy pictures of your little kitten," she answered, reaching from the bed and running a single finger down his lapel and over his crotch, "you yelled at me and told me to get out." She pouted and batted her eyelashes.

"I'm sorry. I didn't mean to yell at you," he replied, hoping to open up further discussions of what had transpired without having to ask her outright.

"It's okay, silly. I understand. I get terrible headaches too. I just didn't like having to find my own way back to the city. It's so far away. That made me *saaaaaad.*" She pressed a little harder into the fabric of his pants. "You can make it up to me tonight."

He realized he must have blacked out after she left, but what concerned him was not having any recollection of picking her up in the first place or the photographs or the headache or how he got from the motel to the *Gazette*.

He stepped closer to the bed so she didn't have to reach as far. "I don't think there'll be any headaches tonight, kitten. But, instead of taking your picture, how about we play a little game?"

"*Ooo*, I *love* games!" she exclaimed, clapping and getting into a sitting position with her knees tucked underneath her.

"Take off all your clothes and stand as still as you can."

"Like a mannequin?"

"Yes, like a mannequin," he affirmed, feeling himself grow braver by controlling his subject.

Luna excitedly complied, ripping off her garments and making sure her bra and panties landed on Smith's head and face. She giggled and lifted one knee to her opposite thigh. He removed the underwear and let them fall to the carpet.

"Lay down."

As Luna assumed the requested position, Smith fished his flask from the inside pocket of his coat draped over the back of the chair. He unscrewed the cap and approached the bed.

"Something to loosen us up?" she asked.

"Something to loosen me up," he replied and kneeled on the mattress next to her naked breasts.

The flask's cap bounced once on the carpet when he let it fall to the floor, and then he touched the opening to her exposed cleavage.

"*Ooo*, that's cold," she exclaimed and arched her back. "But I like it."

Smith tipped the bottle when he got directly between her breasts so the liquid seeped out and sent spider web-like tributaries of booze sprawling across her flesh, fanning out until the trails met the mattress. He tilted the bottle steeper, and her body became covered in a tidal wave of soaking brown alcohol. Haphazardly tossing the empty bottle over his shoulder, he buried his face in her bosom to lap up the liquid.

Luna giggled and placed her hands on the back of Smith's head, guiding his nose and mouth farther into her skin. He felt the alcohol soak his forehead and hairline as he rubbed his face back and forth and slurped the drink, like a dog lapping water from a bowl. He slowly dragged his tongue toward her belly button and felt her push him, urging him to go farther toward her midsection.

"Yes. Yes! Oh, you know what I want, Mr. Arbuckle. And I want you to give it to—"

"What did you call me?" he asked with urgency, snapping up his head to see her face when she answered. He jumped to a standing position, like greased lightning. "Why would you call me that? You know my name! Answer me. NOW, bitch!"

Luna scurried to the headboard and grabbed one of the pillows in fright, using it as a shield and barricade against the madman. She hoped he didn't pull another Jekyll-and-Hyde act on her again. "You—you—you asked me to call you that last time. You said—you said, in here, you didn't want me to use your real name. You said," Luna burst into tears. "You said that, in here—in here we were—we were . . ."

"We were *what*? Spit it out, you stupid broad!" Then he grabbed his temples and grimaced.

Luna lowered the pillow below her chin line, concerned. "Are you okay, Mr. Arbuckle?"

"Don't . . ." He clenched his eyelids closed. "Call . . ." He doubled-over at the waist. "Me . . ." He supported himself by placing his palms on the carpet. "That!" He felt his body tumble sideways but was unconscious before it struck the carpet.

Luna peered over the edge of the mattress. "Mr. Arbuckle?" she whispered. "Mr. Smith?" she asked louder and with more confidence. She swung her body off the bed, feeling the fabric of the carpet underneath her bare feet and between her naked toes. She thought a low grumble escaped from his throat but couldn't be entirely sure, so she bent down and rolled him onto his back.

Smith's eyes were closed, but rapid fluttering occurred behind his lids. Luna reached, hand shaking, to check the pulse in his neck. She screeched when his eyes popped open—eyes not focused on anything. Barren and listless eyes.

Luna stood up and took a step backward. She only had the chance to scream one more time before the beast silenced her.

When he tried to fully extend his arm, his hand got caught on something gooey, but the guck was so strong it wouldn't let him stretch out completely. The material felt like a membrane of some kind. He tried to unfurl his body from the fetal position he was trapped in, but the membrane seemed to keep his posture folded. Then a jarring pulse, beating in a measured cadence, vibrated the clear membrane, and Smith twisted and turned. He frantically outstretched his hands to stop his spinning, but the inside of the membrane was slick, and he couldn't get any friction to slow himself. The violent rhythm accelerated, and he spun faster.

The membrane moved forward through small tubes filled with pulsating red liquid, riding the short, quick pumps like a surfboard. The red stream was visible through the transparent underbelly of the membrane, and his protective bubble was disintegrating around him. An opening filled with light grew larger as he surfed toward it, the membrane dissolving the closer he got.

His body was freed from the confined fetal position, and his face and front side landed into the pulsing flow of liquid, covering him with crimson fluid. He planted his hands into the stream, but his attempt to steady himself was futile. The surge carried him toward the opening ahead, still growing larger. The stream turned into a river, getting exponentially deeper, and Smith thought the surfing sensation had turned into what might have felt like whitewater rafting. The crimson water splashed into his mouth, tasting metallic—mineral-like. Then the illuminated opening widened, like a mouth, and vomited him out. He fell with the spewed liquid, swinging his arms in a circle like a windmill as he free-fell into the nothingness.

His body smashed onto a solid surface hard enough that he was certain the fall had broken all his bones. He instinctively rubbed the small of his back to soothe the pain shooting through his joints and muscles and then rolled over. Soft grass caressed his cheek, and blades tickled the space between his fingers. The pain from the fall dissipated as he sat up and surveyed the landscape: a grassy knoll with rolling hills that seemed to continue to infinity. Then he noticed the bodies and heard the screams. The rolling hills were littered with lifeless figures that Smith was certain were all dead. Hordes of not-dead people ran, slaloming between the scattered dead bodies like a football player escaping defenders, screaming and grabbing and patting their heads. Heads that were on fire.

Smith stood rooted to the spot and turned in a complete circle. The view was the same from every angle. As far as he could see across the rolling hills, for miles and miles, dead bodies and swarms of screaming people tried to extinguish their blazing heads; all men donning the same garb. They looked like the cartoon *Tom and Jerry*, when the characters run for a long time and the background never changes.

Smith gasped when one of these hypnotized screaming men ran by close enough for him to smell the charring hair. He almost stumbled over one of the dead bodies on the ground when he took a step backward. He realized why the scene was so unsettling— never mind the calculated trajectory of each running, screaming male and the countless bodies on the ground; they were all mirror images of Smith, down to even his gray trench coat. He looked at the thousand copies of himself, half lying dead, the other half with their heads on fire, running up and down the rolling hills, careful to not step on the fallen . . . Smiths.

The runners stopped abruptly, as if someone had yelled FREEZE! The deceased slowly rose to their feet, reanimated, like zombies rising from a shallow grave. Combining their ranks, the horde marched to one side of the rolling hill, leaving the other half empty sans the beautifully manicured grass. They turned to face Smith, their archetype, and he saw that all the fires had been extinguished.

One Smith doppelgänger stepped from the front line and approached him, holding out a lit match. He gestured to Smith's head and grunted. Smith shuddered from the sound, resembling too closely the same sounds the Mushroom Cult makes when they communicate with each other. He shook his head, hoping Smith Junior got the gist that, no, he didn't want to set his head ablaze.

Smith Junior turned to face the sea of other Smiths waiting behind them and shook his head to signal that Smith Senior wasn't partaking in their fun. Smith Junior left him standing alone and traipsed back toward the sea of Smiths. Junior stopped a few yards from the front row and raised the match into the air, almost like a silent war cry.

Smith startled when the crowd of Smiths cheered and ran, one by one, toward the flame; their heads spontaneously lighting when they ran by. Handfuls of Smiths dropped to the grass, dead. Other Smiths continued running and screaming. Smith watched as, within a matter of minutes, the rolling hills had reverted to the exact state they had been in when he had arrived; the walkers and their fiery heads maneuvered around the already deceased.

"*Psst!*" Smith heard behind him. When he turned around, he saw George Covington standing on a floating bed covered in roses surrounded by humanoids with disfigured faces. Smith ran to George, zigzagging around the recently expired replicas of himself, waving and feeling relieved to see a friendly face in this nightmarish maze.

George smiled wickedly and pointed to the hump underneath the layer of roses. As Smith got closer, he noticed the hump twitching and convulsing as rose petals detached and fluttered to the ground. Then George kneeled next to the hump and placed his palm over what looked like the tip of a nose peeking through the roses.

Smith reached the levitating bed, and the creatures with the distorted faces took a step backward. "What are you doing? Who is that?" He tried to make out the shape of the body underneath the roses.

"It's your mother, Detective. I'm taking her to the moon, where she can be free of pain and suffering."

"Would you take me with you too? *Pleeeease*?" he begged.

"There's no returning. It's a one-way ticket. Once we get up there"—George pointed skyward—"you can never come back, and you'll never be the same. Are you willing to leave everything you know behind and join me and my insanity? Forever?"

Smith looked at the figure of his dying mother, watched a rose fall from her deathbed, and then glanced at the thousands of Smiths running amok behind him, screaming bloody murder with their heads on fire until they expired and crumpled to the grass of the rolling hills.

"Look what we've become," George said and swept his arm slowly at the disfigured faces, like he was presenting a showcase. "We are the envy of everyone."

"We're like a furious wind in a storm, bringing the hammer down on the low-down dirty rats in the streets," Smith added.

George smiled maniacally. "This could all be yours. And everyone will run and hide."

Smith gasped for air, like a fish out of water, as he awoke on the motel floor with his mouth full of blood.

Smith didn't know how much time had passed since he had blacked out. He scurried backward on his hands and knees like a crab until his back pressed against the wall underneath the window that looked across the parking lot. He sat with his knees bunched to his chin for quite a while, contemplating his next move and recollecting what may have happened in the room.

Luna was dead on the floor. *Not just dead*, he thought. *Mutilated*. Blood had been splattered all over the mirror and bed. Her neck had been ripped open, her guts had been eviscerated, and an eyeball sat on the nightstand, the optic nerve fibers dangling behind it like jellyfish tentacles.

Smith spit again, his saliva swirling with blood. He was fairly sure it wasn't his blood. He grabbed the windowsill and pulled himself up to look out the window. The resident cat hissed through the glass and jumped into a nearby bush as Smith realized the sun was setting.

"How long have I been in here?" His breath fogged the glass as he spoke. Then he directed his attention to Luna and the pool of blood on the carpet. He crawled to her body and inspected the carnage. Rigor mortis and hypostasis had set in Luna's muscles and skin, and most of the blood on the carpet was crusty; the middle of the puddle reminded Smith of molasses.

He looked at himself in the mirror—dots of blood speckled his reflection—and inspected his clothes. He couldn't find any blemishes or soiled patches anywhere in the fabric of his undershirt or vest. His fedora lay innocently where he had tossed it when he and Luna had entered the room. His revolver was still in the holster, and none of the rounds had been fired. No, he had not used his .38 to kill her. Had he used his bare hands? He scraped his tongue along the top row of his teeth. Had he used his . . . *teeth?*

He walked to the window and had to use all his strength to open it. The wooden frame popped and cracked as it glided up its track. He stuck his head out the window and looked across the desert landscape adjacent to the motel. He contemplated the consequences of beating feet and never returning, or attempting to clean the mess and dispose of Luna's body, hoping Clark County's finest would be too dense to tie him to the death. And how would he explain her disappearance to Horvat and Lola? They both knew he was the last one who had picked her up. Hell, Lola had practically shoved Luna into his car.

He turned to look at the severed eye, staring accusingly from the nightstand, just as he heard the raspy hiss of vultures in the distance.

And a knock on the door.

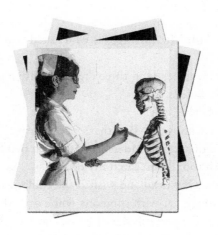

12: Silent Film

Wynn cut the steering wheel sharply, veering her car into the Desert Palms Motel parking lot. The setting sun blinded her for a moment before she swerved into an empty slot. She had hardly shifted the vehicle into Park before frantically jettisoning from the car. Her heart pounded in double time as she left her driver-side door open and sprinted toward Smith's Chevy. She stopped her inertia by placing her palms against the high wheel well and then peered through the windows. No sign of distress. No sign of struggle. But no Smith. She jogged to the front door and entered the lobby like a dust devil.

"May I help you, miss?" Cheryl asked, lowering a copy of the previous day's *Gazette*.

"I'm looking for someone. A friend."

"Most people here already *have* a friend. Or they wouldn't be here, if you catch my drift," she teased and winked.

"I'm not in the mood, you old hag."

"No need to get nasty!"

"Jeepers creepers. I think my friend is in trouble. He's the one who's friends with Mr. Covington, who asked you about the Rolls that night."

"Ah, yes. He checked in three days ago with a girl he had been here with once before."

"Has he checked out?"

"Not that I know of. But that's not unusual. Sometimes our guests like to embark on benders. And not just benders of the booze but of the flesh too, if you catch my drift."

Wynn shook her head and wished she could deal with anyone a little more normal. Or with someone who's drift she didn't have to keep catching. "Do you mind letting me check on him?"

"That's not our usual policy. Here at the Desert Palms we keep our clients protected under a shroud of anonymity. That's how we retain our repeat guests. They trust us with their secrecy. You're not his wife, are you?"

"No."

Cheryl placed a hand over her heart. "Oh, thank Bessie. I thought I had futzed that all up already." She leaned forward across the desk and whispered, "Daughter?"

Wynn smirked. "While flattered, no. I am his . . . business partner. And he hasn't come to work in three days, and we have important accounts to manage right now."

"Well, I'd hate for anything bad to happen to any of our guests during their stay here at the Desert Palms. That would just be a travesty!"

Wynn rolled her eyes and thought, *If you only knew.*

"Come. Follow me," Cheryl finished and grabbed a spare set of keys marked *242* from a hook.

Wynn pointed to the keys. "There's a second floor?"

"Huh?" Cheryl looked at where Wynn pointed. "Oh, the two-four-two. Miss Tierney numbered the second-wing rooms, starting with twos, and the first wing are all ones."

"*Miss*? A woman owns this place?"

Cheryl laughed as they turned the corner. "Miss Tierney is only the most brazen and unrestrained woman you'll ever meet."

They reached Room 242, and Cheryl knocked. After a considerable length of silence, she knocked again.

Smith froze. He swiveled his head back and forth between the open window and the closed door. He didn't know who he wanted to face less: the vultures outside or the inquiring human inside. He wasn't even sure the Desert Palms had a cleaning service. If they did, no one had ever bothered him until now. *Maybe that's who it was,* he thought. *The maid to tidy the room.*

Whoever it was knocked again. The time for a decision was nigh. He looked at Luna's mangled body and quickly glanced at the blood-covered weird mismatched furniture. His fight-or-flight instinct activated, and flight won this time. He bounded toward the open window, noticing the powerful fluttering of the wings neared, when he heard Wynn's voice call his name through the door. He stopped midstep when she screamed his name again, this time sounding like a concerned question. Then he heard her say in a normal volume, "Go ahead. Open it."

He leaped over Luna's decomposing body, unlatched the lock, and opened the door just enough for his left eye to see through the crack. He used his leg and stomach to block the rest of her vision into the room.

"Hot diggity, Smith. What's going on in there? Are you okay?"

"Wynn! I'm fine. I'll meet you outside, okay? Just give me a minute to collect my things."

"Are you alone in there?" she asked, more concerned than accusatory.

"Um . . ." He looked at the floor behind him and almost

slammed the door shut in surprise. "Yeah. Just hold your horses, will ya? Meet me in the parking lot."

He closed the door and spun around. His arms flailed as he scanned the room. Luna was gone. Every speck of blood was gone. Even her eye on the nightstand was gone. A single black feather floated downward and landed on the windowsill. Smith approached the open window and rolled the stem of the feather between his thumb and index finger. He stuck his head out the window and saw the black cloud of wings vanish into the distant horizon. The motel cat jumped onto the windowsill and meowed, startling Smith as he punched it into the shrubbery below with the hand that held the lost vulture feather.

Now it was time to face Wynn.

"Everything okay, sir?"

"Everything's fine, Cheryl," he said as he exited the lobby.

Wynn's shadow sprawled across the entire hood of her car as the sun had almost been consumed by the dunes in the distance. Her arms were folded, and she tapped her foot.

He decided to be upfront and honest. "I had another blackout."

"Another one? Oh, jeepers creepers, Smith. I hadn't heard from you in three days and thought—"

"Why would you hear from me? You told me that *you* needed three days. That I would hear from *you* in three days," he spat. "Wasn't that the last thing you said to me after our little picnic?"

Wynn clenched her teeth and willed herself to not explode. Instead she lunged forward and wrapped her arms around him. "I could only give myself twelve hours. I wanted to surprise you at your office and try to start fresh again. But you were gone, and I waited for you to return all day. The next morning I went to see Hank, and the two of us looked everywhere for you: the bars, every casino. We went downtown, and your buddy, H, told us you had picked up one of his new girls and didn't know when you'd be back. I don't know why I didn't think to check here until about an hour ago."

"Knowing you, I'm surprised you didn't go to the law and report me missing."

She squeezed him to make sure he was really here, to make sure he wasn't a figment of her wishful imagination. "I could never expose you, no matter what evil you got into."

"So how long have you been looking for me total?" he asked, hoping her answer would give him a ballpark figure as to what day it might be.

"Three days. I've been looking for you for three days. Have you been blacked out this entire time? And what happened to H's girl?"

Smith placed a palm to his forehead to slow down the static in his brain. "I've been blacked out for *three days*?"

"What happened to the girl, Smith?" she asked sternly.

"She took off. I didn't do anything with her. We started . . . I was angry. I'm sorry. Oh, God, Wynn. I'm so, so sorry." He pulled her close and put the curve of her skull between the tip of his nose and top lip and inhaled her scent. "I got one of my migraines, the ones that come before I blackout, and I asked her leave. I don't know where she went or how she got back to the city. That's the last thing I remember."

Wynn pulled away from him. "Were you going to . . . you know?"

"Kill her? Nah. It took being in that room with her to make me realize you were right all along. If I'd killed her, I'd be no better than the scum I've put in the slammer. I think I expelled that demon. I know what I want in my life." He brushed a clump of her hair behind her ear. "And it doesn't involve being a comic-book goon superhero for the city."

"Promise me that you'll let me take you to the hospital tomorrow to get these blackouts checked out?"

"You know what I say about hospitals. They're for two types of people: the dying and the—"

"Oh, jeepers, Smith! You just might be dying!"

"Fine. You can take me. But I want to sleep at your place tonight."

She hugged him again, and he absentmindedly wiped a clot of dried blood from the inside of his mouth.

Smith filled out the checklist attached to the clipboard the receptionist had handed him. Questions about family medical history, eating and exercising habits, and previous ailments. On paper, he looked like a dead man walking.

He removed a pack of Smolens from his vest pocket and lit a match from a matchbook advertising the Desert Palms Motel. "How did I get this?" he muttered.

"I don't think you should smoke in here," Wynn suggested as a man coughed behind them.

He nodded and put the Smolens in his pocket, concentrating on finishing the questionnaire.

"Mr. Smith?" a plump older woman called from a small room.

They stood up and walked into the triage cubicle.

"Are you his wife?" she asked, not looking up from her chart.

"Um, no. I'm his business partner," Wynn answered.

"My wife and I are separated. I asked Ms. Deacon to accompany me here, if that's okay."

"Ms. Deacon will have to leave if the doctor decides to admit you. Visiting hours are from nine to noon, and then from five to eight."

Wynn nodded. "I understand, ma'am."

"What brings you in today, Mr. Smith?"

Wynn's presence forced him to be honest and forthcoming. He explained the headaches, the blackouts, and the loss of time—

sometimes days. He neglected to add the blood he sometimes had in his mouth or the committee of vultures that had conveniently removed a dead hooker's carcass within a matter of seconds from his motel room. He was sure those disclosures would get him admitted to a different kind of hospital.

The nurse signed the bottom of the chart and told them to have a seat in the waiting room again. After what felt like an eternity, his name was called again, and they were escorted into an examination room. The bright sterile lights bore down, reflecting off the white walls and white bed. Smith was thankful he didn't have a hangover. He didn't think his drunken brain could handle the room's luster.

A knock on the door brought Smith and Wynn to attention, and then the door swung open. A large man with salt-and-pepper hair and hands the size of baseball gloves entered and shook Smith's hand.

"Good morning, Mr. Smith. I'm Dr. Weber." He sat down on a stool that looked way too small to support his body and flipped through some notes. "Tell me about the blackouts."

The longer Smith spoke to Dr. Weber, the more comfortable he felt. After a healthy back-and-forth of symptoms and possible causes, the doctor asked Wynn to step outside so Smith could change into a hospital gown.

Dr. Weber followed her from the examination room. "You can wait in the reception room if it'll make you feel more comfortable. It's never easy to hear our loved ones talk about such things. It can be disturbing."

"I'm just happy he's finally in here," she answered, wondering if he was patronizing her because she was a woman.

"He'll be back after the radiographs are taken. And we'll discuss a course of action based on what they reveal. If anything at all."

She nodded, and the door opened, revealing Smith standing in the doorway, dressed in nothing but a baby-blue gown. Wynn trapped a laugh with her hand and forced herself to look elsewhere.

"Ready, Mr. Smith? I'll walk you down to radiology."

Smith glared at Wynn. "I dunno, Doc. Are the nurses going to laugh at my getup too?"

Wynn burst into hysterics, and Smith kissed her before walking away with the doctor. Half of her hoped they wouldn't find anything on the radiograph, and the other half of her hoped they did. At least then there might be some answers.

"It's called a pituitary carcinoma—a brain tumor."

Wynn gasped and covered her mouth with both hands. "Are you sure?"

"Common symptoms are blurred vision, headaches, numbness or pain, dizziness, and, most frequently, loss of consciousness," Dr. Weber said. "Now it is cancerous but treatable. We've successfully treated these for over twenty years. I want to admit you, Mr. Smith, and run some blood work. I also would like to observe you over the next few days, to monitor one of these episodes, to give me a better handle on your behavior. That'll also help narrow the diagnosis."

Smith remained stoic, donning what Wynn liked to call his poker face. "So you want me to stay the night?"

"It might be a few nights, if that's okay with you."

Smith looked at Wynn. She smiled and squeezed his hand.

"It's okay with us," she answered. "I won't crowd you. Let me know when you're being discharged, and I'll come and get you, okay?"

Smith nodded, still apathetic and dispassionate. She kissed him on the cheek and thanked the doctor, leaving Smith alone in the building of his nightmares, accompanied by his worst fears realized.

The doctor entered the examination room wearing a white surgical mask, and Smith glanced at his hospital gown. It had mysteriously changed from a jade-green color to a scarlet red. The only part of the doctor's face Smith could see were Weber's eyes—his surgical cap was pulled down to his eyebrows, and the mask covered his nose.

"Well, Mr. Smith. The blood tests and X-rays are clear about one thing," Dr. Weber said.

"What's that?"

"Your results came back terminal. Looks like you're going to *diiiiiieeeee!*"

Wynn screamed, "*Noooooooo!*"

Her voice startled Smith. He didn't even know she was still present until her banshee yell pierced the room.

"Nurse!" Dr. Weber requested through the open door. "Bring the restraints! And remove the wench. She doesn't need to see this procedure."

Smith scurried backward on the hospital bed as six nurses entered the room, all covered in scrubs with their faces blurry. They reminded him of the photographs he had developed from his Kodak of subjects who had moved quickly just as he snapped the shutter. But these nurses weren't moving quickly. They glided into the room as lackadaisical as turtles. And then a nurse without scrubs entered. Her face was blurry as well, but she moved like lightning. She grabbed Wynn and yanked her from the room before Smith could protest. The door slammed shut behind them, leaving Smith alone with Dr. Weber and the six wraith nurses. He could hear Wynn's screams fade until she was either forcefully silenced or had just traveled far enough away to where he couldn't hear her anymore. He prayed for the latter.

"You just told me that you've been successfully treating these—"

Dr. Weber tossed back his head and laughed like an overdramatic stage actor. "Nothing is saving you now! Would you like to declare some final contrition? Huh? Some dark, dirty secret?" Dr. Weber closed one eye and swiveled his head so his opened eye was closer to Smith than the rest of his face. "You'll feel so much better if you just spill the beans!" The doctor lunged forward. "This is your last chance—a deathbed confessional—before facing eternal damnation."

The six nurses stepped forward in unison, and only their eyes came into focus from their blurry faces—as if any real eyes they may have had were now replaced with baby-doll eyes—distinct black buttons surrounded by an oval-shaped blur of a face. Smith darted his head back and forth, undecided which nurse he should concentrate on first. Four nurses grabbed his wrists and ankles while the remaining two applied the shackles, securing his limbs to the bedrails. He couldn't have squirmed or resisted if he had wanted to; his body had become paralyzed once their baby-doll eyes had emerged from the blurry smears of their faces.

Smith wanted to show Dr. Weber and the opalescent-faced nurses he wasn't scared or falling for their antics. He forced himself to smile, hoping to ward off any further scare tactics.

"Don't bother to fake a smile," Dr. Weber said.

The six baby-doll-eyed nurses took a step backward in unison as the door opened, and the nurse who had escorted Wynn away reentered. Dr. Weber swept his arm toward Smith in a he's-all-yours gesture. The nurse grinned and charged the bed. Smith yanked his body backward as far as the restraints would allow him to move. She placed her palm over his face—her pinkie and thumb squeezed his cheekbones while her remaining two digits pressed into his forehead.

He squirmed as voices ebbed and flowed through his brain. Female pleas rushed through his eardrums, like they were screaming from a passing train. Candy's voice . . . *Whoosh!—Please stop!—Whoosh!* . . . Luna's voice . . . *Whoosh!—Don't kill me!—Whoosh!* . . . Then the voice of the one he had been trying to forget echoed down the hospital hallway . . . *Whoosh!—Smith, how could you do this to me?—Whoosh!*

"Stop!" he begged and snatched one hand free from the

restraints to wipe away a tear that had dripped between the head nurse's four fingers still pressing on his face.

The six nurses pounced for his freed hand, and the head nurse raised her other hand to stop them. They froze in place; their baby-doll eyes concentrated on his unrestrained hand as the head nurse lifted her fingers from Smith's face.

She leaned down, her lips gently grazing his as she spoke. "The credits have begun to roll on your salvation, like the closing of a picture show. And you'll never be the same." Her breath stank of spoiled milk and feces. "Your demise will be climactic but so cliché, like love scenes in the rain."

The head nurse kept her eyes open as she firmly pressed her cold lips to his. He thought she would break his front teeth with the amount of pressure she applied. Their gazes locked, and her face contorted into the image of his estranged wife, decomposing and smelling like a mixture of rotting meat and cheap perfume. Smith screamed through clenched teeth and closed lips and then dead silence infiltrated his brain. He squeezed his eyelids closed, counted to five—the world void of sound—and opened them. He was alone in the examination room. The six impious nurses, the head nurse, and the doctor had vanished. The restraints no longer pinned his limbs to the bed. He looked at the clock on the wall and noticed the second hand ticked backward one second, then forward, then backward, then forward . . .

The door opened, and a human nurse entered. Smith sighed in relief when he saw that she wore a normal jade-green scrub and he could make out all the features of her face.

"Oh, thank God. I think I was having a nightmare. A glass of water would be great right about now."

The nurse acted as if she hadn't heard him. She continued to check his chart and compare it to the time of the clock on the wall—the clock that was repeating the same second over and over and over—without acknowledging he was even here. She acted satisfied with the broken time and his chart and reattached the folder to the foot of his bed, then turned to leave the room.

"Wait!" he pleaded.

She stopped but did not turn to face him.

"Could I please get something to drink?"

The nurse slammed shut the door, the *thunk* ricocheting off the walls, trapping both of them inside the room. The defective clock fell from the wall and rolled across the room; the numbers from the clock's face spewed onto the floor, like a silent-film reel unraveling. The nurse turned to face him. She was naked. Blood trickled into her cleavage.

"All we wanted was a good time and to make a little cash," she said. "Is that so bad? We're not naughty."

The door opened, and a pig floated into the room and squealed. A sleeping child materialized and woke up in the chair in the corner and screamed, "Help me!"

Smith tried to speak. "I don't know—"

The child and the flying pig vanished. The naked, bleeding nurse shoved a newspaper into Smith's face, smothering him. She crumpled the paper into a ball and stuffed it into his mouth, gagging him. He bit down on her hand, spurting blood from the puncture wounds, and gripped her wrists. The skin separated and slid off her hand, landing on his chest. Smith lunged from the bed and trapped one of her arms around her back. He spat out the newspaper, and when it landed on the floor he noticed the headline:

LAS VEGAS'S BOULEVARD KILLER CAPTURED;
CONFESSIONS CAUGHT ON TAPE

The nurse wailed in pain from the sharp angle Smith had her arm trapped in.

"If you're a good girl and don't try anything stupid again, I'll set you free."

He twisted her arm again to punctuate his seriousness. She

grunted but didn't answer him. Her flesh-stripped hand dangled lifelessly by her side. Blood dripped onto the newspaper lying on the floor. He looked at the headline one more time and then to the naked and bleeding nurse he had tangled up like a pretzel. This was all her fault. All of it. All the filth on the streets was because of her and her opportunistic marketability for the weak and horny.

"Be a good girl. Stop tainting the waters. And I'll set you free."

He felt her relax under the pressure he applied to her arm.

"I'm just kidding. None of it's true," he said and bent her arm backward as hard as he could, snapping it off at the elbow. "None of it's true!"

He stumbled backward with the bloody stump of her forearm in his hand, and she barked at him. She charged, her right arm severed at the elbow and gushing blood, with her left hand—stripped to the bone and tendons—held straight out, fingers splayed to trap whatever piece of him she came in contact with first. He got into a baseball batter's stance, holding her severed forearm at the wrist, ready to swing-batta-batta-batta-hey-batta-batta-*SWING!*-batta-batta . . . And that's what he did.

Smith swung the nurse's arm and connected with the side of her head so hard that she dropped to the floor, twitching. The skin on the wrist slipped off, and the arm sailed across the room and struck the far wall, leaving a bloody splatter. He stepped over her lifeless corpse and headed for the door. Headed for where the door *should* have been.

The walls were seamless now. The doors and windows were gone. From floor to ceiling, the walls did not contain any breaks. Screaming, he ran his hands along the white padding of the walls, his fingers burning from the friction of the fabric that protected the cushioning. He noticed the blood splat from the severed arm was gone from the wall. When he looked behind him, he saw that all the hospital apparatuses had been replaced with a single mattress tossed haphazardly on the floor without sheets or blankets. The nurse was gone, along with her arm and any evidence she had been here at all. No remnants that the room had ever existed inside a medical hospital remained. The single, solitary mattress was the only item in the padded cell—or what felt like the gates of Hell.

Smith, defeated and discouraged, traipsed to the mattress and sat down. He closed his eyes and ran his fingers through his hair. Swinging his feet onto the mattress, he rolled over into the fetal position to get comfortable. He smacked his lips and tasted that familiar metallic tingle. Vomit clenched his stomach as he recalled biting into the nurse's hand when she had choked him with the newspaper, her vile blood squirting everywhere. He spun around on the mattress and almost tumbled to the floor. If he hadn't reacted as quickly as he had, he would have rolled right off the hospital bed.

He gripped the bedrails and looked around. Everything was back, intact. The once-broken clock hung on the wall, keeping accurate time with a second hand that made its appropriate tick-tick-tick. The walls had shed their padding. The door and window had returned. And the blood splatter from the nurse's severed arm shone bright and red for all the world to see.

Smith looked at the floor, and his heart jumped when he saw a bloodied, dead nurse. Her arm was detached, lying carelessly on the chair in the corner where he had seen the small child materialize. He slid off the bed and kneeled beside the nurse. She was a young woman, blonde, and dressed in her jade-green scrubs. The skin on her left hand was still attached, and the only blood he saw was from her right arm being severed from her elbow. Her nametag read SABRINA.

Thoughts rattled his brain as he tried to figure out what had happened. She hadn't been a naked, murderous nurse. She was Sabrina—a night nurse just attending to her rounds. Had it been a hallucination? Another blackout incident? Whatever it was, it didn't change the fact a dead nurse lay on the hospital room floor.

He checked her left hand for teeth marks. None. He wiped his mouth with the back of his hand, confident the taste of blood was an illusion, but red liquid stained his skin.

Smith quickly collected his clothes and changed out of the gown. He stepped over Sabrina's body to get to the door. The hallway was empty, and the nurse's station by the staircase to the right was unmanned. He wondered if that was Sabrina's post tonight. He noticed an electric elevator to the left. Slipping from the room, leaving Sabrina's corpse behind, he shuffled like a crab toward the elevator doors, keeping his eye on the nurse's station. He reached the elevator and pressed the Down button.

"C'mon, c'mon," he begged as he continued to tap the button, like sending a Morse-code SOS distress signal.

He ducked his head when the elevator dinged, as if the sound would be the one thing that gave him away. The door opened, and he pushed the button donning the number *1*. He tapped his foot in nervous anticipation of what would be on the other side of the door when it opened in the lobby. The elevator dinged again, signaling the end of the ride.

A receptionist smiled and nodded at him as he walked past the desk. "Have a good night, sir."

"Thank you, ma'am. Same to you," he replied without looking at her as he passed through the exit doors and into the freedom of the cool Las Vegas nighttime air.

Smith shoved a few coins into a three-slot pay phone he found a few blocks away from Las Vegas General and dialed the only telephone number he had ever memorized due to his many inebriated nights at Rippetoe's: the local taxi-meter service. He advised the dispatcher of his current location and final destination, and she informed him that it might be upward to half an hour before a cab could get to him. He stated that the wait was reasonable and finished the call by describing himself so the driver could easily identify him.

The taxi arrived under schedule without Smith being noticed—he was sure hospital staff and the Las Vegas Police and the Clark

County Sheriff's Office and the Nevada State Police were involved in a full-fledged manhunt by now—and drove him to his office. He needed to make some phone calls and couldn't risk using the party line at his house; so the private line in his office was the only option he felt comfortable using. He dialed Las Vegas General's number and requested to be transferred to the ward. He held his breath as he heard a long tone and then the receiver connected.

"Inpatient," a female answered.

"Is . . . Sabrina there?" he asked and closed his eyes. The sound of her name escaping his lips was as startling as a pile of ceramic plates crashing to a cement floor.

"This is Sabrina. How can I help you?"

His eyes snapped wide, and his mouth fell open. He couldn't seem to formulate any words or coherent response as he wondered if it all *had* been a hallucination from another blackout: the wrong diagnosis of terminal results, the silent-film-reel clock, the levitating pig and the pleading child, the six henchman nurses, bludgeoning the demonic head nurse with her own severed arm, the padded cell, and then finding the murdered Sabrina, who now sounded happy and chipper on the other end of the line.

"Hello? Sir? Are you still there?"

Smith lowered the receiver and placed it on the cradle, disconnecting the call. Sabrina was alive. And he had voluntarily admitted himself to the hospital, so he knew the staff wouldn't be searching for him. He realized neither would the police now that Sabrina was not lying in a pool of her own blood. He wondered how he could possibly know her name if he hadn't looked at her name tag while she lay beaten and expired?

He needed to find George, but Wynn had talked Smith into leaving his car at Wynn's apartment complex so she could drive him to the hospital that following morning. And he knew she would accept no excuse in the world as to why he had fled the hospital before being rightfully discharged.

He must covertly find a way to retrieve his car.

I WAS ALWAYS EASILY INFLUENCED...

13: Mature Audiences Only

Hank's voice cracked when he answered the phone.

"Hey, buddy. I'm truly sorry to wake you up, but I need a favor," Smith began, finding comfort in a friendly voice.

"Yeah, yeah. Of course, love. What time is it?"

"Umm . . . eighteen minutes 'til three. I need a ride from my office to Wynn's apartment to get my car."

"Why can't Wynn come get you?" Hank cleared the sleepy tone from his voice and sounded normal.

"I left the hospital without being discharged, and she'll be hot under the collar about it."

"Hospital? *You*? I thought we'd see pigs fly before I'd ever hear of Detective Smith entering a hospital still conscious and with all his faculties."

"I'll explain on the ride and give you all the juicy details if you'll come get me."

"Give me half an hour, love. Wait for me outside. I hate getting out of my auto in the dead of night. I get the heebie-jeebies."

Smith rolled his eyes. "I'll be waiting outside."

Hank hung up, and Smith took a long drink of his favorite brown alcoholic beverage.

Smith shut Hank's passenger door and thanked him.

"I don't want thanks. I want the story, love," Hank said and merged onto the roadway. "And you gotta give me directions."

"Remember when you found me outside the *Gazette*, all dazed and confused?"

"Yeah, if you weren't such a raging drunk, I would've assumed you were having a stroke that morning. But you told me it was some kind of blackout."

"I was coming out of one of those blackouts and didn't know where I was or where I had been or for how long."

"Have these been going on for a long time? Left or right up here?"

"Left. And, no. They started as migraines and then progressed to blackouts. Right around the time . . ." Smith looked at Hank, focusing on the road. They were the only vehicle on the road.

"Around when?" Hank asked. "When the bad juju with Wendy started?"

Smith nodded. "When I caught her and What's-His-Name having lunch together at Monks' Seafood, and then the blackouts started the night she eventually took off with him."

"Still no leads on her whereabouts?"

"Honestly, Hank, I've stopped looking or caring."

"You know, love? Sometimes, when life gets you down, you gotta fucking pick yourself up by your bootstraps."

Smith gawked at Hank in disbelief. "I don't think I've ever heard you cuss before."

Hank giggled. "Oh, bugaboo, there's a lot of me you've never experienced!"

Smith shook his head in an attempt to stop any unsavory

images of Hank forming in his head and continued. "The Boulevard Killer has consumed my every waking thought, so I took a drive downtown—you know, just to look for him. I thought I was hot on his trail. I became sick to my stomach with all the filth walking the streets." Smith cautiously said the next part, monitoring Hank's reaction. "The filth *he* was helping exterminate."

Hank swallowed hard but did not look at his friend. He kept his attention on the roadway. "Straight or right?"

"Stay straight. I picked up that lady in the pictures I was telling you about—the photographs I found in my pocket the morning outside the *Gazette*."

"You said one was of a streetwalker blowing you a kiss and the other was of the same woman naked, standing on a bed."

"Yeah, those. While I was downtown looking for the killer, I saw her again. So, I picked her up in the Chevy and fucked her. Her name was Luna—well, her street name was Luna. I killed her at the Desert Palms Motel. The bitch didn't know what hit her."

Hank gasped and slapped an open hand over his mouth. For the first time during the ride, Hank looked at Smith, and he was sure he saw Hank slide closer to his driver-side door to put even just a few more inches between his longtime-friend-turned-confessed-killer.

"There's a certain amount of enjoyment in watching someone die," Smith continued, slightly enjoying how uncomfortable his story made his friend. "When I woke up from my blackout, she had been dead three days. Blood was everywhere."

Hank's hands shook, and his knuckles turned white as he gripped the steering wheel. Smith decided to bring his friend's angst down a notch before Hank popped his top. Smith placed a hand on Hank's shoulder, and Hank flinched, like someone had bit him.

"Then the fuzziness of the blackout faded, and I realized I hadn't killed her. She wasn't dead. There was no body, no blood. But three days *had* passed. Wynn had tracked me down to the motel. It was the longest blackout I can remember ever having. That's what prompted her to make me check in to the hospital. But I snuck out a few hours ago, after I must've had another blackout in the hospital. I had an extremely violent dream involving a menagerie of demonic nurses and then a real nurse, who I thought I had beaten to death with her own arm. But again, come to find out, none of it was real. No real deaths, no unholy characters trying to eat me."

He saw Hank relax when his friend realized the carnage and murder had been contrived.

"And these blackouts seem to surround sexual urges. I think they stem from finding Wendy with that bastard. I didn't realize how often I was visiting downtown until some of the girls called me by my name. And I guess I picked up a few of them, although I don't always remember it."

"So you think, in order to fulfill these dark sexual urges, you saw the prostitutes?"

"Yes, and I acted on every twisted and sadistic fantasy I had ever had. I began to change. I must've made Luna pose naked for my own personal pornography. Why else would I have naked photos of her in my pocket? Then, the night of my blackout, I emptied an entire bottle of whiskey on her body and lapped it up like a dog in heat. And there's one more thing."

Hank glanced at him through the corner of his eyes, suspicious of what further confession might be made.

"I watched the Boulevard Killer murder one of the girls through his motel window. Her name was Candy. I had tailed him to the Desert Palms and took photographs of the whole thing. And he drilled her first before killing her. I became aroused, not during the sex or during the murder, but during the anticipation of knowing what was about to happen."

Hank slammed the vehicle's brakes and let the car idle in the middle of the street. "You *watched* him kill a girl and didn't report him? Smith, you used to be a sheriff's *deputy*! And you branched out on your own to *help* the people you said weren't being helped by the so-called corrupt department you worked for."

"Could you keep driving please? We're just sitting in the middle of the road."

"I'm concerned about your mental state," Hank added and pressed the gas pedal with the tip of his cowboy boot.

"I had an obsession with power and control over others. That's why I took this case and basically closed my services to any additional clients. Tracking the Boulevard Killer was the ultimate rush, to track someone who had complete power and control over their victims—victims who I felt would make the world a better place if they were no longer corrupting it. I didn't realize, by immersing myself in this case, my sexual appetite would increase and become violent."

"You idolize him. You commend his actions! Does Wynn know this is going on?"

"Yes. In fact, she helped me develop the photographs from the night I watched him kill Candy."

"That girl is a saint. Don't do anything to futz that up, love. You shouldn't be sneaking under the cover of night to retrieve your auto from her place. You need to reach out to her and let her in. Really let her in. I don't know what your status with Wendy is anymore, or if she's ever coming back, but Wynn is a keeper. I can tell she truly loves you."

"Wendy isn't coming back. I have many demons I face every day, and she is one of them. Along with this thing that emerges when I blackout. And now, like I told you, the blackouts are coming with vivid nightmares. I mean, where does it end? Will it just keep compiling until I go full-out mad and sacrifice every fiber of who I am to keep these thoughts and urges well fed? Take a left up here, and Wynn's place is on the right."

After a few moments of silence, Hank turned the wheel and steered the vehicle into Wynn's apartment complex parking lot and sighed heavily.

"What's wrong?" Smith asked.

Hank stopped beside Smith's Chevy. "I'm just disappointed in you. I thought you were better than this, as an ex-deputy and a man."

Smith exited Hank's vehicle and thanked him for the ride, ignoring Hank's proverbial one-two punch. He closed the passenger door and leaned down to look through the open window. "I'll stop by and see you at the *Gazette* in a few days. Maybe after I have some more answers."

Hank nodded but wouldn't make eye contact.

"What's wrong? Why are you so disappointed in me? You're the *only* person I've ever been able to count on, no matter what's going on in my life. And right now, I feel like a dog chasing its own tail."

Hank stared forward through the windshield, focusing on nothing in particular, and looked downtrodden. "You sound as if you've become the very evil you have set out to destroy."

"I was always easily influenced—"

Hank mashed the gas pedal and left Smith standing in a dark parking lot next to his vehicle before hearing the rest of what Smith had to say.

"I was always easily influenced," Smith whispered to himself as he watched Hank's taillights fade from sight.

14: The Hitchhiker

The headlights from Smith's Chevy stabbed into the night sky as he careered out of Las Vegas on Interstate 515 toward George in Boulder City. Smith's hands gripped the steering wheel so tightly his knuckles turned white. Then he felt all the tension from the night's events and his palaver with Hank dissipate as he noticed a figure's silhouette in the headlights. The man had his thumb pointed at the road and a newspaper tucked underneath his other arm. Smith thought he would love some company to take his mind off all his misery and to stop this feeling like everything was spiraling downward.

Smith pulled his vehicle to the shoulder just past the man and leaned over to unroll the passenger window. "Where ya headed?"

The man stuck his head through the opening. "White Hills, Arizona."

"I'm stopping in Boulder City. That'll get you almost halfway there at least."

"Halfway is better than no way."

"Get in, and we'll be on . . . our way," Smith said, adding some lightheartedness to his mood.

"Much obliged, partner," the man said and slid into the passenger side of the bench, not giving any indication he had found it amusing how many times they had just used the word *way* in their initial exchange.

Smith pulled onto the roadway without as much as a glance at the hitchhiker. He already regretted picking up such an obvious party-pooper.

"Beautiful night, isn't it?" the man asked and unfolded the newspaper.

Smith tuned out the hitchhiker and glanced at the man's copy of the *Gazette*.

"What do you think of these Boulevard Killers?" the man continued.

"*Killers*? As in plural?" Smith asked, quickly jetting his focus to the hitchhiker and feeling his stomach drop. "Are the papers saying there are more of them now?"

"No. They aren't privy to what I know. And it's two men. As far as I can tell right now. Do you think the coppers are ever gonna catch them?"

Smith nervously rubbed the steering wheel with both hands while he concentrated on the road. "I think it's only a matter of time before he—they—get careless and leave an incriminating clue."

"Spoken like a copper. You a copper, mister?"

"PI now. Ex-deputy in another lifetime."

"Then I guess you can understand how bad most people want these sonsofbitches thrown in the slammer. But not me. No siree, Bob."

Smith eyed him suspiciously and decided to just let the man explain his theory of the two men without being coerced.

The hitchhiker leaned across the bench to whisper, as if he were afraid someone else would hear his confession. "I'm gonna kill the bastards. Good and right. Look at today's headline! Two more girls found in unmarked graves in the desert near that sleazy motel out in Mesquite. The coppers aren't hunting men. They're hunting monsters."

Smith gripped the steering wheel again. "I'm glad *someone* is taking an initiative to get these guys off the streets."

"Oh, I'm not just gonna get them off the streets, bub. I'm gonna remove their heads from their necks and scatter them in so many different locations that their own grandmas won't recognize them."

"I'm just as outraged as the next guy, but that sounds a little harsh."

"My niece was one of his victims. Sure, she wasn't the most stand-up lass and has been in and out of trouble her whole life. But she was *family*! Snatched right from downtown. Me and my sister—her mother—were working to get her to move in with me in White Hills. You know? Help build her self-esteem and get her back on her feet. Maybe even get her a job at the dam with me. A job she could be proud of. We're always looking for tour guides. But there's no helping her now, is there? She was found in one of those desert graves. Her high heel was what tipped off the coppers."

Pum'kin, Smith thought.

"That's why I collect all the newspapers with stories about the victims. It helps feed my motivation and anger. Gives me a purpose again. Keeps me close to Amy."

Damnit, I didn't really need to know her real name, he thought. "What's your plan? If you don't mind me asking?"

"No, not at all, partner. Glad to be getting a lift by someone who shares my enthusiasm. Name's Tim," he said and extended his hand.

Smith hesitated for a moment before shaking it. "Arbuckle."

"You got a first name, Mr. Arbuckle?"

"You got a last name, Tim?" he replied.

Tim sat quiet for a moment. "Fair enough. I already have their license plate number. They drive a black Rolls Royce Phantom with a metal Shit Happens sign wired to the back fender but I've yet to get a solid look at their faces. I could spot the automobile a mile away, but, if I had walked past them in the street, I wouldn't know it."

The car passed the Henderson city limits marker, and I-515 turned into Route 93.

"But then I got close enough one night to finally see inside the Rolls—this was the night I discovered there were two of them—and the driver looked familiar. I couldn't put my finger on where or how I knew him. I racked my noggin all night about why he looked so gosh-darn familiar. They picked up a young dame, dressed to the nines. Definitely didn't look like one of the normal working girls. Almost like she was trying too hard to be some kind of movie star."

Greta. He was spying on us the night we picked up Greta. The only night I have ever picked up a girl with George is the one night we get spotted. Fantastic.

"I followed one of the men, the owner of the Rolls I assumed, to his house. He lives in Boulder City, smack-dab right where you're headed, partner. Get this—he has a wife and two little children. But that's not the best part. You wanna know the best part?"

Smith didn't really want to know the best part. He didn't want to hear Tim say anything more. Smith certainly didn't want to hear if Tim knew anything about Smith's personal life too. What if Tim knew Smith had been the other man in the car and was toying with him to watch him squirm before pulling the trigger? What if Tim knew about Luna? Or worse, what if Tim knew about Smith's relationship with Wynn and went after her too? Smith tasted bile in his mouth with the realization that not only did this stranger know where George lives and that he is the Boulevard Killer, but that he'd have to kill this guy to keep him quiet, to save Smith and George from a possible gruesome demise.

Smith made a committed decision: Tim had to die. And Smith only had a short amount of time to concoct and execute a plan. The length of Route 93 before reaching Boulder City wasn't too long.

He instinctively pushed his elbow against his rib cage to ensure his revolver still sat in the holster.

"What's the best part?" Smith asked, engaging in the conversation like he cared, setting Tim's mind at ease while he looked for the best spot on the route to kill the hitchhiker.

"I work with that rotten snake at the dam! Can you believe that jazz? I've been working side by side for months with one of the Boulevard Killers—one of the men responsible for Amy's death—and never knew it! That's why he looked so familiar. Oh, the irony!"

Smith surveyed the long and winding road in front of them as the car bounded along the asphalt. He could see the intersection of Veterans Memorial Highway in the distance beneath the pale starlight. If he was to silence this stranger forever—and how could he not at this point?—the time would have to be now.

Movement in his rearview mirror caught his attention. He took his gaze off the road and saw he and the hitchhiker were not alone in the car anymore. In his mirror, Anya, Luna, and Pum'kin sat in the backseat. Anya sat in the middle, between her two ghouls, and made eye contact with Smith through the reflection in the rectangular mirror. The other two girls watched the landscape through their respective windows, like youngsters on vacation, gaping at an unexplored countryside. Anya smiled, revealing her squared teeth. She raised a single finger to her lips, signaling Smith to be quiet, and a searing pain stabbed through his head. Smith yelped in agony and took his hands off the wheel to put pressure on his temples.

"You okay, Mr. Arbuckle?" Tim yelled, grabbing the unmanned steering wheel.

Smith turned to tell Tim to get his mitts off the wheel, but instead he found himself standing in his bedroom, looking at Wendy and her beau in disbelief. Smith was frozen, his hand still clasping the doorknob. Wendy's boy toy grabbed the discarded bedsheets to cover his privates.

"Baby, I can explain," Wendy said, scurrying backward as Smith lunged for the man in Smith's bed.

Smith felt a calmness and an odd sense of déjà vu envelope him as he flung himself at the stranger who had been drilling Wendy. Smith couldn't remember where he had been coming from, or why he was home, but he felt as if he had been talking to someone right before he had opened his bedroom door. Then all his thoughts went blank as he wrapped his arms around the man, and they tumbled off the other side of the bed.

Wendy screamed and ran for the telephone in the living room. Smith stood up, grabbed the olive-colored lamp from her nightstand, and hurled it at the back of her head. The lamp shattered as it hit its target, sending her sprawling to the floor.

The naked man folded his hands and brought them down like a hammer on the base of Smith's neck. The adrenaline surging through Smith's body was enough to withstand the blow and just made him angrier. He spun around and grabbed the sheet covering the man's genitals, pulled it taut, and wrapped it around the man's neck. The naked man tried to snake his fingertips underneath the sheet, but it was futile. Smith had the sheet too tight, and the man was running out of oxygen. Blood vessels in Smith's forehead bulged and pulsed with anger as he pulled the sheet tighter. He felt the man relax and go limp and let him crumple to the floor.

Smith stepped over the man and stormed toward his cheating wife—his childhood sweetheart—the bitch. She lay facedown, and he lifted her head by a handful of hair. Her chin rose off the floor, and she moaned as she regained consciousness.

Smith grabbed underneath her armpits and forced her to her unsteady feet. "Get up, you whore."

Her head wobbled as she regained control of her muscles. She rubbed the back of her head where the lamp had struck her.

"How long have you been seeing him this time, Wendy? I thought you had ended it after I caught you guys at lunch together. How long have you been fucking him in our bed?"

Wendy's chin flopped to her chest, and she closed her eyes again.

"How long?" he screamed and shook her by the shoulders so hard that he thought her head would come free—*wished* her head would come free. "How long, you lying, cheating, good-for-nothing piece of shit? Did you think you could get away with it? Do you think I'm stupid?"

Wendy smacked her lips and opened her eyes. "You're dumb as a rock. He's been drilling me since last year."

"You're mine. Always have been and always will."

"Ha! You're too in love with your booze and solving everyone else's problems to notice your own wife's hoochie went cold. And I found a nice young man willing to warm it up. And, oh, boy," she finished, chuckling defiantly, "did he ever warm—"

Wendy toppled to the floor in a bloody heap as Smith kept his elbows locked, still holding his smoking .38. He looked down to confirm his wife was dead and found Tim squirming in the dirt on the roadside, one hand holding his wounded leg and his other hand extended upward at Smith.

"Please, mister. Don't shoot again. Don't kill me!"

Smith noticed the blood seeping between Tim's fingers that gripped his leg. Smith's revolver still smoked.

"Whatever you want, I'll get it for you! Just, please. I have a family!"

A rattling sound from inside the Chevy diverted Smith's attention briefly to his car. The headlights were like two eyes shooting white beams into the pitch blackness of the highway as the car idled behind the two men. Something moved inside the vehicle's cabin, and Smith thought he saw Anya's pale complexion whoosh from the backseat into the front passenger seat and disappear. Tim's incessant whimpering redirected Smith's attention to the man on the ground, pleading for his life.

"Calm down," Smith began in a soothing voice and kneeled, still gripping the revolver.

Tim squeaked and shuffled backward a few feet.

"Close your eyes. It was all a bad dream."

The car radio turned on, and the smooth jazz of Benny Goodman's "Puttin' on the Ritz" poured from the speakers and through the open window. The melody and arrangement of the instruments floated over the silence of the desert. Then the song faded, and a hissing noise from the radio replaced the music. A new song faded in—Louis Armstrong's "Basin Street Blues"—then faded out, the radio hissing like static again. Smith was sure this time he saw Anya whoosh back into the rear of the car after Frank Sinatra sang "My Love for You" clear and strong. No more fading in and out, no more hissing.

Smith placed his hand on Tim's perspiring forehead and then straightened up. "Now go back to sleep. This'll all be over when you wake up."

"Who *are* you?" Tim screamed.

Frank Sinatra's majestic crooning stopped abruptly as the sound of the gunshot echoed through the vast desert surroundings, followed by almost complete silence—just the sound of the Chevy idling behind Smith. He holstered the .38, stood over Tim's dead body, and smiled as he stared at the half-missing portion of the hitchhiker's skull and brains.

"Allow me to introduce myself. I'm the man you've been looking for. The front-page news. Your cold-blooded killer."

Black feathers and menacing beaks encased Smith, swarming past and around him, like a rock bisecting an incoming tide. He raised his arm to shield his eyes from being slapped by a flapping wing. He looked behind him, and, over the funnel of vultures, he saw Anya, standing on the roof of his Chevy, slowly clapping her hands in congratulations.

"What do you want them to do with him?" she called out. "I can't use him. He's all yours. Show me what you're made of."

The vultures had now formed a perfect swirling funnel over Tim's body, waiting for their orders. Tim's ultraviolent description of what *he* would do to George and Smith when found resonated in Smith's mind.

"Paint the highway with his blood!" Smith yelled to the black-feathered tornado. "In the morning, no one shall recognize him."

Anya raised her hands with her palms facing upward, as if she were releasing an invisible dove into the air. The whirlpool of vultures collapsed downward, and, for a moment, Smith couldn't see any part of Tim's body. Then a detached finger was launched into the air from the melee. And another separated finger. Followed by a single toe. Afterward a severed hand. Then an ear. As each extremity was pecked free and flung skyward, the vultures immediately ignored it, letting it fall where it may.

Within minutes, body parts and copious amounts of blood trailed from one side of the highway to the other, littering that stretch of Route 93.

The first sunrays had grazed the horizon by the time Smith pulled into George's driveway. Even if Covington had worked last night—either at the dam or at his extracurricular job downtown—Smith knew George would have been home by now. The Rolls was parked in the driveway, just as Smith assumed it would be.

He rang the bell and took a step backward when Maggie opened the door.

"Good morning, Mr. Arbuckle. Everything okay?"

"Everything's peachy, Mrs. Covington. Is George home?"

Smith heard two sets of pitter-pattering feet running through the house toward the front door.

"Who is it, Mommy?" Rose asked.

"It's Mr. Arbuckle. Could you see if Daddy is up yet?"

"Oh, I don't mean for you to wake him," Smith said. "You don't have to get him. I can just see him later at work or something."

"Oh, poppycock. Come in and make yourself at home."

Smith thanked her and entered the house. He heard Rose and Raymond upstairs, clearly not using their library voices to wake up George.

"How's everything going at the dam? Are you settling in nicely?"

"Yes, ma'am. Everyone there has been just swell. I'm touched by everyone's hospitality."

George tied his bathrobe as he walked down the stairs to the living room. A look of concern swept over George's face when he saw Smith standing in his house.

"Everything okay, Todd? Sorry I wasn't at work last night. Touch of the bug and all," George said without wasting any time.

Smith was thankful for the hint. At least now they were on the same page regarding George's reason for not going to work, and Smith wouldn't accidentally blow the whistle on the façade they had created.

"I'll leave you boys alone," Maggie said and looked at Smith. "Bath morning for the wee ones."

Smith nodded, and George waited until she had disappeared upstairs to speak. "Everything okay?"

"Can we talk outside?"

George led Smith to the front porch and closed the door behind them. The Nevada sun had already burned the dew off the front lawn grass. George produced two cigars from his bathrobe pocket and offered one to Smith. "You seem tense."

They both lit their cigars quickly, and Smith puffed on his before speaking. "I need to ask you something. Do you ever feel like someone else is living inside you? Especially when you're with Anya and her girls? Have you ever felt another *you* emerge? Maybe take control and make you do things you can't remember after you wake up?"

George rested his hand holding the cigar on the porch rail and looked quizzically at Smith. "Who else lives inside you?"

"I assume, by your choice of words, this happens to you also."

George brought his cigar to his lips and paused. "Someday,

when we have ample time to really get down to brass tacks, I'll show you the puppet master that's really pulling Anya's strings."

"Oh?"

"She's governed by a higher force." George leaned in and lowered his voice. "By that book I told you about in the desert."

Smith gulped and wrung his hands. "Oh yeah, the book," he repeated, hoping George couldn't hear the nervous tremble in his voice.

"When the time is ripe—you and I will both unequivocally know when that is—I'll ceremonially pass the book to you and officially be relieved of my duties, and you'll be the one *blessed* with Anya's fellowship until the cycle dictates when your turn comes one day to relinquish the book to your inheritor. Remember, as intimidating as she can be sometimes, she still always needs a *living* caretaker to safeguard the book and to collect bantlings for her. Her abilities haven't reached complete divinity yet, where she'll be able to kill and act on her own accord. She needs to kill what an amendment in the book calls a *Chosen Virgin*. God help us all when she attains *that* pinnacle of power."

Smith rubbed the back of his neck and thought he was safe for the time being. It didn't appear George even knew the book was missing, never mind that Smith was the one who had temporarily borrowed it without permission.

"How can she kill this so-called Chosen Virgin if the book controls her limitations and states that only a caretaker—someone like you or me—can kill for her?" Smith asked, already knowing the answer but wanting to thwart any possible suspicions George may have that the book might not be safe and sound in his closet.

"The book isn't flawless. The restriction placed on her doesn't apply if she wholeheartedly believes she has found the Chosen One. Whether she's right or not seems to be irrelevant to the book. Perception is everything, and unfortunately it rides on *her* perception."

"So what stops her from just killing every virgin, one by one, until she finds the Chosen One?"

"The book is very clear that killing virgins is . . . noxious—I believe that's the specific word used. I interpret it to mean that with each *wrong* virgin she kills by her own hand in the quest to find the Chosen One, her influence over the Mushroom Cult diminishes slightly. Too many wrong targets and Anya's control over her flock could slip through her fingers."

Smith nodded. Everything George was schooling him on coincided with what he had read and understood himself.

"When Anya first arrived with this book—and what a sneaky, sinister way she got the previous caretaker to weasel himself into my life to transfer ownership of the book—I experienced periods of time I couldn't remember. Usually when I was about to grab the next girl. I wasn't always so neat and tidy with my method. When I started, it was a mess. I got better at it, and the periods of missing time grew longer. Sometimes I would hallucinate grisly deaths that didn't really happen."

"Yes!"

"But I always knew it wasn't me. I had acquired a transient parasite, if you will. One I had unwilling allowed in but didn't necessarily want to leave. We came to a compromise, me and him, and I got to know this dark entity inside me a little better—to understand him, I should say. Then, the more I learned from Anya's book and the more I put those methods into practice, the less and less he reared his head. Until eventually he left me alone completely and stopped coming around. With that, I was in charge of all my actions and kills. So, I ask you again, who else lives inside you?"

"We haven't met—not like you're describing with yours—but he shows up from time to time, and it's almost as if I black out when he takes over. Well, I *do* black out, but the last two times I've remembered everything while he was in control. But on the way over here, I killed a man who had solid proof that you're the Boulevard Killer and that I'm involved. Hot nuts, he was even convinced we've been a team all along."

"Where did he get this idea?"

"He's been following you. He even followed you home. Told me about Maggie and Rose and Raymond. He works with you at the dam!"

"And you took care of the problem, I presume?"

"Yes, I neutralized the threat. I even think I got some silent weird permission from Anya. She and two members of the Mushroom Cult appeared in the backseat."

"Looks like she has more faith in you than I thought."

"I blacked out right when I made the decision to kill him and then entered this weird flashback of the night I found Wendy in bed with the same knucklehead I had already caught her seeing once before."

"Wendy . . . your wife, who has been missing?"

Smith nodded.

"I get the feeling that she's not missing. Not really. That you know exactly where she is. Where she's . . . buried."

"I don't! That night was my first blackout. The last thing I remember was opening the door and seeing my wife in bed, naked, with another man. Up until tonight, that's where my memory has stopped. The next memory I have is sitting in the Chevy in my driveway with a sandy shovel in a backseat covered with blood. I had blacked out from the moment I had opened the door until she was dead and buried somewhere and I had returned home."

"What about the guy?"

"He was still in my bedroom with a sheet wrapped around his neck. I had to take care of him. But, up until just a little bit ago, I never *really* knew what had happened with Wendy. My blackout dealing with the hitchhiker somehow unlocked that night with Wendy, and I relived it, as if I was back in my bedroom and in control. But I know I wasn't. I was just a marionette, going through the motions."

"How do you know that's what really happened with Wendy? Couldn't it be false memories emerging purely as a hallucination?"

"I don't know. Has this ever happened to you?"

"Not like that. What happened when you woke up?"

"This was obviously the shortest blackout. I don't think it lasted more than a few minutes. But I had shot the hitchhiker in the leg, and, when he started pleading, I shot him in the head."

"Well, at least we don't need to worry about being outed by him anymore."

"That's when Anya called the vultures and let me choose what they did to him—"

"Whoa! Hold everything! The vultures were summoned without *me*? And then obeyed *your* instructions?"

Smith nodded, then gulped. He wasn't sure if he had just made a major blunder, exposing how he must have the book now. *What if only the caretaker who is in possession of the book has the authority to direct the vultures? Did I just inadvertently confess to stealing the book? Who really knows how all this pizzazz works anyway?* Smith stiffened his body and prepared his wits for a possible combat situation, although he did not want to go toe-to-toe with the Boulevard Killer on the man's own front porch.

"Well, I guess we'll just have to add that cog to the wheel of Still Figuring It Out as We Go. Just when I think I have the workings of the book locked down, I'm thrown a curve ball, like this. I honestly thought the vultures only listened to the possessor of the book and Anya. I didn't mean to interrupt or digress. Please, continue. This is fascinating."

Smith furrowed one brow and spoke slowly, remaining cautious as he eased back into his story. "I wanted to see the hitchhiker torn limb from limb and scattered all over the road. Anger grew inside me when I remembered how he had said that's what he would do to us, when he caught the two Boulevard Killers. I felt vindicated, passing down an eye-for-an-eye retribution."

"Why are you telling me this, Smith? I can't imagine it's because you're looking for some advice or my adulation."

"Because my parasite reminds me a lot of you."

"What happens after you wake up from these blackouts? When you take control of your thoughts and actions again?"

"The people are dead, and I'm covered in blood. Sometimes there's blood in my mouth."

"Could you have cut or hurt your mouth?"

"No. It's not my blood. Whoever takes over me has a thirst for blood, it seems. Like my parasite has always had a taste for violence and enjoys seeing the fear in our target's eyes—whether my whoring wife, her knucklehead boyfriend, or the scheming hitchhiker—before we snuff them out."

The two men stood in silence, puffing their cigars. Smith could hear Maggie wrangling Rose and Raymond out of the bathtub upstairs.

"And to tell you the truth," Smith added, "I'm beginning to like it myself."

15: Envy the Vultures

"I'm heading to work," George called up the stairs later that evening.

"Have a good night! See you in the morning," Maggie replied.

George, dressed in his Hoover Dam technician overalls, entered the Rolls and pulled out of the driveway. He headed toward the dam on Nevada Way and then steered the vehicle onto Route 93 westbound, toward downtown Vegas instead.

Maggie smiled as she shut off the light to the children's room. For one lingering moment, she studied their sleeping cherub faces. She'd held on to the dream that George might get promoted at the dam and move to day shift. However, she couldn't help feeling he had sabotaged his chances himself. She didn't think he particularly liked graveyard shift, but he wasn't rushing to get off it either.

With her children tucked snuggly in bed, Maggie went downstairs to start a load of laundry. She turned on the small radio in the kitchen for company and retrieved her and George's personal laundry basket, and then carried the hamper designated for his work clothes to the wash basin. She spun the hot water knob all the way to the left and dumped their personal clothes onto the floor, sorting them by color and checking all the pockets for loose change and other tchotchkes.

Next she grabbed George's work overalls. Maggie found it peculiar that her husband's work attire came home less and less soiled as the weeks went by. She had justified it by thinking he was probably doing more clerical work and less technician-type activities. That seemed logical and kept her overly paranoid mind's suspicions at bay . . . until she found a pack of matches in his pocket. A pack of matches advertising the Desert Palms Motel all the way out in Mesquite. A motel Maggie was certain charged by hourly increments. She clenched the matchbook so tightly the cardboard edges dug into her skin.

"No wonder he likes working nightshift," she said aloud, not wanting to think about how many nights he had kissed her goodbye, only to partake in an all-night detour.

She stepped over the small hump of unsorted clothes on the floor and shambled to the sofa. Sitting down on the middle cushion, she fingered the matches, absentmindedly flipping them around and around while staring blankly at the small fireplace. A plethora of questions flooded her: How long has he been unfaithful? Who is she? Is *she* more than one person? Was he planning on leaving? What should she do about it?

She pocketed the matches and stormed to the telephone. The operator patched her through to George's department at the Hoover Dam.

"Hello, this is Maggie, George Covington's wife."

"Good evening, Mrs. Covington. How's ol' Georgie feeling? Had a mighty bad touch of the bug, did he?"

Maggie felt a little better hearing his boss confirm George's illness. "Yes. He's doing much better. In fact, he's on his way to work now. Just left a few minutes ago."

"Glad to hear it. We've missed him around here. He's been gone so long we were taking bets whether he was retiring or just faking."

"How . . . How long is *so long*?"

"Oh, jeez, Mrs. Covington. We haven't seen George once all month. Good thing he had a bunch of sick time saved up so he still got a proper paycheck."

Maggie felt a ball descend into her stomach. She made a last-ditch attempt to hear anything that wouldn't signify the possible end of her marriage and happy household. "He came home from work a few mornings ago with a new fella. Said he just started working with him, a Mr. Arbuckle."

"I'm sorry, ma'am, but we don't have anyone working here by that name, and we haven't hired anyone new in months. With the country being all postwar gung ho, most of the good prospects are applying at the Lechner factory, where they're making the gun parts and stuff. Would you like me to have George call home when he gets here, since you said he's on his way and all?"

"That would be splendid. Thank you."

Maggie pressed the switch hook and held the receiver close to her chest. She knew she had to act fast if she wanted to see firsthand what shenanigans her husband was really up to when he left for work every night. Calling her parents, she asked her mother if she could come by and stay with the children while Maggie went out.

"Is everything all right, dear?"

"Yes, Mom. Fine. I want to get George a surprise for our anniversary, and it's so hard to do when he's home sleeping during the day while I have the kids. I don't know how long it'll be, but they're both sleeping."

Maggie's mother agreed, and Maggie paced impatiently close to the front door for the chance to leave and catch him red-handed, engaging in whatever indiscretions he had been getting away with lately, or for however long the wool had been pulled over her eyes. Unless she begged him to confess, and he complied, she realized she'd have no way of knowing how long he'd been two-timing her. Maggie wrung her hands to the point where she might rub the skin off her fingers, while continuing to wear a path in the hardwood floor by her figure-eight strides. She pinched the outside of her pants to again feel the outline of the matchbook tucked snuggly in her pocket.

The headlights of Maggie's mother's car swung into the driveway and approached the house, signaling what possibly might be the beginning of the end.

The Desert Palms Motel's red VACANCY sign spewed cartoonlike hues over the parking lot and the parked vehicles. Maggie pulled into the lot ninety minutes later and cruised slowly to find her husband's unmistakable Rolls—the one with the distinctive vulgar sign hanging from the rear chrome fender. She placed her index finger into the crease of her two closed lips as she studied each row of cars, hoping she was wrong and his car wouldn't be here. Then she spotted it tucked around the corner, and her heart sank. Exiting her vehicle, she spied the rooms with their lights on—occupied rooms, even if only for a few minutes depending on how "quick" the customers could perform—and wondered which one contained her husband and his call girl.

Maggie swallowed hard as her trembling hands gripped her blouse's collar. Her stomach stormed like a monsoon as nervous adrenaline shot through her body with the realization of what she had to do to get into that room, but wasn't sure if she even had it in her moral compass to play the part of the ruse. Thinking, *That's my husband in there!* got her feet moving toward the motel's entrance. She ripped open her blouse to expose as much cleavage as she could. Buttons snapped and clanked onto the asphalt of the parking lot as she walked.

"May I help you, miss?" Cheryl asked, looking up from the day's copy of the *Gazette*.

"I hope you can, darling," Maggie said, putting on her best sleazy voice but sounding more like an overzealous student auditioning for a high-school play. "I'm supposed to be meeting a . . ." She snapped her fingers to accent her ploy about not easily remembering his name. "Mr. Covington. Yeah, that's his name." She paused to see if he had even checked in under his real name. If he hadn't, she didn't have a contingency plan, except to go from window to window.

Cheryl leaned backward in her chair and folded her arms.

"He . . . um . . . ordered a . . ." Maggie quickly looked over Cheryl's head at the small postcards thumbtacked to the wall from cities all over the world. Her gaze fell on a depiction of a busy London street. "Double-decker. He ordered a double-decker," she finished, hoping the receptionist didn't catch on to her spur-of-the-moment neologism.

"And what, pray tell, is a double-decker? Is it a sex position?"

"It is," Maggie said, now standing erect with confidence. "And Mr. Covington has asked me to be the bottom deck, if you know what I mean." She punctuated her new identity with a wink.

Cheryl giggled. "Oh, I know, child. I know. That Mr. Covington certainly has some"—she closed her eyes and smiled—"fun tricks up his sleeve for us girls."

Maggie did her best to suppress the vomit rising from her gut.

"Yes, he's always been one of my favorite . . . clients"—*Was client the right word?*—"and I don't want to keep him waiting. So, could I please have a key to his room?"

"I'm really not supposed to give the spares to guests. In case of emergencies—fires and such. Can't you just knock if I give you the room number? Isn't he expecting you?"

Maggie didn't think that would suffice. Her husband would probably hide the dame before opening the door. "He was explicit in his directions. He wants me to role-play, acting as the room maid and entering to service the linens. He always says cleanliness is paramount." Maggie winced at how lame she sounded and became nervous about how much of this scenario sounded undoubtedly embellished. She felt the more she talked, the more the odds were that she would fall into one of the many holes she had dug to keep up the charade.

"He certainly is a kinky one," Cheryl said giddily and reached behind her. She handed Maggie a large red key with gold lettering. "You kids have fun!"

Maggie snatched the key from Cheryl and cantered down the corridor. She pointed to each door as she passed them, whispering each room number in cadence, until she found the one matching the key. She took a deep breath, held the air in her lungs, and exhaled through pursed lips.

She knew it was go time.

The crepe fabric tickled Rose's nose, and Rose instinctively rubbed her face in her sleep. When her arm flopped onto the mattress, and she didn't wake up, Anya lowered the veil more, draping it over Rose's forehead, nose, and chin. Rose attempted to scratch the multitude of itches, but her fingers got trapped in the black fibers.

She sleepily opened her eyes. Anya's hidden pale face hung inches from her, the decaying ghoul's putrid breath exhaling in perfect timing with Rose's inhalations. Rose tried to scream but gagged on the hot, stale odor of death expelling from Anya's mouth. Anya clamped a hand over Rose's mouth and nose to silence her. Rose looked sideways to Raymond's bed to see if he had woken from the disturbance inside their bedroom. Her little brother hadn't even flinched.

Rose gazed at the ghoul, and Anya smiled, revealing her square yellowed teeth. "Didn't I tell you, child, that I'd kill you the next time you touched my book?"

Rose remained silent except for the short bursts of whimpers escaping through her lips and out the spaces between Anya's fingers.

Anya pressed Rose farther into the mattress with the hand covering the girl's mouth. "Didn't I?"

The pressure practically broke Rose's nose and vomer bone, and she tried to scream through the compression, but all that came out was a back-throat gurgle.

"But you didn't just touch it this time, did you, wench? No! This time you had to steal it! Tell me where you hid it, and I'll let you live."

Rose's eyes grew large, and she did her best to shake her head, hoping the demon woman on top of her would understand she meant she didn't know where the book was. Anya pressed harder on Rose's face, and the girl screamed so hard, her larynx felt like sandpaper vibrating inside her throat.

"So, you're gonna be difficult. How about I kill him instead?" Anya asked, turning her head toward Raymond, sleeping in his bed. Her veil rubbed over Rose's long eyelashes.

Rose blinked furiously as dust fell into her eyes, and she made *uh-uh* noises with her voice.

"Didn't think so. C'mon. We're going somewhere to chat, woman to woman, and let your sleeping dog of a grandmother lie downstairs."

Rose was yanked from bed, her neck whiplashing backward.

Anya positioned Rose's body in her arms, like a groom carrying his bride over the threshold—or a lover carrying a dead spouse to their grave—and tiptoed toward the doorway, keeping Rose's neck supported on her forearm while wrapping her hand around Rose's mouth to muffle any screams. Anya exited the bedroom without waking the little boy sleeping in the bed on the other side of the room.

She glided with Rose in her arms down the staircase, Anya's feet never touching the wood, and passed the old lady sleeping on the couch. Anya stopped and squatted, stabilizing her center of gravity, and tilted her head at the old lady.

Rose noticed her grandmother and squawked in short bursts—between gasping for air from sobbing and Anya's decayed hand covering Rose's mouth and nostrils.

"This old hag must be Grandma," Anya whispered. "Maybe she'll help you remember where the book is, as I slice off her toes, one by one."

Rose shook her head and flailed in Anya's arms, trying to find a weakness in the witch's grasp.

"Nah. Let's let Granny sleep. This is between you and me," Anya said and carried Rose out the back door and into the side yard.

Darkness and the stillness of night shrouded the street. The chirp of cicadas dotted the encompassing silence surrounding the house's curtilage. Nothing moved. The leaves on the trees didn't have any wind to make them dance.

Rose darted her gaze around the area to anticipate where the demon wanted to take her. Anya entered the shadows of the trees on the far side of the property, and Rose saw the figures step forward. She bucked, tensing and arching her back, to escape from Anya's hold as legions of pale white, sickly thin female creatures revealed themselves from the canopy of branches.

"Ladies! This here is Miss Rose Covington. Little Miss Rose thinks it's okay to steal from us. She thinks it's okay to take the very power that gives you all life."

A murmur of disapproval swept through the Mushroom Cult.

"A witch, everyone. Little Miss Rose fancies herself a witch. And has stolen the good book from us."

Cyana stepped forward and gurgled a few unintelligible syllables.

"Why? Why, you ask? Good question, Cyana. Now fall back in line. Because"—Anya raised her voice, like a pastor reaching the patrons in the back row of his congregation—"Miss Rose Covington wants to learn our secrets so she can control us all."

The flock grunted in aversion.

Rose squirmed and thought, if she could spin and knock Anya off balance, she might have a chance of being dropped. Then she'd run into the house and wake Grandma, and she would know how to get rid of the monsters.

"Miss Rose Covington wants to learn how to control your vultures to use your pets against you!"

The figures hiding farther back in the trees stepped forward, and the front lines approached Anya and Rose. Rose grabbed Anya's arms, like a terrified toddler grabbing a parent. She buried her face in Anya's shirt—her forehead pinning the bottom of the black veil to Anya's chest—to hide her eyes from the advancing army of shuffling ghouls. Her body's twisting slid Anya's hand off her mouth, and Rose burst into tears.

"Not so brave and pompous anymore, are you, wench? Where's your bravado now?"

"Please stop," she begged between hiccups. "I'll help you find your book. I *promiiiiiiiise!*"

Anya leaned down so her mouth hovered right above Rose's ear. "I don't care about that daft book anymore. I have you now. I've been waiting for the Chosen One to be revealed for centuries. It makes perfect sense and is almost bittersweet how the book picked *his* daughter to award me with divinity. In a few minutes, needing that book will be futile. And so will relying on mere mortals to kill for me."

"But I didn't take your book!" Rose screamed, her voice momentarily silencing the cicadas' chirping.

"This time curiosity killed the rose," she whispered, then spoke louder. "Miss Rose's sins include stealing our book! Her sins include wanting to know our arts. Her sins include wanting to control us. And she can't wash away all the sins she's made to this day. There'll be no last rites given to her, and we can hand down only one judgment for a crime of this magnitude against the Mushroom Cult."

Groups of clawing fingers scraped Rose's body as she clung tighter to Anya's frail and decaying body and screamed.

"Take her."

The disciples swarmed Anya and pried Rose from her arms. Multiple ghouls held each limb tight, while others held her head and supported her back. Rose was transported horizontally across the rest of the yard toward the tree line, like pallbearers carrying a casket down a church's center aisle toward the altar. They controlled her bucking and flailing by keeping her taut with the sheer number of hands and arms wrapped around her as they approached the edge of the lawn. One ghoul—who some called Nikki—pushed through the crowd and sauntered toward the terrified Rose, ripping off a strip from the bottom of her short nightgown and stuffing the cotton into Rose's mouth to stifle her screams.

The procession entered the darkness of the trees, and Rose saw a cross hanging from one of the thicker tree trunks, reminding her of something that hung in their living room and in her and Raymond's bedroom—something her mother had called a *crucifix*—where they would get down on their knees every night and thank Jesus for keeping them safe and healthy.

Then she saw another one of the ghouls standing underneath the cross, holding a burning torch, a yellow-toothed smile splayed across her face.

George thrust wildly inside the girl, her cascading brown hair whipping his face as she grinded and bounced on top of him. He knew he was close to finishing—she was close to yet another fake finish for the paying customer's benefit—so he discreetly reached for the hammer he had hidden underneath the mattress. He had been fantasizing about the *thunk* and the vibration that would be sent down the tool's handle when its metal head connected with her temple in one solid blow. His fingers clasped the wooden handle as she rode him like she wanted to break him in half.

George had freed most of the hammer when the motel room door flung open. He bucked like a steer, throwing the girl off him, and she flung the red sheet over them to cover her breasts and hips—turning the bed's topography into a sea of crimson—leaving her long silky leg exposed. George propped himself up with his left hand, the red sheet sliding and stopping at his midsection.

Maggie turned her back to them. Tears fell from both her eyes and traveled over her blushed cheeks. She used her forearm to wipe the snot from her nose. She refused to look at them when she heard George say something. She couldn't decipher his words— didn't *want* to make out what he was saying. Instead of giving him the satisfaction of seeing her cry, she strained her eyeballs to their corners to see him in her peripheral vision. George held out his right hand in a plea, and the tramp—still covering her bosom and privates with the red sheet—lifted and placed her exposed thigh over George's stomach. Either he hadn't noticed or he didn't care because he made no effort to swat her away. Maggie would swat the floozy, like the infesting bug she was.

"There's nothing you can say right now to make *any* of this better," Maggie said through a mouth filled with thick saliva.

"Is this your girlfriend?" the slut asked George.

Maggie heard George say *no*.

"Oh. Hi! Are you another one of his girls downtown? Nice to meet you. My name's Trixie."

Maggie turned around, her gaze shooting daggers at the bed. Trixie leaned forward with her hand extended for a truce handshake and the red sheet fell to her hips, revealing her breasts. George grabbed Trixie by her other arm and yanked her back into a sitting position. Maggie threw the room key at George, striking him in the left eye, and stormed toward the door.

"Babe, wait," he said, sliding from underneath the covers and stumbling into his discarded pants.

Maggie flung open the door and disappeared down the corridor. George tripped while putting on his shoes and stumbled behind her, leaving the room door open.

"Are you coming back? You weren't finished," Trixie called from the bed, but she never received an answer.

Rose flicked her tongue and stretched her cheek muscles to expel Nikki's makeshift mouth gag. She couldn't get enough power behind the fabric to even move it around her palate. The Mushroom Cult repositioned her vertically and lifted her upward to the cross attached to the tree. Rose tensed all her muscles in panic and screamed from the back of her throat so hard that little black dots invaded her vision. Her curly blond hair fell in her face; her pigtails had been removed before bedtime—*She didn't want to get an* owie *in the middle of the night, did she?* her mother had asked her— and she could only blink to keep the strands from stabbing her eyes.

"Our work is righteous and good, isn't it, my children?" Anya said, stepping into the tree line.

The cult murmured their affirmation.

"And our work is for the good of all humanity, isn't it, my children? You've all been resurrected—baptized—into warriors against the unjust, terrorists against untruths," Anya continued and noticed louder murmurs and a few more nods were added in response as they bound Rose's wrists to the cross with thick ropes. "But you weren't always pure. Everyone carries some contamination. Because no one is innocent, and no one will be spared." Anya levitated and hovered restlessly in front of Rose. Anya caressed Rose's cheek and smiled, revealing her squared teeth. "Not even little Miss Rose Covington."

Rose almost gagged on Anya's hot breath as the witch leaned in closer.

"I envy the vultures who're gonna peck out your eyes after your body stops baking."

Rose thought about those *Hansel and Gretel* books again and willed herself to find her own safe gingerbread house inside her imagination as the flock below shoved each other, like wolves defending a fresh kill, for a chance to be the one who ties Rose's ankles to the bottom of the cross.

"This sacrifice is for all humanity, so our mission won't be interfered with or interrupted by this imp."

The ghouls stepped backward, and Anya floated to the ground. She glanced up at a sniveling and sobbing Rose. Anya smiled proudly at her brood's handiwork; the girl looked like a true martyr, suspended in a T-shape and transforming an ordinary cross into a proper crucifix. It was time to burn the Chosen One in effigy so Anya could reclaim her place among the deities, the Forevers.

"Light her up."

Candy nodded and took a step toward their sacrifice.

George stepped in front of Maggie's car as she started the engine. "C'mon! Let's talk about this!"

She rolled down her window. "It's hard to want to talk to you about cheating on me when you're standing there bare-chested. I can't take anything you say seriously. It's like you're flaunting it while apologizing for it. Now get out of the way so I can go home and take care of *my* children!"

"Maggie, I love you. You need to understand—"

"Go to Hell," she said and accelerated from the parking spot toward the exit; she would've hit George if he hadn't sidestepped out of her way.

He jogged to the Rolls, dug his car keys from his front pants pocket, and opened the driver-side door. His shirt and the broad in the room had already become an afterthought—Trixie should count her blessings that she'll live to see another day. He mashed the gas pedal and fishtailed from the parking lot onto Route 15 westbound, in hot pursuit of the one person he never expected to be chasing: his own wife.

Candy touched the bottom of the cross with the torch, and Rose immediately felt the tips of the flames lick her toes. She flexed her muscles as far as the ropes would allow and tried to wiggle her feet free. The baby-soft bottoms of her feet tingled at first; then she felt like small safety-pin needles had been jabbed into her flesh. She bore down on her throat and screamed through the torn shirt stuffed inside her mouth to wake her grandmother, but, no matter how hard she tried or for how long, she couldn't muster enough volume to raise anyone. The flames grew like an emerging monster, its teeth of fire gnawing on the wood, famished for flesh.

Anya reached upward through the flames without flinching, unaffected by their devouring heat, and grabbed one of Rose's bare knees. "This is all your fault, child. If you hadn't meddled with the book, I wouldn't have known the book had picked you to be the Chosen One, and you wouldn't be burning alive. I want you to take to your grave that you are the cause of all this. But first I want to thank you. After you burn, and I'm choking on nothing but smoke and ash, I will emerge a deity."

The flames touched Rose's toes, and her gag-muffled scream carried such power that the capillaries in her cheeks exploded and filled her face with a reddish blush.

Anya kept her hand on the little girl's knee as the fire crackled and popped, eating the wood to the left and the right of her body. "Look at you, little wench. Holding on to dear life, like it's something real."

Then the flames caught the fabric of her white nightgown with the pretty little pink baby elephant print—the nightgown she had begged her mother to buy when she saw it displayed in Ensminger's Basement the day before her last birthday.

Are you sure you're ready for big-girl sleepwear, sweet pea?

Yes, Mommy, I'm a big girl tomorrow!

Yes, you are. My little girl is gonna be a big girl!

And, Mommy?

Yes, baby?

Elephants are my favorite.

I know, baby, and you know what?

What, Mommy?

You're my favorite.

Rose and her nightgown were obscured from the cult's vision, trapped behind a barrier of orange flames that now extended past the top of the cross. Her screams had stopped, and her wiggling had since turned into random muscle spasms. Black smoke poured upward through the trees and polluted the sky above the street with the stench of burning wood and flesh.

Anya released her hold on Rose's charred knee and pulled her hand from the fire. She smiled at the beauty of the dancing flames, pirouetting around her poisonous possession: Rose. The only one who could have brought Anya down—*if* she had been interpreting the book correctly for all these years—was the one who had now bestowed the ultimate gift to Anya.

"You look so pretty now," Anya whispered to the incinerating corpse and impatiently waited for the reward to be crowned upon her. She wasn't sure if she would feel any different or would know the exact moment when her rightfully earned acquisition of divine permanence would commence.

She still hadn't noticed any monumental change within her

when two sets of headlights pulled into the Covingtons' driveway a few seconds apart.

Maggie saw the roaring flames and plumes of smoke bellowing from her house's vicinity when she turned onto their street. She pushed the car as fast as it would go, the chassis vibrating and bouncing her around the cabin. She glanced in the rearview mirror, not only to see if her husband was still behind her but to see if he had reacted to the spectacle as well. At first she couldn't see him in the mirror and then noticed his Rolls overtaking her car in the opposite lane. When George had cleared the front of her car, he dipped back into the correct lane and created distance between the cars as he sped toward the house.

George slid the Rolls into the dirt driveway, almost overshooting the entrance and launching onto the side yard. He regained control of the steering and guided the car up the driveway. He felt somewhat relieved the flames weren't near the house; then fear almost rendered his muscles useless when he saw Anya's silhouette facing the driveway with hordes of shadowy figures behind her, like a Spartan army lined up for war. Maggie veered diagonally behind George's car so her front tires landed on the grass. She kicked open her door and sprinted toward the house to check on her babies.

George took a step toward the congregation hiding beneath the flaming tree. He stopped when Anya extended both arms outward—reminding him of a crucified Jesus statue—and rested her left ear on her shoulder. He had never seen her imitate that pose before and wasn't quite sure what it meant, until she listlessly raised one finger and pointed to the tree. George's gaze followed her directional and squinted to make out the shape in the fire better.

His voice cracked as he screamed his daughter's name and broke into a full sprint toward the hanging fire-engulfed cross.

Maggie was a few paces from the side door when her husband's voice pierced through the gentle sound of twigs crackling as they turned to kindling. She spun around and saw him racing toward the large tree on fire.

He never stopped screaming, "NO! NO! NO! NO!"

Her heart dumped a stream of adrenaline into her veins, and she propelled her feet toward the tree before she realized she had even moved. George was going to reach the tree first, but that didn't stop her from yelling to tell him that she was right behind him.

Anya dropped her Jesus Christ pose—*Demon, be driven,* traversed through George's mind—and her attention was diverted to the woman running toward her. Anya smiled when she knew the exact moment the little wench's mother—her cohort's wife—saw her daughter's charcoaled remains hanging from the now-extinguished cross. The hag started screaming, SCREECHING, her daughter's name, and then there weren't even formulated words wailing from her throat, just incoherent bursts of noises that sounded like syllables constructed purely of vowel sounds. Anya saw a light turn on somewhere inside the house. The hag had caused too much of a ruckus by screaming for her charred daughter and woke the grandmother.

Anya decided that drastic times called for drastic measures. "Cyana! Pum'kin! Take care of that noise, please!"

The two ghouls sped past George with lightning speed—faster than he ever believed any member of the cult could move—as he reached his blackened daughter. He looked back just in time to see the fear in his wife's eyes as Cyana's and Pum'kin's stiff, outstretched arms decapitated Maggie without breaking stride. Maggie's head rolled a few yards, her blond hair and freshly cut bangs tangling with the grass, before coming to rest on her left ear. Her body stayed upright for a few seconds before crumpling to the ground, blood erupting like a geyser from the gaping hole where her head should be.

George screamed something that sounded like *GAH!*, but Anya couldn't be sure. The meanings behind mortals' expressions could be so hard to decipher sometimes. And concerned her even less now that she was sure she had attained deity status, even if nothing felt different quite yet.

George turned his back on his headless wife's corpse and continued to cover the remaining few yards to his crucified daughter—her white nightgown with the pink baby elephants had fused with her seared flesh. He reached the tree, and the Mushroom Cult backed up a few paces to give him room as he tried to untie the ropes, but his skin singed as soon as he touched them. He noticed they were almost completely burned through, so he swatted at them, slapping the knot as hard and quick as he could before the heat singed his hand with each swipe. After a few passes at the rope, it unraveled from around his daughter's ankles. He wrapped his arms around her legs to use his torso as leverage to free her from the cross.

The side door opened, and he saw the outline of his mother-in-law, standing in the doorway, looking over the yard, and surveying the black smoke bellowing from the tree line. He froze, his arms still around his daughter's legs, and glanced at the pool of blood encircling his wife's body.

"George? George, is that you? Who was screaming?" she called from the stoop. "Are you both home? Looks like it put itself out, but I already called the fire department. Come inside before you get hurt. They should be here any minute. Where's Maggie?"

George scanned his immediate surroundings. *She can't see the carnage from there*, he thought. *She has no idea her granddaughter has been burned alive by a cult of the living dead and her daughter lay decapitated on the other side of her car.*

As if on cue, the sirens became audible in the distance. He knew it would only be a few moments before the cavalry arrived; most likely the fire department would be accompanied by the sheriff's department. He focused into the depths of the trees and noticed Anya and every single one of her sheep disciples were gone, vanished. Not a single trace remained that any of them had ever been here.

George was all alone, with two brutally murdered members of his family on his property. He was shirtless and had just chased his accusatory wife for over an hour from a pay-by-the-hour motel to the house. He had called out sick to work for almost a full month now. He was solely responsible for a trail of dead hookers, scattered in more places than he could ever remember. And the sirens got closer.

He released his hold of his cremated daughter's legs and stepped backward and looked at his hands. They were covered in soot and blood. Then he looked at his wife's body and her head staring into the night sky.

"Are you coming in? I haven't checked on the children yet. I'm gonna see if they woke up from the commotion. Hope you two lovebirds had a nice time tonight."

George heard the door close. He knew he was down to only a few seconds before she climbed the stairs, walked to the nursery, and discovered Rose's bed was empty. She would certainly come running outside after that. And then what? Find George by himself with his family slain in the side yard? *The ghouls did it. Riiiiiiight.*

He could now hear two different tones of sirens—the fire trucks and the black-and-whites—getting closer to the intersection leading them down his street. Any second now he was sure he would hear Grandma's frantic screaming from upstairs. The sirens grew closer. The wind sent a shiver across his bare chest, now decorated with the soot and ash from his daughter's legs. Blood and death and ash covered everything. The rotating emergency lights now bounced off the neighboring trees and roadway. They were close. Responding to what they think so far is just a tree fire. Oh, what a gruesome surprise awaits them.

Maggie's mother's scream carried through the closed nursery window and reached George at the tree line, surely waking his son. George realized he hadn't even considered Raymond through all this—the sirens were even closer—and could just *feel* his mother-in-law scampering down the staircase. In a few more seconds, she'll explode through that side door, looking for Rose, finding a scene well beyond her worst nightmare. With George standing in the middle.

He saw the top of the fire truck over the front hedges. He heard Grandma's screams reach the bottom step. He knew this moment might come someday, but he never could have imagined it would be under these circumstances. The side door opened at the same time the front fender of Ladder 1 cleared the row of hedges beside his driveway. George knew it was *act right now* or face a completely different fate—one that ended with him wearing a gray-and-white-striped jumpsuit in a six-by-eight-foot cell, waiting for his special day on the gallows.

He crouched down and made a beeline for the woods just as Maggie's mother stepped from the side porch onto the dirt and the first firemen turned the corner from the street onto his driveway. As soon as George hit the tree line, he heard Maggie's mother howl in confusion and grief as a firefighter yelled for George to halt. He didn't halt. He didn't even slow down. He heard the babbling chaos and befuddled yelling from all the arriving units as they came upon the slaughter George had left behind. Twigs and thorns hiding in the thicket slashed his bare chest and ripped his pants as he ran. A pair of flashlight beams bounced over his head like searchlights. They had entered the tree line to hunt for him.

George looked behind him and could make out two deputies hot on his trail. The twigs and fallen logs did not slow down their pace. They powered through the trees with urgency, their flashlights creating funnels of surreal shadows.

"Anya, if you have any power to help me, this would be the time," he pleaded, calling for the very entity who had just torched his daughter and decapitated his wife. "I think you owe me at least this favor."

Silence was in front of him, two pairs of footfalls behind him, getting closer.

"Have you abandoned me, you cunt?"

The two searchlights landed on his back.

"Freeze! Put your hands up!"

George stopped running and raised his hands.

"Turn around slowly and no funny business."

George shuffled in small pivoting steps as he investigated the pathway between himself and the two deputies, aiming their service weapons at his chest. One of the deputies didn't look a day over eighteen and seemed scared as all get-out, and his partner was an obvious salty and disgruntled old-timer. George snickered. As soon as he laid eyes on them, he had already chosen which one would go home as a hero today.

Once George had decided in which direction he would charge them, he took a deep breath and committed to carry out this his final act. It was important he picked a path that had the least possible debris; he couldn't risk tripping and being vulnerable enough to be handcuffed. A one-way ticket to the slammer just wouldn't do. Heroes don't go to death row and take it from behind. Heroes live in infamy as martyred saints of civilized society.

"Stay put! Don't do anything stupid," the old-timer commanded and then said to his rookie partner, "Go cuff him, Olli. I'll cover you."

George thought the rookie—Deputy Olli—looked terrified and laughed. *Of course the old man is sending in the fresh meat to do the dirty work.* George imagined this whippersnapper hadn't been out of the academy for very long, and this could possibly be the most action he's seen yet. Maybe even the first time he'd drawn his weapon. To test the rookie's jitters, George quickly lowered his right hand and scratched his chest.

"We told you to keep your hands up!" Olli ordered, his gun shaking from the suspect's sudden movement.

Perfect, George thought. *I have you exactly where I want you.* He inhaled until not another single iota of oxygen could fit into his lungs, held the air until it felt like it would burst through his chest, and released the longest, loudest war cry he could expel as he beat on his chest like a gorilla and charged the rookie. In his peripheral vision, he saw the old-timer close his left eye and level off his weapon. He hoped the rookie deputy wouldn't let George down before the geezer pulled his trigger first. George's confidence in the rookie waned when he staggered backward and fumbled to get both hands on the grip of his gun.

George leaped over the only shrubbery separating himself from Deputy Olli and worried the old-timer would shoot before his partner did. George realized he didn't have a plan if he actually *did* reach Deputy Olli. He had assumed this whole scenario would have already been over by now. Surprised he had made it this far, George purposefully slowed his attack toward the rookie.

"Freeze!" Olli repeated.

George did not adhere to the deputy's order. He continued to move forward, closing the distance between them, hoping the rookie would do what he had been trained to do and would save George the anguish of death-row life and the nightmares of his slaughtered family.

"Oh, for crying out loud. Get out of the way, kid!" the old-timer yelled.

George knew those words has just signed his death warrant, but he refused to be taken out by some grizzled, end-of-the-road copper. George wanted to give some young buck bragging rights to the pretty dames—how he had single-handedly taken out the Boulevard Killer in an act of valor—although George figured it might be years, maybe decades, before Clark County's finest would connect the dots to pin all the bimbos' murders on him.

If only the kid would put his nerves aside and stop hesitating.

George only had a few more steps before he would be on top of Deputy Olli, and he was pretty sure the old-timer wouldn't let George get that far. He realized, if he could just get more traction in the soft dirt, he'd launch himself at the rookie and go out in a blaze of glo—

16: 100 Suicides

"So you're really not mad?" Smith asked as he played with her hair.

Wynn nuzzled her head into the crook of his arm. "I just have to realize you're a man set in his ways." He lifted her head so she could look him in the eyes, the sheet falling away and exposing their naked bodies. "But I do wish you had called me to come get you. You were there voluntarily. You didn't need to sneak out and have Hank drive you here to get your car. I would've gone to get you, fuzzy slippers and all."

Smith laughed and pulled her toward him, locking his lips on hers. "I'm gonna head into the office a bit."

"Do you need me to come with you?"

Smith stood and buttoned his pants. "Nah, doll. You stay here and catch up on your beauty sleep."

She threw a bed pillow at him. "So now you're calling me ugly?"

"Ugliest mug I've ever seen."

She walked on her knees across the mattress. "*Hmm.* Well, this ugly mug loves you."

Smith absentmindedly rubbed his chest. Images from his

newfound memories reeled through his brain, like a silent film in fast forward.

"Are you okay?" Wynn asked. "Was that too soon? Oh, I'm such a nincompoop. I *knew* it was too early. I knew you weren't ready to hear that from me. From *anyone* actually."

Smith shook away the violent images of Wendy's murder. "Huh?"

"Smith, did you even hear me?"

"What? No. Sorry. I was somewhere else for a minute. I'm back."

Wynn shook her head. Maybe it was better he hadn't heard her this time. He still wouldn't open up to her about Wendy, and, until he got a good handle on his emotions about her taking off with some other guy, Wynn felt it might be safer to not verbalize her feelings just yet.

Smith slipped his arms through the straps of his shoulder holster and twirled his fedora before placing it on his head. He made two finger-guns with his thumbs and index fingers and pretended to shoot her with both of them. "Here's looking at you, kid."

Wynn giggled. "All right, Mr. Bogart, get out of here! And, hey, will you even be back for lunch?"

"I sure hope so. Another picnic?"

She threw the other bed pillow at him. "Get outta here!"

Smith tugged his desk's center drawer by its metal handle, but it didn't budge. He pinched the lip underneath the drawer and strained the muscles in his fingers. The drawer finally released and slid out faster than he expected, cocking sideways on the track. He cussed under his breath as he tried to set the drawer straight, but it was futile. He knew he'd have to crawl under his desk with a screwdriver and remove the metal brackets. He squeezed his hand into the small opening of the crooked drawer, the slack skin on his hand bunching up and rippling as he pushed farther inside to feel around for the box.

His pressed firmly on the edge of the small felt box, flick-jumping it closer to the opening to grab it easier. When the box danced toward the front of the drawer, he pinched and extracted it, like tweezers surgically removing a splinter from a child's foot. Smith opened the box, and the sunlight glistened off the one-carat mine-cut diamond set in a yellow-and-rose gold engagement ring. He snapped the box shut and tucked it in his trench coat pocket.

He picked up the phone and dialed George's number. Wynn didn't need to know his only purpose for visiting the office was to retrieve the engagement ring and to call George to see if he was home so Smith could return the book to his friend's closet—hopefully undetected—and then bait him into a discussion to explain and clarify some of the entries he had read.

Smith let the phone ring an exorbitant amount of times before he admitted defeat and hung up, disappointed. He could wait a while and try George's number again in a few hours—Wynn wasn't expecting him to return for at least another four or five. That would still give him enough time to replace the book in its rightful location in the closet before heading to Wynn's. He glanced out the office window over the city skyline, patted the ring box in his pocket, and headed for the door.

He turned the doorknob, and the phone rang. He paused and looked behind him at the telephone on his desk. It might be George, coincidentally, trying to get a hold of him too. More likely it was some dame whose husband was cheating on her or some father whose daughter had run away or some sibling trying to locate their long-lost twin. He knew he wasn't ready yet to take on new clients and caseloads. Even if it was George, the book could wait another day. He'd been waiting for someone like Wynn his whole life. And it was time Detective Smith, private eye extraordinaire, finally got what he felt he deserved.

He closed the door behind him and could still hear the phone ringing when he exited the front doors of the building that led to the busy Las Vegas sidewalk.

Smith reached underneath the front bench and located the book. It was right where he had hidden it when he had parked in the back lot. He didn't need any peepers noticing the ornate-looking artifact and breaking into his car to steal it. He flung it onto the passenger seat and adjusted his rearview mirror. The pale widow, hidden behind her black veil, and two of her cronies—he wasn't sure of their names; George was the one who had those memorized—filled his mirror with their reflections.

"Jesus H. Christ, Anya. You have to stop popping up like that. You're gonna give me a heart attack."

"Just shut your yap and drive."

Smith made eye contact with her through her reflection and refused to drop his glare. He wasn't ready to allow her to be the alpha if they were to work together. She might hold some control over George, but Smith wasn't about to become some lackey she could order around. And sending that message started with standing his ground right now.

His hands fell off the steering wheel to his thighs in an overt act of defiance. "No, Anya. Tell me what you're doing in my car again, or we don't go anywhere."

She grabbed the top of the front bench and pulled herself forward. "If we are going to be successful, we need to get—" Then she stopped.

Smith furrowed his brows at her unexpected silence and peeked behind him. He knew immediately this impromptu meeting had just taken a turn for the worse.

Anya's quivering finger pointed at his passenger seat. "Where, in the hell, did you find that?"

Smith slid the book toward him, like an old lady protecting her handbag from a stranger on a park bench.

"Don't touch that! It's mine!" Anya said frantically and flung herself over the front bench.

Smith gagged on her putrid breath of rotted meat and curdled dairy. "Fine, fine. Take it." He handed it over his shoulder.

Anya grabbed the book and lovingly patted its cover as she scooted into the back bench between the two ghouls.

"I'm driving to someone's apartment now. Just want to ensure that's okay with everyone in the car," he said sarcastically.

"Take the long way," Anya replied. "I have much to brief you on."

Smith pulled the Chevy into traffic and joined the morning commuters. A low guttural yell from the backseat startled him. He glanced in the rearview and saw one of Anya's girls pointing at the book and making a noise that reminded Smith of a frightened cat.

"I know!" Anya replied to the ghoul's outburst. "What? You don't think it wasn't the first thing that went through my head too?"

The servant answered with a series of moans that sounded to Smith like *HURGH, HURGH, HURGH . . . HURGH!*

"I *told* you that I was concerned about that, since I still haven't felt any difference yet. Now shut up. Children are supposed to be seen, not heard." And then to Smith she said, "So you're the one who's had the book?"

He glanced at her in the mirror. "Why? Has George been looking for it? I was planning on returning it today."

"No. I don't think Mr. Covington will need it anymore. Although knowing you were the one who had it may have saved some people a lot of unnecessary tragedies."

"I'm not following."

"It's nothing to concern yourself with anymore."

"Anymore?" he asked, stopping at a red traffic light.

"The cult belongs to you now. You're the rightful guardian of the book, safekeeping all its secrets. The protector of the one thing that protects me, and, in turn, I protect you. So, you see what a complicated circular relationship we've entered into with each other?"

Smith vowed he would not fall for that trap. He did not buy Anya's decree; it was all smoke and mirrors to win his unequivocal devotion. Once he let down his guard, he knew she would find a way to stick her hooks in him, and then he'd eventually become a slave to her as well—no better than her disciples and no better than George had become.

The traffic control light turned green, and Smith accelerated with the normal flow of traffic. "Go head, Anya. Play hardball with me. I plan on seeing George sooner rather than later. I'll get my answers. Plus I know more than you think I know. George told me that the book must ceremoniously be passed from one caretaker to their successor. You can't just knight me your new caretaker because it suits your needs. I'm not ignorant to the power we *do* hold over your making brash decisions against the book's constitution."

"Mr. Covington has gone into"—Anya's shoulders drooped—"forced retirement from our line of work."

This time Smith looked over his shoulder instead of using the mirror to peer into the backseat. "What do you mean, *retired*? He didn't mention anything to me about stopping any of his—" Smith's voice grew louder. "Are you implying something has happened to—" Now he yelled, "What have you done to him, you conniving bitch?"

Anya remained cool, calm, and collected. "They always go into retirement the same way. You know, Mr. Smith? I've never had anyone, through all these centuries, ever retire properly. Why do you think it is that not a single partner of mine has ever hung up their hat, so to speak, through natural causes or voluntary resignation?"

"God, Anya, I really hate your damn cryptic riddles. I'm aware that George was just one caretaker of a whole slew in a long line throughout the years."

"Not just through the years but through the *ages*."

"And you're implying every single one has committed suicide? That *George* has killed himself?"

"I'm implying none of them were committed to a bright future for our children and couldn't hack the pressure and weight this responsibility demanded of them. They were cowardly sheep, hiding in wolves' clothing, the mental and emotional magnitude of what the book accomplishes driving them to their ends. And, yes, George's wolf laid down and died last night, and his inner sheep panicked. If you don't believe me, call your friend Hank. I believe his boyfriend has already spilled the beans and given Hank everything he needs to make quite a splash at the top of the *Gazette*'s front page."

"If all your previous caretakers resigned by suicide, how is the book ever passed down properly, as dictated in its passages?"

"It's a living document. It can rewrite itself to fit its needs, to safeguard its survival, to ensure our mission's success."

"How can you know all that but not know where your precious book was?" he asked mockingly.

"The book works in mysterious ways," she answered.

"Some people say the same thing about God."

"I know. That's because they are synonymous."

"Are you telling me that the book and God are one and the same?" Smith waved his hand back and forth. "Don't answer that. I don't want to know. That's a slippery slope I just emotionally can't go down right now. So how many have there been so far? How many Georges? How many Smiths?"

"Mr. Covington was the Mushroom Cult's ninety-ninth caretaker."

"That makes me the nice-and-tidy even-numbered one hundredth. Well, you can put *this* in your pipe and smoke it. I will *not* be your one-hundredth puppet or your one-hundredth future suicide victim. You can take this job and shove it."

"You'll learn to play nice with us. Then you'll learn to love us. Then you'll realize you need us. Don't worry. It's the same for everyone. You're not any different than the ones who've come before you. You'll see. And then, one day, you too will accept your fate, just as the previous ninety-nine have done before you."

SALEM, MASSACHUSETTS; 1984

17: ADULTERY

Smith rolled over and pulled his sleeping wife's body close to him for warmth from the frigid Salem winter air. He felt the wrinkles and coarseness of her skin, but he didn't care. He loved her as much today as he did the day he had returned to her apartment with the engagement ring. Time may have altered their bodies but not their passion.

Wynn stirred, opened her eyes, and glanced at the digital alarm clock. "It's not even midnight yet. Go to sleep."

"I have too much on my mind."

"Well, try, please. Tomorrow will be hectic. You always get pooped so easily when Travis brings the kids over. And what eight-year-old wants a grandfather who can't go outside and play catch with him because Grandpa's too tired?"

"Play catch outside? There's three feet of snow on the ground. I don't know how you ever convinced me to retire in New England. It's like a punishment. Plus the kid would rather sit around and listen to those damn cassette tape thingamabobs all day anyway," Smith huffed. "Never seen a kid rather sit and listen to something called a boom box than go outside and run around. Back in my day—"

"I know about your *day*. Now go to sleep. You've kept me up long enough. I need my beauty rest too, you know?"

"I'm going to make myself some chamomile tea. Might take the edge off and warm me up," Smith said and slipped from bed, his bones creaking with each step. He entered the kitchen and put the teakettle on the stove burner so Wynn could hear the appropriate sounds—it was the attention to the little details that had kept him in business for so many decades without raising any suspicion from his wife or his children through the years. And now he must skirt around his grandchildren too. They're getting too smart for their britches.

Ten minutes later, he sat at the kitchen table with a coffee mug full of whiskey and the teakettle's scream simmering down against the blustering wind coming off the ocean outside. Their mustard-yellow touch-tone telephone sat in front of him, the cord stretching from the backside of the phone, over the edge of the kitchen table, and along the linoleum flooring to the jack in the wall. Smith lifted the receiver, waited for the dial tone, and punched in the phone number—one that began with a 1-900 exchange—that would set tonight's coup de grâce in motion.

After he had dialed the number, he heard a series of clicks as he connected to the hotline.

"Hello,"—sweet and sultry; even after all these years, just how he liked them—"my name's Crystal. What name would you like me to scream out while you're pounding me so good tonight?"

Smith trapped the receiver between his shoulder and cheekbone so he could light a Smolens. "Master."

"Yes, Master. I'm your dirty, dirty slave tonight. Let me tell you what makes me so wet—"

"Shut your mouth, dirty whore. I know just what I want."

"Yes, Master. I'm just *dying* for you to tell me how you like it."

He took a swig of whiskey from his faded and well-worn TOP GUN FOR HIRE coffee mug and puffed on the cigarette. "I want you naked—"

"Uh-huh."

"Taking all of me in your mouth."

Smith heard Crystal moan. Realizing she was probably just some middle-aged overweight housewife from Parkview named Judy or Karen or Denise playing the masquerade just increased his sinful urges for violence and dominance. He finished the whiskey and decided to play the Devil in her land of make believe.

"Tell me how the view is, whore. Down there on your knees."

"Oh, Master. Show me yours, and I'll show you mine." Crystal made overly exaggerated moaning sounds—he even thought he heard her lick her finger and smack her lips when she reached the tip. "You're so big and hard. I like being choked by your throbbing cock. I don't think I can fit you all in my mouth."

"I want you to beg and plead."

"Please, Master, let me suck your dick. I'll let you do anything to me if you just let me swallow all—"

CLICK!

Smith replaced the receiver on the base switch hook and looked at the clock. Under ninety seconds. Not enough time for the credit card to be billed. Straitjacket Seductions offers the first 119 seconds free, an advertising gimmick to set them above the plethora of sex lines cropping up recently like wildfire. He didn't need any more than ninety seconds. He had this down to a science. He needed just enough to get his blood boiling and then to deny feeding his urges—keeping them hungry kept him fueled and motivated for his trips downtown. It had been years since he had hunted all night purely on ambition. The girls at Straitjacket Seductions acted as his pregame activity—his shot in the arm for a night on the prowl.

He knew his time playing this vigilante game was nigh. He

just hoped Anya would release him without consequence—without suffering the fate of his predecessors. He had, after all, helped supply her with enough bantlings over the past forty years, between Nevada and Massachusetts, to build her Mushroom Cult army into a grand empire.

Smith wasn't ready to die by his own hand. He wanted to watch his grandkids grow up. And have an opportunity to find a worthy apprentice, just as he had been to George Covington four decades earlier.

Smith sat in the driver's seat of his Pinto, cursing with each turn of the ignition key that failed to start the car. He slapped the steering wheel with a frail and scarred hand while he turned the key again with his other hand. The engine turned over, and Smith looked at the clock on the dashboard. Plenty of time to make it to the clubs on Pickering Wharf before last call. They hadn't closed the VIP rooms yet.

He turned the dial of the car radio to find something to calm his nerves. Old age seemed to have brought the jitters sometimes, and the bitter cold air rattled his joints. He scanned the stations, looking for the one that only played smooth jazz—no Anacostia Trio, but a good mix of the hits from the heyday of big bands, jazz, and swing. The hits from his time.

He stopped when he heard the familiar opening note progression of a song that had been played in excess in his house. His oldest granddaughter had gone through an obsessive phase—borderline unhealthy—with the movie about the seniors of Rydell High. Smith didn't care if he ever saw the movie again; although he did think the dame who played Sandy looked like a knockout when she danced in that black leather number at the end of the movie and sang to her greaser boyfriend. He felt a morose sense of nostalgia hearing the theme song again, after his granddaughter had eventually lost interest in watching the movie every day and even listening to the soundtrack on the gramophone they had at the house. He knew death was just around the corner for him, whether it was by the will of the book or by natural causes. He felt it in his bones. Yes, grease certainly is the word.

He pulled the Pinto into the side lot of Hypnotic Encounters—recently plowed and outlined by towering snowbanks—and parked underneath the flashing neon sign of the profile of a cartoon-style woman floating on her back in a large martini glass. The bouncer nodded at Smith and let him enter the club without paying the cover. Smith chuckled, believing the hospitality was because the club was closing in an hour, even though the real reason was probably because the bouncer had given Smith the Senior Discount.

Smith sauntered between the tables and toward the stage, where the dancer only utilized one of the three poles. The girl wore red vinyl boots that stopped halfway up her thigh and nothing else. He moseyed to a table up against the stage and sat down. He glanced behind him and counted three—no, four—other patrons in the club. A slow night for Hypnotic Encounters. The song ended, and Vinyl Boots trotted offstage, her hair and surgically enhanced breasts bouncing with every step.

"And last but not least," a man spoke, his voice booming over the house speakers, "please give a warm Hypnotic Encounters welcome to our newest edition, making her maiden stage-voyage tonight. Let's help her pop that cherry, fellas, shall we? Give it up for Aurora!"

The music grew louder—some terrible new-wave song with a synthesized beat—and the new girl, donning nothing but a cowboy hat and two tassles hanging off her nipples, sashayed onstage and approached the pole. Smith remained stoic while the four drunk perverts behind him whooped and hollered. Smith would have been convinced she was no older than thirteen if it wasn't for the Celtic trinity-knot tattoo on her lower back, putting her *at least* at the mandated age of eighteen.

She stopped a few feet before the pole and remained motionless. The music blared, and the lights strobed, and Aurora didn't move. The horny bastards behind Smith quickly turned from catcalling to yelling insults and obscenities. Smith tilted his head, like a puppy hearing a shrill noise, intrigued at her grand entrance and then sudden bout of stage fright.

Aurora stared at the pole, stared as if it would bite her the moment she touched it, stared as if—once she wrapped her legs around it—she could never return to any semblance of innocence. Stared as if it were the most frightening and mesmerizing thing she'd ever seen.

"Dance, you fucking slut!" one of the *gentlemen* behind Smith yelled. "Don't you want your dollar?"

Aurora broke her stare with the pole and looked at the empty club, clearly intimidated by the heckler. Smith glanced at his watch; time was running out for tonight. Aggravated, he looked at the exit. Maybe, if he left now, he could pick up one of those two-dollar whores downtown before even they were all spoken for. The longer he stayed in Hypnotic Encounters, the longer he realized this hoofer probably hasn't collected enough transgressions yet to be worth sacrificing to the cult—another Greta White, Greta who had come from right here in Salem. Tonight felt like a bust.

"C'mon, sweetheart, give them what they want. Do what you did for me this morning," the faceless man spoke in his booming voice again.

Aurora sighed and fixed her attention on the pole again but still didn't move.

"This is just pathetic," Smith whispered. Then louder he said, "Hey! Aurora! Come here a sec."

She peeled her terrified stare from the pole and looked at Smith. He saw her face relax—sometimes his age either gained sympathy from the girls and worked in his favor, or added an additional level of creepiness and made his interactions more challenging. Aurora walked across the stage and stopped in front of Smith's table. She flung her cowboy hat on the unoccupied chair, like a small child throwing a tantrum. Smith made the come-here gesture with his hand, and Aurora knelt down.

"Oh, what's with this happy horseshit?" another heckler yelled.

Smith shook his head in disgust before he spoke. "Don't listen to those bastards. You don't really want to do this, do you?"

Aurora shook her head.

"What's your name?"

"Auro—"

"Your real name, doll."

"Caitlin."

"Listen, Caitlin—"

The music stopped abruptly. "Sir, please stop talking to the dancer, or we'll be forced to remove you from the establishment," the man boomed overhead again. "Aurora, those dollars aren't gonna fly on stage by themselves. Right, fellas? Now shake that ass and press your titties together and give them a show!"

"Listen, Caitlin. You seem like a nice girl, and I don't think this is the life for you. Just get dressed and go home. Vultures out there would love to prey on the likes of you. But you have the power to keep them at bay with each life decision you—"

Two sets of hands scooped Smith under his biceps and yanked him from his chair with such force that it toppled to its side. The handful of drunkards behind him clapped and cheered as the bouncers dragged Smith through the club and out the front door, the soles of his sneakers scrapping like rudders. He caught a glimpse of Caitlin, covering her exposed body with her arms as she headed for the backstage area, leaving the stage empty and the few customers unsatisfied. Before the door closed, and he was left alone on the sidewalk, he heard booing and what sounded like a cocktail glass shattering as it hit the stage.

Smith slipped on a patch of ice while getting to his feet and admitted defeat for tonight . . . maybe forever. He turned the corner of the club to the side lot and thought that, after giving Anya four decades of his life, it might finally be time to hang up his hat—or fedora—on their lowlife-extermination business.

He whistled the tune of his favorite song, about dressing up like a million-dollar trooper and trying hard to look like Gary Cooper, as he unlocked the Pinto. When he turned to look out the rear window to reverse from the parking spot, he stared directly into the pale widow's eyes—blurry behind the black veil—sitting in the backseat. Smith sighed and stopped the car.

"I can read your thoughts, Smith. You've gone soft. The Smith I know would never have let that bitch go with some fatherly advice. He would've done her in real good." She spat on the floorboard to punctuate her disgust with his actions. "I know you're coming to the end of your days. And, of all my caretakers, you've been the most splendid and fruitful to building the cult. I can never repay you for what you've created for me."

"I'm tired, Anya. I'd like to enjoy my grandkids. I'd like to sleep next to my wife in however long we've got left in our golden years, without constantly sneaking out of the house to scavenge the streets. I don't have it in me anymore."

"You lost your way a long time ago, Smith. I noticed your lack of motivation shortly after you dragged us all to Salem. I'm not sure the book was happy with you either."

He placed his wrinkled and shaky hands on the steering wheel. "Wynn thought it would be safer here to raise kids and grandbabies than Vegas. The influx of casinos and gangsters really scared her after Travis was born. But it's all been for naught, Anya. The city is worse than it's ever been, despite all the efforts I've wasted on cleansing the streets over the years. What was it all for? I'm just worse for wear because of your mission."

"It's the book's bidding."

"Oh, to Hell with your book, Anya. It promised you divinity, and you still have not been able to obtain that."

"I was close once. I made one fatal error in my calculations, and that child died in vain. And not only did I fail to reach divinity but my powers diminished because, well, *virgins are noxious.*"

Smith removed his hands from the steering wheel and pointed his index finger at her face, his fingertip grazing her black veil. "She was a fucking *child!* You killed . . . no, you *torched,* an innocent baby because you had such tunnel vision with the signs you thought the book was sending you. Maybe the book doesn't have a consciousness. Maybe the book isn't executing some greater master plan for humanity and your beloved Mushroom Cult. Maybe, just maybe, Anya, it's a doggone ancient book written by charlatans and snake-oil salesmen."

He shifted the car into reverse and journeyed home as Anya remained silent in the backseat. The Pinto left the wharf area and entered the residential neighborhoods.

"I think I've found him," Anya said, breaking the silence.

"Found who?"

"Your successor. Would you stay on par until we can get him to bite? For me?"

Smith shook his head so slightly that Anya didn't notice. He glanced at the dashboard clock and felt relieved he would be home at such an early hour. It would be nice to have every night be a stay-sleeping-with-Wynn night. He didn't think Anya would release him unless someone could take his place. Her caretakers might all get tired eventually or get caught, but, unless a replacement was on deck, he knew he belonged to her. For the good of the cult. What's a few more weeks of exterminating the roaches who fed on the city's innocence if it meant peace and quiet until death do him part?

Smith navigated the Pinto into his driveway. "All right. Do your magic. Bring him in."

18: Love Song For a Witch

He flipped the light switch, and the room illuminated with a sickly fluorescent glow. He took a step toward the Mr. Coffee on the wet bar, and his toe caught the corner of a bookcase. He stumbled forward and caught himself on the corner of his desk, keeping the liquor sloshing around in his stomach from escaping through his mouth. He dumped yesterday's grounds and filter and replaced them with new ones. Then he filled the reservoir with water and turned on the Mr. Coffee.

"Excuse me, Mr. Stepp," the intern secretary said, opening the door without knocking. "You have a walk-in. I think you need to talk to this one."

"Already? I just got here. Wait. How long have you been here, Vicki?"

"Sir, I came in at eight. When we open."

Stepp waved her off with a you're-being-ridiculous look on his face and tossed a handful of pills into his mouth—the blue ones helped with the ups and downs; the white ones were intended for the ins and outs.

"She said something about her grandfather being the Wharf Killer."

Stepp stopped midswallow. "Are you fucking kidding me?" he asked, his words garbled by the pills in his mouth.

"Should I send her in?"

"I'll come out to meet her. Thank you, Vicki. Good job."

She blushed and suppressed a giggle before returning to her desk. Stepp cleared his throat and poured himself a warm, black existence from the Mr. Coffee. With mug in hand, he stretched his neck as he straightened his tie and headed for the lobby to meet his next potential client. Stepp winked at Vicki as he passed her desk and thought she would pass out right there.

"Detective Stepp," he announced—his introduction competing with the radio station's commercials filtering through the speakers in the lobby—and extended his hand to the visitor sitting next to the gaudy fake Christmas tree.

The woman, with a face so free of blemishes Stepp thought she could pose as a mannequin, accepted his greeting and shook his hand. "My name's Eva. Eva Smith. And I think my grandpapa might be the one killing all those girls on Pickering Wharf."

"Let's talk in my office, Ms. Smith."

Stepp escorted Anya past Vicki's desk, placing a hand on the small of Anya's back. Vicki craned her head, hoping she might hear just a little bit more of the woman's story before Stepp's office door closed. Vicki knew, once that door closed, she wouldn't be privy to anything else about the case, whether he took it or not. Vicki crooned about how mysterious her boss acted.

"I have a picture I think you'll be interested in," Anya said as she and Stepp neared his office door. She handed Stepp a Polaroid. "This is the most recent photo of what my grandpapa looks like."

"I don't understand," Stepp replied. "When was this picture taken?'"

"Last week, when we were on vacation."

Stepp inspected the picture.

Vicki wished for nothing more than to see what he saw.

"With all due respect, Ms. Smith—"

"Please call me Eva."

"With all due respect, Eva, I don't appreciate jokes like this. I'm very busy and don't have time for gags."

Vicki leaned backward in her chair to eavesdrop better over the disc jockey's voice coming from the lobby speakers.

"I assure you, Mr. Stepp, that this is far from a joke."

"This is a picture of an old man standing in front of the Desert Palms Motel near Las Vegas. A motel that burned down before I was even born. I should know. I grew up just outside Mesquite."

Anya pointed at the Polaroid. "Look at the date on the back."

Vicki strained her ears, intrigued and excited they might have an honest-to-God mystery case on their hands for once.

"How is that possible?" Stepp said when he looked at the date the Polaroid had been taken.

"Find my grandpapa," Anya said, "and I'm sure all the answers will become clear."

"Sit down, Eva. I wanna hear what makes you think he's the Wharf Killer."

Vicki watched Stepp close his office door, isolating her boss and his mysterious client from Vicki's prying eyes and nosy ears. She knew she wouldn't find out anything else about the strange Polaroid. Her boss was so guarded and elusive. Maybe it was better that way.

Vicki pulled open her desk drawer and removed a bottle of Pampering Pink nail polish, already mentally moving on with her day, daydreaming about her blind date later that evening at Gardenia's on the wharf. Maybe he looked like Fabio, and they would ride away from this ugly city together on horseback.

"Next on our holiday countdown of this year's top fifty songs," the DJ said to an empty lobby, "is Billy Idol's 'Rebel Yell,' coming in at number forty-six!"

Detective Stepp's intern secretary had already forgotten all about the woman with the bizarre Polaroid in her boss's office and closed her eyes as she blissfully drummed along with the eraser end of a pencil to the beat of her favorite song.

Just another day in Detective Stepp's office . . .

CPSIA information can be obtained
at www.ICGtesting.com
Printed in the USA
BVOW06s1251121217
502636BV00001B/3/P